"What is it, Tannis? What are you so nervous about?" Zachary probed.

Her heart pounded. "I told you I don't want to get involved."

"Too late. When I kissed you last night, you can't deny that you kissed me back, that you enjoyed it, that you thought about it long after you got home."

"Okay! I enjoyed it! I thought about it so much that it nearly drove me mad!" Admitting the attraction still didn't help her accept it.

"You've awakened feelings in me that I have no right to acknowledge," she added quietly.

"Why not?"

She held his gaze in silence, unable to tell the truth, unable to lie. "I just can't."

Secrets! She'd told him last night she was full of them. Now she saw him search her eyes—looking for betrayal? For the damning evidence that he was walking blindly into a setup?

Dear Reader,

Welcome to the Silhouette **Special Edition** experience! With your search for consistently satisfying reading in mind, every month the authors and editors of Silhouette **Special Edition** aim to offer you a stimulating blend of deep emotions and high romance.

The name Silhouette **Special Edition** and the distinctive arch on the cover represent a commitment—a commitment to bring you six sensitive, substantial novels each month. In the pages of a Silhouette **Special Edition**, compelling true-to-life characters face riveting emotional issues—and come out winners. Both celebrated authors and newcomers to the series strive for depth and dimension, vividness and warmth, in writing these stories of living and loving in today's world.

The result, we hope, is romance you can believe in. Deeply emotional, richly romantic, infinitely rewarding—that's the Silhouette **Special Edition** experience. Come share it with us—six times a month!

From all the authors and editors of Silhouette **Special Edition**,

Best wishes,

Leslie Kazanjian,
Senior Editor

SUZANNE ASHLEY
Bittersweet Betrayal

Silhouette Special Edition

Published by Silhouette Books New York

America's Publisher of Contemporary Romance

SILHOUETTE BOOKS
300 East 42nd St., New York, N.Y. 10017

ISBN: 0-373-09556-2

First Silhouette Books printing October 1989

Printed in the U.S.A.

SUZANNE ASHLEY,

a former community college reading instructor, adores music, from Wolfgang A. Mozart to George Michael, and reading, especially books that surprise her. As for her own writing, she says her mind never stops thinking in romantic terms. She currently lives in Florida with her husband and two children.

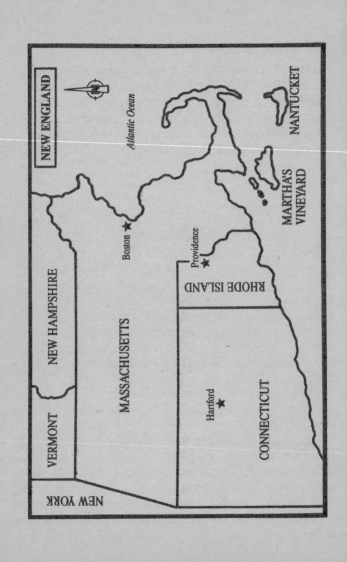

Chapter One

Tannis Robbins sat in the tiny cubicle she jokingly referred to as her office. Hunched over her computer terminal, she was scanning the data that rolled across the screen. When the telephone rang on the cluttered desk beside her, she simultaneously pressed the computer's scroll-lock key with one hand and lifted the telephone receiver with the other.

"Research and Development. Robbins," she said impatiently as her eyes still skimmed the image frozen before her in a green glow.

"Richard Conway, Ms. Robbins. Would you meet me in my office in ten minutes, please?"

Before Tannis could even form a reply, the harsh click of the disconnection echoed in her ear. Richard Conway may have made it sound like a request, she thought as she tapped the keys to log out on the terminal, but he meant it as an order.

Walking down the hallway to the bank of elevators, she tried to recall how many times the owner of Conway Electronics had summoned her to his office in her five years of employment with the company. A dozen maybe. A few times to commend her for her work, but more often to point out problems that he wanted her to solve.

Which was it this time? she wondered as she looked out the smoked glass window that offered an indistinct wedge of Boston where Conway Electronics housed its main offices. Noting the fine powder of snow that brushed against the pane, she sighed and turned to the elevator when the chime announced the car's arrival.

The doors closed noiselessly after she stepped inside and pushed ten to take her to the executive floor. Alone in the confining space, she ran her hands along her hairline to be certain that no stray tendrils escaped from the all-business bun at the nape of her neck. As she smoothed wrinkles from her navy skirt, she wished that she had known she'd be seeing the president today. She would have worn a different outfit. This one was beginning to show its age and wouldn't take many more washings, but there was no space in her ever-tightening budget for new clothing.

A few minutes later, Tannis entered the hushed, muted sanctum of upper management.

"He's expecting you," the receptionist said with barely a glance at her.

The son of the company's founder, Richard Conway had inherited his position when his father retired several years ago. In his late forties, he could have been a handsome man if he'd allowed his features to settle into the pleasing lines nature had intended for them, but his almost-constant scowl lent his face an expression of dissatisfaction.

He didn't rise when she walked in, nor did he speak right away. Instead, he motioned for her to sit in the chrome-and-leather chair in front of his desk. Refusing to feel intimidated, Tannis didn't speak, either, but settled where he indicated and folded her hands neatly in her lap.

"What electronics firm has come up with the most sought-after product for the past two Christmases?" he asked without preamble.

Tannis answered promptly. No second thought was necessary. "Wizac."

"Correct." Conway leaned closer to her across the wide expanse of his desk. "But not again. I want Conway to beat all the competition next year."

"Of course," she agreed, but wondered what this had to do with her.

"Certain sources indicate that Wizac is working on something very innovative."

Nodding, she still didn't understand.

"I want to know what it is!" He pounded his fist on the desktop for emphasis.

I'm sure you do, she thought wryly. Every computer-related firm in the country wanted to know what Zachary Spencer and his company, Wizac Electronics, were up to. And Richard Conway, more than anyone else. Conway had a personal vendetta against the man. "What does this have to do with me?"

A sly smile played on his lips. "You, Ms. Robbins, are going to find out."

He's lost his mind, Tannis decided. That's it. The competition finally got to him. "How do you expect me to do that?"

Taking his time to study her thoroughly, Conway leaned back in his chair. "Zachary Spencer is looking for a personal assistant to help him coordinate his many projects. If you were to apply for that job—and get it—you'd be in the perfect position to find out what he's working on."

First Tannis's mouth dropped open in disbelief, then snapped shut in indignation. "What makes you think he'd hire me?"

"You're good. He'll hire you."

Tannis held his gaze and met the challenge, guessing her job was on the line. "I won't do it."

"I thought you'd say that. I'm prepared to make it well worth your while. It would be very lucrative for you. We'll call your debts to me even. And there will be a bonus for you if the situation turns out profitable for this company."

Almost against her will, Tannis found herself turning the offer over in her mind. She imagined a life free of crippling debt. It wasn't just the money. She longed to be rid of her obligation to this man. If he were paid off and she had a little extra cash, she could take the time to find another job and never be under his thumb again. But if she didn't do what he asked . . .

Conway pressed harder. "How is your sister?"

Tannis's eyes frosted to blue ice. He had hit her weak spot. They both knew it. "The same."

"Still in that expensive health-care facility?"

Her mouth went dry. Her voice was a hoarse whisper. "Yes."

A hint of menace flickered in his eyes. "I'd strongly advise you to do this for me, Ms. Robbins."

Struggling with strong emotion, Tannis knew she would hate herself if she agreed. "I could go straight to Zachary Spencer and tell him what you've suggested."

"Maybe you could." He shrugged. "But you won't."

"What's to stop me from getting the job and then telling him your plan?"

"Your knowledge that I'm capable of turning the situation around to make it look as if you came to me offering to sell his secrets. Then you won't have a job at Conway or Wizac. And you'll still owe me a sizable sum of money—money I'd be prepared to go to any lengths to collect."

She knew he could do it. And he would. "Then if I don't do what you ask, I'll be unemployed?"

"That would be the least of your problems. I can ruin you." Conway met her eyes with no indecision or shame, as if he'd asked her to do something as mundane as stamp the mail. "I have no use for employees who don't follow orders. Particularly those who owe their position to my generosity."

Generosity! Although he'd paid her college tuition, she knew it was because he relished putting his employees in exactly this position. She needed every penny of her income. She barely made it as it was. Conway held the power to keep her from getting any job in the industry. And he was ruthless enough to do it. How long could she stall him until she figured out some other solution? "May I have some time to think it over?"

"Of course." Opening a drawer, Conway pulled out a thick manila folder. "I've prepared a dossier on Spencer for you. Spend the weekend studying it. I'll expect your answer Monday morning."

Several hours later, in the security of her one-bedroom apartment, Tannis pulled a hand-knit afghan around her and sipped from a steaming mug of hot chocolate to counter the damp February chill. She wore thick knee socks under her jeans and a bulky wool sweater over her blouse. She couldn't afford to raise the thermostat on her electric heater. The previous month's utility bill had cut into her grocery budget. She'd rather use extra blankets than skip lunch.

Spread before her on the coffee table was the dossier on Zachary Spencer, the man they called the Wizard, and the corporation he headed, Wizac. After a thorough study, she was familiar with every aspect of the man. Zachary Spencer *was* a wizard. He'd gone to MIT, obtaining his bachelor's and master's degrees in electronic engineering. Conway Electronics had snapped him up before the ink on his diploma had dried.

Quick to recognize Zachary's genius, the company had rapidly promoted him to head of R and D, but after five years, Zachary left Conway to open his own company. His Wizac I cracked the home-computer market wide open. The simplicity of the machine's operation had appealed to even those most reluctant to join the computer age.

The television advertising hadn't hurt, either, Tannis decided as she recalled the commercial. A timid-looking guy with his hair slicked back, wearing horn-rimmed glasses and a plastic pocket protector leaned on the computer terminal and promised, "You don't have to be a nerd to understand the Wizac." Then a voluptuous blonde dressed in a sexy black evening gown slinked into view and sat down at the keyboard to prove it.

Sales had skyrocketed. Zachary Spencer became a multimillionaire and branched out into other areas. And Richard Conway had never ceased to despise the man for leaving his employ. It was common knowledge at Conway Electronics that the owner thought Spencer had stabbed him in the back by taking advantage of his job to perfect the design for his own gain.

There had been talk of a lawsuit, but Conway had never followed through. Perhaps because he knew he couldn't win. However, his quest for revenge against Spencer ruled many of his business decisions. And now Tannis had the dubious distinction of being the one chosen to help Conway cheat the Wizard.

Tannis stared at the eight-by-ten photograph of Zachary Spencer that Conway had provided. Just the expression on his face said a lot about the man. Impatience. "Hurry up and take the picture," he seemed to be saying to the camera. "I've got other things to do."

Dark blond hair fell across his high forehead in tousled disarray. The angular planes of his square jaw relaxed a bit as his sculpted lips formed a smile. The slightest suggestion of dimples creased his cheeks.

But the feature that struck Tannis the most was his eyes. The color of polished jade and fringed with long lashes, they were a harbinger of his intelligence. This was a man she wished she could meet under different circumstances. Perhaps across a candlelit table.

Thrusting that notion from her thoughts, Tannis scooped up the papers and stacked them neatly in the drawer of a small table under a pile of magazines and crawled into bed. She hated the fact that Conway had her in this position. When she'd been young and rash, she'd signed an agreement tying her to Conway Electronics in exchange for college tuition. Though her time was up, her obligation had increased. He'd made her substantial personal loans in the early months of her sister's illness before she'd made the necessary changes in her life-style. She'd sold her new car with the astronomical monthly payments, moved from the upscale town house to the low-rent apartment and given up lunching with the staff for brown bagging.

She didn't even have any savings to fall back on. Even without the unending cycle of debt, she knew she couldn't meet her sister's expenses if she lost her job and had to start all over again. What on earth was she going to do?

Seized by an uncommon restlessness, Zachary Spencer stared unseeingly out a second-floor window of his sprawling, six-bedroom, century-old home in the Boston suburb of Chelsea. For the first time in his life, he had no direction. He knew he should be well into the experimental stages of some new gadget if he wanted to saturate the market by Christmas. But he had no plausible ideas. At the very least he should be involved with the updated model of the Wizac computer that his team of engineers was working on, but even that didn't spark his interest.

Maybe I came too far too fast, he thought, running a large hand through an unruly shock of dark blond hair. Maybe I should consider the offer to sell and retire.

Retire at thirty-four? Some of his classmates had retired already. He knew it was not uncommon for an MIT graduate to be a millionaire by the age of thirty. But for him the money had just been one of the perks. All he had wanted to do was build a better computer—the best computer. And the American public had agreed.

His next major venture, the Wizac doll, had been a gift of love, and again the American public had agreed.

Now what? he wondered. What did he want to do? Money allowed him freedom of choice. But to choose what? He didn't know.

"What is it, Amber?" he asked, turning at a sound behind him. "Hungry?" He dropped his hand to stroke the soft fur at the nape of the cat's neck. "Me, too, but not for food. I've got a hunger in my soul that defies explanation."

Clutching Amber to his chest, he smiled into her vivid blue eyes. "Maybe what I need is a woman."

As if she understood his words, the golden-coated Siamese let out a mew of protest, leaped from his arms and padded haughtily toward the kitchen.

"Okay," Zachary said, chuckling softly as he followed her down the stairs. "Food first, a woman later."

"So I don't really see that I have any choice," Tannis said to her sister at her regular Sunday afternoon visit to the Greenbriar Health-Care Facility. "I owe Conway so much, I have to do what he says. And I'm certainly not in a position to move or to job hunt. That is, if anybody would even hire me after Conway finished spreading his lies." She sighed. "I guess I could agree and then stall every time he asked me for information. Or maybe just make something up."

Reaching out, she touched Meredith's arm reassuringly. "Oh, well. No point in worrying about it. You know how I've always loved a challenge." Her forced optimism faded, and her voice softened. "I've certainly had enough challenges lately."

Meredith lay unhearing in the hospital bed, deep in a coma. For a long sad moment Tannis studied her sister—the dark auburn hair that spilled across the pillow, the relaxed lids covering eyes as blue as the summer sky, the narrow, slightly upturned nose, the soft pink lips that had always formed a sparkling smile. Tannis knew that to the casual observer Meredith appeared as normal as any other twenty-eight-year-old woman as she slept. But Meredith's sleep had lasted for almost two years.

Hearing the tread of rubber-soled shoes in the hallway, Tannis looked up to see the rotund figure of Dr. Elliott Moore enter Meredith's room.

"Tannis!" he greeted. "After all this time, it still gives me a start to see you sitting beside Meredith. The likeness is amazing."

"Identical down to the crescent-shaped birthmarks on our left hips." Tannis cast an affectionate smile toward her twin.

"Still talking to her?" The doctor moved forward and placed a comforting hand on Tannis's shoulder.

"Constantly. I don't know if it does anything for her, but it's great therapy for me. We always shared all of our thoughts." She looked up at the elderly man. "It's a hard habit to break."

"Who knows? Maybe she hears everything." He frowned at the uncommon sadness in Tannis's eyes. "Something wrong?"

"Just a problem at work. I worry about what would happen to Meredith if I lost my job."

"You could save money if you would eliminate the physical therapist."

"No, Meredith needs the muscle stimulation so she can resume a normal life when she wakes up."

"If she wakes up—"

"*When* she wakes up." Tannis interrupted with stubborn insistence. "Meredith is the only family I have left. I will not give up on her. I'll do anything I have to, to help her get well."

At precisely eight o'clock on Monday morning, Tannis crossed the lobby of Conway Electronics, still not certain exactly what she would tell her boss. She'd spent a tortured weekend trying to find a way out of the demand Conway had made on her.

Maybe Spencer really had cheated Conway, she thought. Maybe corporations spied on others all the time. Then she remembered Zachary Spencer's eyes in the photograph. She had seen a lot of things in his expression, but not dishonesty. A man of his genius would not need deceit to succeed.

On the tenth floor, Richard Conway's cool, efficient receptionist was not yet in place, so Tannis pushed open the double doors and went inside unannounced. Her decision was made. She had to tell him before she lost her nerve and changed her mind.

Conway was on the phone, listening intently. He noticed Tannis and motioned her to a chair, but she stood before his desk, her feet firmly planted, waiting.

"I don't care what it takes," Conway barked into the instrument. "Do it. I'll expect your report before the day is out." He slammed the receiver down and glared at it for a few seconds before he looked at Tannis. Then he smoothed his features into a more controlled expression. "So you've reached a decision?"

"What decision? You've left me no choice. As much as I hate it, I have to go along with your directive."

Conway's face lit victoriously. "I thought you might." He opened a drawer and pulled out a file folder. "I've prepared your résumé for you and written a glowing letter of recommendation."

He'd known she'd had to agree, the bastard! But she wasn't beaten yet. Tannis scanned the papers in the file. "This letter says I left for personal reasons. What am I going to say if he asks me to elaborate?"

"You could tell him that we were having an affair and I fired you because I was ready to end it but you weren't."

That thought turned her stomach. "I'm sure I can think of something more believable," she said icily.

"Whatever." Conway glanced at his watch. "Go to his personnel office. They can set you up with an interview. After you're hired, don't call me here. Someone might recognize your voice. I'll contact you."

Sighing, Tannis turned and left the office. With any luck at all, she thought, Zachary Spencer would be an antifeminist who wouldn't want a woman on the job. If that were the case, would Conway simply order her to have a sex change operation?

Apprehension seized her as she drove the short distance from the Conway offices to the Wizac building. She'd stopped in R and D to clean out her desk and give her supervisor the brief explanation that she'd quit her job over an altercation with Conway. It had been hard to lie to the man she liked and respected, but it was a necessary evil. Something she'd have to get used to, she told herself. There wasn't much room for honesty in the field of espionage.

Stepping from the car in the Wizac parking lot, Tannis craned her neck to take in the building. It was constructed of red brick that managed to look old though she knew it wasn't, and dark, smoky glass. It didn't look high-tech or futuristic like the Conway building, but comfortable, familiar, at ease with its surroundings. And maybe it was, with MIT barely more than a stone's throw across the river.

The feeling of warmth increased when she entered the lobby. A waterfall sprang from natural stone and cascaded down one wall, surrounded by lush plants and blooming— yes, blooming—flowers in the middle of winter.

Twenty minutes later, Tannis had been shuffled through personnel and was on her way to see Zachary Spencer in his office on the top floor. She worked at calming the nerves that undermined her composure. He was, after all, only a man. Certainly no more threatening than Conway. But Conway was ruthless and villainous. She didn't think Zachary Spencer was.

In contrast to the lush formality of Conway's office where the president sequestered himself away from all employees save the single receptionist, Zachary Spencer's executive floor was teeming with activity.

A huge room was filled with about twenty or thirty desks, arranged in an order that approached straight rows, but didn't quite make it. Each desk held at least one computer terminal, and behind almost every terminal, someone sat tapping away at the keyboard. The haphazard lines of desks broke for an aisle that led to a large oak door. If she'd had any doubt that the president sat behind that door, it was dispelled by a large yellow sign reading, Genius At Work, which pointed the way.

Tannis smoothed her hair in a habitual gesture and took a deep breath as she walked toward the president's office. Just outside the door, at the last desk on the left, a raven-haired woman wearing a clinging white sweater and curve-hugging knit skirt eyed Tannis suspiciously.

"May I help you?" the woman asked. She swept a disapproving gaze over Tannis's two-year-old pale blue skirt and matching jacket.

"Tannis Robbins to see Zachary Spencer."

"You don't have an appointment."

There was no trace of question in the words, but Tannis had dealt with obstinate secretaries before. This one obviously hadn't been hired for her typing skills. "No, but I was just in personnel and Mr. Williams told me to come up here."

The woman's gaze met Tannis's and held steady. "Mr. Williams didn't call me."

Shifting slightly, Tannis explained patiently. "Nevertheless, I was instructed by Mr. Williams to come up here to speak with Mr. Spencer about the position of personal assistant."

"Mr. Spencer can't see you now. Leave your résumé, and I'll call you if he wants to set up an appointment."

Tannis hesitated. She'd gotten the impression from the personnel director that Zachary Spencer would be interested enough to see her right away. Apparently his secretary wasn't going to give him the opportunity. Richard Conway's directive aside, she took getting past this woman as a personal challenge. "Why don't we let him decide?"

"Leave your résumé," the woman repeated. "If he wants to see you, I'll call you."

From the coldness of the woman's expression, Tannis speculated that her résumé would be in the wastebasket ten seconds after she left the building. She knew if she went back to Conway, he'd simply order her to try again. Though not defeated, she knew when to retreat. Clutching the file folder that held her employment history and letter of recommendation, she assumed as much dignity as possible. "I'll try another time."

Tannis marched with deliberation back to the elevator and punched the down button. While she waited, she stole another glance around. Corridors led away from the office to the right and left. No one was paying any attention to her leaving.

With a sudden flash of inspiration, Tannis moved quickly. Knowing that any company that used computers would have an interoffice electronic mail system, she ducked down the hallway in search of a vacant terminal.

After walking down only one corridor, her efforts were rewarded when two women came out of a small conference room, empty coffee cups in hand. As soon as they turned away from her, Tannis slipped into the vacated room. Two terminals sat on a table, still logged in. She knew she had only a few minutes, but if she was lucky, she would need only a few minutes.

Settling in the nearest chair, Tannis placed her fingertips on the keyboard. Within seconds, she was in.

Zachary choked back a curse when the intrusion came on his screen. He hated interruptions, but accepted them as part of the responsibilities that came with his position. Relaxing the stiff posture he'd had as he concentrated on his work, he took off his steel-framed glasses, wearily rubbed his eyes and typed, *Go ahead.*

He watched as the amber letters came up on the screen. *Need to see you immediately.*

Who is this? Zachary typed, frowning.

As soon as the words appeared, he felt an uncomfortable shiver course up his spine, as though he'd been invaded. *You don't know me.*

His fingers pounded furiously on the keyboard. *Then what are you doing in my system?*

Need to see you.

"Hackers!" Zachary grumbled. Though he'd been one himself in his younger days, they were a nuisance when he was too busy to applaud the skill they displayed by penetrating his security. But it had been a long time since anyone had gotten in. He had designed the intricate maze of codes himself. Forgetting his work for the moment, he let curiosity take him as he typed, *Where are you?*

Down the hall. Zachary read the words and this time the curse exploded from his lips. Computer whiz kids playing in a lab somewhere were a nuisance, although a tolerable one. But if someone had the nerve to walk into his building and sit down at one of his terminals, that was another matter entirely. No longer irritated, Zachary was angry.

With purposeful strides, he crossed the room and flung open the door to the outer office. Ignoring the startled glances of his secretary and the other people in the room, he stalked to the corridor.

When he saw the two women returning from the coffee room at the end of the hall, he deduced that the nearby conference room was the most likely location. He went swiftly to the door, prepared to grab some precocious high school student by the scruff of the neck and toss him toward the elevator. But when he rounded the doorway and met the largest, most beautiful blue eyes he'd ever seen, he froze.

The slight tremble of fear that had flickered in Tannis as she awaited discovery fled the instant she saw Zachary. Good Lord! The photograph didn't do him justice. He was more attractive, more vital, more powerfully masculine in person. Restrained energy radiated from him as he stood in the doorway. His intelligent eyes scanned and filed every detail of her appearance.

"I tried the more conventional method of getting in to see you." Tannis held his gaze with hers and forced coolness to dominate her unsteady nerves. "But your secretary is very protective."

"She's supposed to be," Zachary grumbled. Then, remembering his anger, he strode across the room. Despite the cool beauty and the exquisite eyes, she was a trespasser. He would do best to forget the female form and concentrate on the threat. "My office. Right now."

When Tannis hesitated at the anger in his voice, Zachary gripped her arm and pulled her to her feet. "Now!" he barked again, prodding her to the door.

Though his grip relaxed, he still kept his long fingers around her arm as he steered her down the hallway and into the outer office. Sweeping past his surprised secretary, Zachary growled a command. "No interruptions, Delilah."

What an appropriate name, Tannis thought as she shot the stunned woman a killingly sweet smile.

Zachary slammed the heavy wooden door behind them and unceremoniously dumped Tannis in the chair closest to his desk. As he moved around to his own chair, she took a quick look at the president's office. Here was a trace of the organization that had been lacking in the outer office. A massive bookcase along one wall held numerous volumes in precise alignment. There was a comfortable sofa in muted gray. Tall plants framed a long window. The huge desk was cluttered, but there was a sense of order to it. She guessed that he knew exactly where everything was and that before he left for the day, each stack of printouts, each overflowing file folder would be put carefully where it belonged.

Zachary sat facing her. "Who do you work for?"

My, but the boy wonder is touchy about his system, Tannis thought as she studied the aggravation evident on his face. "At the moment I'm free-lancing."

"And you needed to see me?"

"Yes." There was the impatience she'd seen in the photograph. "I came to apply for the position of your personal assistant. Mr. Williams sent me up here, saying that you'd want to talk with me yourself, but your secretary wouldn't let me in." Pausing to draw a breath, she noted that his anger was fading, replaced by a curious interest. "So I found my own way to get your attention, proving both my computer skills and my ingenuity."

Taking the file folder that she'd been clutching, she laid it on his desk. "My résumé."

A curious smile formed on his lips, softening the dark intensity of his eyes. He gave her a long, thorough look, then picked up the folder. After he'd studied the file, Zachary again studied her, taking in the determined set of her jaw, the intelligent cast in her deep blue eyes, the sleek defeminizing hairstyle. He felt a sudden urge to pull the pins from that tidy little bun and see if her hair felt as silky as it looked, but he stifled it and concentrated on business. "Tell me about your career at Conway."

Sliding open a desk drawer, Zachary pulled out a pipe. He filled it from a leather pouch while she outlined her rise up the ranks to her position in educational software. When she listed the names of programs she had assisted with, she expressed her surprise that he seemed familiar with them.

"I wouldn't be much of a businessman if I didn't keep up with the competition, would I?"

"I guess not." Tannis watched the smoke curl up from the bowl of his pipe as the rich aroma of cherry tobacco drifted to her.

"I haven't advertised this position. How did you hear about it?"

She'd anticipated that question. "Industrial grapevine. A lot of people at Conway still talk about you." That, at least, wasn't a lie.

Zachary chuckled with amusement. "I can imagine. Why did you leave Conway?"

Tannis drew a slow breath. She'd anticipated that question as well and had worked out a plausible explanation. "I'd gone as far as I could." That certainly was no lie, either.

He glanced at her résumé. "There are several positions there above yours."

"Not for a woman. Not at Conway." That, too, was true.

"What makes you think I'm more liberal-minded than Conway?"

"I was under the impression that you were far more intelligent than Richard Conway."

For a moment he stared at her, sensing a fragility beneath the spunk. He wondered why he didn't simply send her on her way. It couldn't be the wide blue eyes, could it? He decided to go with instinct and ask himself the questions later. "Charlie Haskell replaced me as head of R and D when I left. Is he still there?"

"Yes."

Reaching for the phone on his desk, Zachary punched the numbers of Conway Electronics from memory. "Charlie Haskell, please," he said into the phone. "That's all right. I'll hold."

"Would you like me to leave the room while you talk?"

His eyes drifted back to Tannis. "No, but if you're uncomfortable, you could make us some coffee while we wait." He indicated a folding door on the far side of the office. "Everything you need is over there."

Under any other circumstances, Tannis might have balked at the presumptuous order, but her situation wasn't usual. Silently she rose and crossed the deep pile of the forest-green carpet to the door. Pushing it aside, she found a well-stocked mini kitchen and started the simple task.

With boring music humming in his ear from the telephone, Zachary watched her. He studied the staunch rigidity of her spine in direct contrast to the alluring feminine curves only barely discernible beneath the suit. As he wondered how she'd look in clinging silk, he felt a tightening in the pit of his stomach. Settle down, Zach, he cautioned himself. Just because you admitted you needed a woman doesn't mean you should put a move on the first interesting one who walks through your door.

Interesting? Was that all it was? How about intriguing? How about the fact that in seven years of business, no one had ever walked into his building and sat down at one of his terminals to get his attention? He'd rarely interviewed anyone who spoke so animatedly about her work as she did. He'd talked with her long enough to ascertain her intelligence and her enthusiasm. She was exactly what he was looking for in an assistant. And beautiful to boot.

Tannis prepared the coffee machine and switched it on, trying not to dwell on the physical pull she'd felt the moment Zachary Spencer's large frame had filled the doorway. The eyes had gotten her first, not just the unique color, but the intelligence in them, the quick assessing feel of them. He seemed to take in things that weren't visible to normal eyes.

Turning around, she found him watching her and felt a momentary panic at the intensity of his gaze. Then he relaxed his stare and smiled briefly at her. The hint of dimples framed his mouth.

"Cream and sugar?" she asked with a smile in return.

"No cream. Three sugars," he answered. Then in response to a voice on the other end of the phone, he grinned. "Charlie, you old goat! Zachary Spencer."

Trying to ignore his conversation with her former supervisor, Tannis crossed the large room to study the collection of books that lined the opposite wall.

He had everything from computer-science textbooks to Stephen King, Kurt Vonnegut to Jean-Paul Sartre. She had half expected to find Isaac Asimov and Robert Heinlein, but guessed that science fiction held little attraction for a man who created his own fantasies. Also on the shelf, oddly out of place among the volumes, sat a baseball secured to a small brass pedestal.

Before she had time to speculate on the significance of that, Zachary had hung up. She returned to the coffee maker to fill two mugs, stirring three packets of sugar into one.

Zachary reached across the desk to take it. "Charlie misses you."

Tannis sank back into her chair. "I felt badly about leaving him, but I thought it was the best action for me."

Zachary nodded thoughtfully. "Charlie also said that he'd give his right arm to have you back and I'd be a fool not to snap you up immediately." He saw a surge of what might have been relief in her eyes. "Why don't we give it a two-week trial period? We can find out if we get along all right before I start you on any of my big projects."

"That's fair." Tannis wondered if two weeks would be long enough to solve her problems. "What will I do?"

Wrapping his hands tightly around the coffee mug, Zachary brought it slowly to his lips, his gaze never leaving hers. "Various things."

Something about the intensity of his stare touched off a flicker of fear in Tannis. "You call this position personal assistant. Just how personal did you mean?"

Over the rim of his cup, he regarded the expression of panic in her eyes. "This is a purely professional offer. Charlie told me what you were paid at Conway. I'm willing to match that to start with because he said you were worth it. You needn't worry about my intentions."

A crimson flush spread upward from Tannis's neck and seared her cheeks. She hadn't meant to be insulting, but there was something unsettling about the way he looked at her. Regaining control was a struggle, but she managed. "I didn't mean to imply that you were less than reputable."

"No problem. I have a few personal projects that I'd like to see move more quickly. Nothing I want to market, so I don't bother R and D with them. Since you've worked in educational software, I'll give you a math program that I've been thinking about." Rising, he gestured to the door. "Now let's get you formally employed. You'll need to complete all the paperwork."

Following him across the room, Tannis waited as he opened the door, then preceded him through it.

"Where should I put you?" He scanned the large room, then turned to the secretary. "Delilah, I've just hired Ms. Robbins as my personal assistant. I want her close enough to me that I can summon her with a shout."

Delilah frowned, displeased. "I think one of the conference rooms down the hall has an extra desk."

"Great! Get someone to move it in here, and we'll put it right across from you."

"No!" Delilah protested. "I meant—"

But Zachary had already turned back to Tannis. "I feel that communication between departments is essential, so each division has a representative that works here.'' He pointed out a few people. ''Word processing, marketing, accounting. Well, you get the idea. They're all connected to their departments by the internal system. Pretty much the opposite of Conway.''

''Yes.'' Tannis thought of the cubicle where she'd worked. Employees there were encouraged not to talk to each other, presumably so no time would be wasted. ''This sounds like a good idea.''

''It's worked so far.'' Zachary turned back toward his doorway. ''Go back down to personnel. I'll have some work for you by the time you get back.''

Tannis willed her feet to walk slowly when she had an overwhelming urge to run for her life.

How had she pulled it off? she wondered in amazement. One thing that she hadn't counted on had happened. She liked Zachary Spencer. How was she going to betray him?

Simple. She wasn't. She'd never intended to. She would just bide her time, making Conway think she was spying until she came up with a better plan. But she'd better come up with one soon.

Chapter Two

Tannis spent most of the first week observing Zachary in action. Not because of the mission Conway had sent her on, but because he was fascinating to watch. He'd been incredibly involved in one crisis after another. Amidst the comings and goings through the office door beside her desk, she'd marveled at the speed with which he worked. He rarely sat still except for occasional times when he seemed to be deep in thought. It appeared that he could block out the rest of the world while he concentrated on a problem, almost in a trancelike state.

Unless he was in private conference, he kept his office door open. When he wasn't facing his computer terminal, Tannis was directly in his line of vision. Several times, she'd felt uncomfortable and had swiveled her chair to find him watching her.

As Zachary had explained Monday morning, her first assignment was to develop a software program that explained prealgebra in an interesting and entertaining way.

Because that subject was too many years in her past, she'd spent most of her time making notes as she reviewed basic textbooks.

He'd yet to give her an access code for the computer, though there was a terminal on her desk. So far, that hadn't posed a problem. It had provided a convenient excuse when Conway had called her at home to find out whether she'd learned anything yet. Now, however, at nearly five o'clock on the last day of the week, she was ready to start on the program. She couldn't do that until she was familiar with the system.

As the others around her began covering their terminals and clearing their desks, preparing to leave for the weekend, Tannis looked at the heap of notes on her desk. The extra ten or fifteen minutes it would take to organize them would be worth it, she decided.

With the exception of Zachary's personal secretary, everyone in the office had been friendly to her. Delilah had been cold and resentful. Tannis doubted that it had to do only with the slight altercation outside Zachary's office on Monday morning. Thankfully, Delilah had left at noon for a weekend ski trip in Vermont.

Now, with the last person saying goodbye, she was alone in the suddenly quiet office. Except for Zachary. Without turning she knew from the sporadic click of the keyboard that he was at his terminal. Not without effort, she tuned out the sound and concentrated on finishing her task.

In a moment the raspy squeak of Zachary's chair penetrated her thoughts. She heard a muttered oath and then, "Delilah!"

Turning only her head, Tannis saw him sorting frantically through a stack of papers on his desk. "She's not here."

Zachary glanced up, frowning. "Ask Karen to come in."

Tannis stood and walked toward his desk. "Everyone's gone."

Still frowning, he glanced at his watch, raised his eyes to Tannis, then lowered them to his desk, muttering under his breath as he went through the pile of papers again. "I gave Delilah a letter to type that has to go out today. She didn't bring it back."

"I'll go look on her desk." She located the printed letter and the longhand version Zachary had written. "Is this it?" She placed it on the desktop before him.

"Yeah, thanks." He scanned the letter quickly and swore again. "Damn! The figures are wrong."

Placing her hands on the desk, Tannis leaned over to look at the paper. "Can we fix it?"

"Probably." Lifting his head, Zachary found her eyes inches away from his. "Go out to a terminal and see if she saved it when she printed it."

Backing away slightly from the intense green gaze, Tannis shook her head. "I can't."

Impatience furrowed his brow. "It's only a few minutes after five."

"Oh, it's not that. I don't mind working late when it's necessary."

Zachary stared at her, noting the allure of the sparkling eyes that had plagued him all week when he'd struggled to keep his mind on business. They pulled him even now when an important piece of mail had to be corrected. "What is it then?"

A smile pulled at the corners of her mouth. "I don't have an access code."

"Oh." Shifting his eyes to the paper, he picked it up and rose from his chair. "Then I guess I better give you one."

Tannis followed him to her desk and waited while he punched in the keys that would allow him to enter a new access code. The amber cursor blinked in readiness. "What would you like for a password?"

How about victim of circumstances? Tannis thought. Mata Hari? "Just 'Tannis,' I guess."

"Boring." Zachary angled his head to gaze at her. "Where's your imagination?"

"What code would you give me?"

Briefly, he let his gaze drop to her mouth. Temptress? Femme fatale? She'd sufficiently filled his thoughts for the past few nights to warrant either name. "Just 'Tannis' for now." He turned back to the keyboard. "We can change it later when we think of something appropriate."

After locating the letter in the word processing program, Zachary rose from the chair and gestured for Tannis to sit. She settled at the terminal and placed her hands on the keyboard. The oxford cloth sleeve of Zachary's shirt brushed against the fabric of her navy blazer as he leaned over to show her which keys to press to correct the figures. It was impossible for Tannis to ignore the burst of electricity that she felt at the contact, but if Zachary noticed her involuntary shiver, he made no comment.

Though his eyes were on the computer screen, his face was close enough for her to see the stubble of five o'clock shadow on his cheek, close enough to smell the lingering cherry tobacco scent that clung to him. She forced her eyes to the screen and concentrated on his instructions.

"Then type Print," he finished. "I'll take it to the post office when I leave."

As Tannis started on the correction, Zachary turned and went back to his office, but he knew any further attempt at clearing the paperwork from his desk was hopeless. How could he think about business when the delicate fragrance of her perfume still permeated his senses? He had not missed her reaction when their sleeves had brushed together. She'd been jolted just as he had. How long could they both ignore this maddening, inexplicable pull that they had toward each other? He'd felt it the moment he'd stepped into the office down the hall and caught her at the terminal. And he was certain that she'd felt it, too.

Tannis finished the letter and took it into Zachary's office where she found him sitting at the desk with his elbows resting on the arms of his chair, his fingers steepled in front of him, deep in concentration. "All done." She placed the letter before him. "Anything else?"

"No. You can go." He stretched his arms over his head, causing the fabric of his shirt to strain across his flexed muscles. "I just have to clean up this mess, and I'll be gone." Dropping his arms, he indicated the array of printouts and file folders that littered the top of his desk.

As eager to find some tidbit of useless information that would hold Conway off as she was reluctant to return to her lonely apartment, Tannis leaned over his desk and reached for some of the papers. "I'll help you."

With fluid agility, one hand shot out to circle her wrist. "No."

His swift command stilled her. For a brief second, they both stared at the contrast of his large, dark hand against her smaller, whiter one. Then their eyes met. Slowly his fingers unclenched. "I'm sorry. That's just one of my eccentricities. I don't like anyone to touch my work."

Withdrawing her hand to a pocket of her blazer, Tannis spoke softly. "I was just trying to help." Unable to move, she kept her eyes on his. Her mind still held the image of that masculine hand on hers. She still felt his heated touch.

God, what was that look in her eyes? Zachary wondered. It was almost panic. A reassuring smile eased across his lips, giving Tannis an up-close glimpse of the twin creases that framed his mouth. "It has nothing to do with you. If you knew me better, you'd understand that I don't allow anyone to clean my desk." Though the frightened vulnerability on her face slowly faded, he felt an urge to soothe her further. "Why don't we have dinner tonight and talk about some of the projects I have in mind?"

Dinner! Good Lord, she would love it. But she couldn't do it. The only thing keeping her sane in this insane situation was forcing an impersonal distance between the two of them. Dinner together would destroy her resolve, even if it were ostensibly a business meeting. "I can't."

"There's no Mr. Robbins, is there?"

"No, I . . . I just don't think it's a good idea."

"Because you work for me?" He quickly assumed that his guess was correct. "Then if I fired you, you'd go?"

Smiling at the glint of humor in his eyes, Tannis shook her head. "If you fired the best computer specialist you've ever met just to have dinner with her, you'd be stupid. I don't have dinner with stupid men."

"How about if I fire you now and rehire you Monday morning? I hate to eat alone."

So do I, Tannis thought, but I don't have much choice. "Maybe some other time."

"When?"

Damn! He was persistent. He rose from the desk and walked around to stand before her. It wasn't often that she had to crane her neck to look at someone. At five foot eight, she found that even moderate heels put her at eye level with most men. Zachary stood several inches above her. There was a look on his face that said he wouldn't let her go until she gave him an answer. "I'll surprise you," she said.

A sensuous light flared in his eyes as he smiled. "Good. I like surprises."

"Have a nice weekend, Mr. Spencer." She turned to leave.

"You, too, Ms. Robbins." Was there a hint of irony in his voice?

On her way to the elevator, Tannis lectured herself to remember her reason for being there—to steal from the man, not to feel outrageous tingles at the touch of his fingers. How long had it been since a man had touched her? Not since Mark. And she remembered precisely the day that he had walked out of her life. Christmas. Over a year ago.

Had it really been that long? When the elevator arrived, she stepped into the car and sighed. Over a year since she'd been on a date. Not that there hadn't been invitations. She just hadn't been interested. The pain was too strong. And the thing that had chased Mark away was still there. Would always be there.

Stepping into the lobby, she passed the gray-haired security guard who took up his post every evening. He sat leaning back in his chair, his feet propped on a portable table, idly flipping pages in a sports magazine.

"Good evening," he called with a friendly smile as she passed.

"Good evening," Tannis returned, and pushed open the heavy glass door.

The late-winter night was clear and crisp, though chilling as Tannis crossed the asphalt to her car. When she pulled out of the parking lot, she cast one last glance at the building. Solid, like the man.

She'd learned some things about Zachary Spencer this week. The legendary intelligence was there. She'd seen it and been impressed by it. But there was more. She'd seen him powerful as he'd haggled over price with a parts supplier. Then in the next minute, she'd seen him unexpectedly sensitive as he'd stopped by the desk of a woman in the office who had just returned from an out-of-state trip to bury her grandmother.

More recently, in their brief encounter, she'd learned that he was meticulously guarded about his work. Not just with her, she suspected. Yet he entrusted the security of his building to an aging, friendly man who according to the rumor mill, spent most of his shift asleep.

She'd also learned that he wasn't accustomed to being told no. What would she do if he asked her to dinner again? She regretted she'd missed the opportunity to supply herself with a husband. Maybe she could invent a jealous boyfriend.

Again, she wished that they could have met under different circumstances. He was everything she looked for in a man. Intelligent, quick-witted, persevering, comfortable with himself and not hard to look at. Not hard at all. Yes, she'd learned a lot about him, she thought, remembering that large dark hand as it circled her wrist. And she'd learned something about Tannis Robbins, too. She could still be excited by a man.

Pondering that thought, she turned her car into the parking lot of her apartment building. Mark's leaving her had closed off emotions that she didn't think would ever open again. Zachary had done it with just a touch of fingertips. She found herself wondering what those strong, tanned fingers would feel like on other areas of her skin. An unwelcome shiver sped through her body at the absurdity. She was *not* going to get involved with Zachary Spencer, of that she was sure.

Zachary was having some unsettling feelings of his own as he opened a can of cat food and plopped it into a dish on the floor beside the kitchen table. Despite his last-ditch effort to make Tannis change her mind about having dinner with him, he was not eating alone.

Amber padded elegantly over to her dish and sniffed its contents experimentally.

"Don't be so picky," he said to the cat. "It's all you're getting."

Deciding he wasn't going to offer anything else, she dipped her whiskered face into the bowl.

"You're probably not going to like this, Amber, but I've decided that I'm more than casually interested in the new woman that I hired, and I'm not sure why."

It never occurred to Zachary that anyone witnessing the scene might find it odd that he talked to a cat. The habit was born of necessity. Since childhood, he'd found it easier to talk to animals than to humans. By now, of course, he'd learned how to communicate with just about anyone, but still preferred the silent companionship of his cat.

Most of the time. There were moments, usually late at night, when he longed for someone who wasn't intimidated by his extremely high IQ or by the fact that his thoughts raced as though they were played on a VCR that was stuck on fast forward. Rebecca hadn't been intimidated. She'd understood. But she had left to take a job in Silicon Valley, swearing that the distance from one coast to the other couldn't cool their relationship.

His precise memory called up with haunting clarity the day he'd helped her load her belongings from the apartment they'd shared into the U-Haul hooked behind her car. Although she'd smiled and promised to come back for a visit very soon, he'd known from the look in her eyes that she wouldn't.

Soon after that, the Wizac hit the market and success had seized him. Burying emotions to throw himself into his work, he'd stayed too busy to dwell on her. Fame and fortune had brought a steady stream of women. Plenty he'd spent the night with, but none he'd liked enough to bring to his own private castle.

Looking back, he doubted that he'd really loved Rebecca. He'd thought so at the time, but his analytical mind, so quick to unravel problems and puzzles, had a difficult time with emotions. And love, the most complicated of all feelings, had never really been mastered.

Zachary looked at his empty plate and realized that he hadn't tasted the food. With a weary sigh, he lifted his dishes and went to the sink to wash them, leaving distant thoughts of Rebecca for more vibrant ones of Tannis. He remembered the feel of her narrow wrist when he'd gripped it. He'd felt her pulse leap at his touch.

Asking her to dinner had been a spur of the moment decision. Though he'd been disappointed when she refused, he realized it was probably for the best. He'd always made a point of avoiding personal relationships with women who worked for him. Still, something about Tannis made him want to throw that policy out the window.

No, he decided as water from the kitchen faucet ran down the drain unheeded, it was better to ignore the attraction and concentrate on business.

Studies indicate that identical twins share far more than physical characteristics. Tannis had years ago accepted the fact that she could finish a sentence that Meredith had started. More than once, they'd gone off on separate shopping trips to come back with matching sweaters or identical pairs of shoes. High school and college had been a series of pranks that involved switching places. If one twin accepted a date then got a better offer for the same night, the other twin took her place with the first young man, and he'd been none the wiser.

It wasn't until they finished college that they ever really went in different directions. While Tannis had opted for the research end of computer science, Meredith had chosen a more practical application of her skills. A job with a major hotel chain had taken her to a remote South Pacific island to set up the systems at a new resort. It was the first lengthy separation the twins had ever experienced, but it was the final one. Meredith had returned to Boston comatose.

Yet even as her sister lay in the hospital bed unmoving, unspeaking, unaware of the world around her, Tannis sometimes felt an eerie sense of communion with Meredith. All through their lives neither twin had found it odd that they were able to send each other their thoughts and feelings mentally. On the contrary, they found it odd that no one else could do it.

It was this unusual bond that brought Tannis to Meredith's bedside every Sunday afternoon. And it was for this reason that she talked to her.

"Well, I've had one of my more eventful weeks," Tannis announced upon entering her sister's room. "I went for

Conway's ultimatum. I had to, didn't I? Just until I figure out something else to do."

She dragged a chair to the side of the bed and settled comfortably beside Meredith. "Zachary Spencer hired me as his personal assistant, and you know what? The killer is that this is a job that I'd really like to have."

Uncommonly restless, Tannis rose and paced the small room. "You should see the man, Meredith. He's gorgeous. Remember how we used to rate guys on a scale of one to ten? Zachary Spencer is an eleven."

When her circuit brought her to the bed again, she paused, resting her hands on the back of the chair. "He asked me out to dinner Friday night," she said softly. "And I wanted to go."

Moving to the side of the bed, she sat down and took her sister's hand, stroking it in silence for a long moment. "I really wanted to go," she whispered.

Minutes ticked by in the quiet room as Tannis sat with her sister, thinking of the lifetime they had shared. It never occurred to Tannis to resent the financial strain Meredith's condition had imposed on her. It was simply a fact that she had to take care of her. And while it may have been a burden, she'd never for a moment regretted the choices she had made in the past two years.

Sure, it had cost her the relationship with Mark, but Tannis firmly believed that she was better off without him. Yet the rejection had hurt. Still clasping Meredith's hand, her thoughts drifted back to Zachary and the powerful attraction she felt. And the danger pursuing that attraction could cause her. She could not afford to become emotionally involved with the man she'd been sent to spy on. Could she?

Go for it, Tannis.

The message came to her so forcefully that she jerked her head up with a start. "Meredith?" she questioned in a trembling voice.

But her sister remained silent. Still pale, still unmoving, still deeply asleep. Shivers started at the base of Tannis's spine and accelerated as they traveled up her neck, "Meredith? Are you trying to tell me something?"

Though Tannis sat for what seemed like hours, staring at her sister, gripping her hand until trickles of sweat dampened both of their palms, nothing else came to her. Finally, she bent to kiss Meredith's cheek and started off down the hall to find Dr. Moore.

Just outside his office, she saw him, holding a medical chart as he spoke with a nurse. He looked up when he heard Tannis approaching and smiled. "I was just coming to look for you, Tannis."

A cursory glance at her too-pale face alerted him to her distress. "Go on in my office." He waved a hand at the open door. "I'll be right there."

Clutter. Framed medical degrees. Citations from various organizations for service to the community. Pictures of grandchildren in different stages of growth. Tannis had sat in this office numerous times over the past two years. Always, she absorbed every detail of Dr. Moore's wisdom. Always, she pleaded for some hope that Meredith would regain consciousness. Always, she exhibited unwavering faith.

Dr. Moore entered and eased his plump body into the chair behind the desk. "Still worried about your finances, Tannis?"

"No, that isn't a problem. I've changed jobs." Resting her elbows on the arms of the chair, Tannis laced her fingers together. "Do you know much about identical twins?"

"A single fertilized egg splits to form two embryos, identical in genetic structure. The subject of many fascinating studies."

"Yes." Tannis nodded. "You know, Meredith and I used to be able to communicate without speaking. Oh, nothing sophisticated. Just a brief thought or feeling. Sometimes a picture. It wasn't anything we could consciously control. It just happened sometimes. Especially if one of us was in a highly emotional situation.''

Dr. Moore dipped his hands into the pockets of his white coat and tilted back in his chair. "I've read about it."

Swallowing nervously, Tannis tightened her interlocked fingers. "It happened just now. I felt that Meredith was sending me a message."

Displaying neither skepticism nor belief, Dr. Moore leaned forward. "Tell me about it."

Without embarrassment, Tannis described her conflicting feelings about her dinner invitation from her new employer and related the mysterious sensation she'd experienced while sitting on Meredith's bed.

"Could it have been your subconscious telling you what to do?"

"Yes, of course, it could have." Tannis moved in her chair, crossing one leg over the other. "Or it could have been a message from Meredith."

"And you say this happened often when she was well?"

"The night before Meredith's supervisor called me to tell me that she was ill, I was very sick. I had shivers so powerful that my bed shook, followed by flashes of heat that left my bedcovers wringing wet. I didn't have the strength to get up and look for the thermometer, but I know that my temperature was extremely high." She paused, watching the reaction on the doctor's face. "The next morning I was fine."

"Twenty-four hour virus?" Dr. Moore suggested.

"Maybe. I thought so, too, at first. But maybe I was experiencing the symptoms of the tropical disease that gripped Meredith."

A lifetime of understanding the unique relationship she shared with her twin afforded Tannis the patience she needed to explain the import of what she was feeling. "The point is, Dr. Moore, that if Meredith is capable of communicating with me, then she must be alert and aware of what's happening around her. Maybe it was just my own optimism. But if it truly was Meredith's thought that I picked up, then she hears and understands everything I say to her."

Losing the control that had kept her emotions in check, Tannis shouted, "I've got to find a way to wake her up!"

Dr. Moore removed his glasses and ran a gnarled hand over his face. "As chief of staff here, my main objective is to see that all of the patients are comfortable and well cared for. I know a little bit about a lot of areas of medicine, and not very much about brain damage. Do you want to call in a neurosurgeon?"

He believed her! Tannis's eyes brightened. "Then you think this means something?"

"I don't know." He sighed wearily. "We've had her examined by specialists, and they say nothing can be done."

"But if there's a chance at all that her condition has changed, I have to do whatever I can."

Dr. Moore ran a hand across his tired eyes before repositioning the plastic frames of his glasses. "I have contacts at various hospitals in the area. I'll see who they recommend and set up a meeting for you."

Reaching across the desk, Tannis took his hands in hers. "Thank you, Dr. Moore. Thank you for not laughing at me. Is there anything else we can do?"

"I don't want to give you false hope, but if you think she hears you, then we'll do whatever we can to find out. Keep talking to her."

Tannis did. For the remainder of the afternoon, she sat beside Meredith, relating the conversation with Dr. Moore, desperately hoping to receive another message. But just as when they had tried to force the telepathy in their youth, nothing else came.

* * *

"What do you mean 'nothing'?" Richard Conway's voice raged across the phone wires. "I want some results, and I want them soon!"

Tannis took a deep breath, trying to quell the fury that this disgusting man stirred in her. The phone had rung almost the minute that she got home from Greenbriar, and she was in no emotional condition to deal with Conway's lunatic rantings. "Mr. Conway, I have explained that I haven't yet had the chance to look for anything. I only got computer access late Friday. You want me to be discreet, don't you? If Zachary catches me, it won't take him five minutes to figure out I work for you."

"Zachary? You're on a first-name basis with him?"

Tannis screwed her eyes shut and tried not to scream. She forced her voice to quiet. "Everyone calls him Zachary."

"That's good. Maybe you should be extra 'friendly' to him. A woman like you shouldn't have any trouble luring him to confide in you."

"A woman like me shouldn't be doing this at all!" she snapped, unable to control her quick flare of temper.

"Do I have to remind you of your motivation?"

"No," she said quietly. "You don't. It never leaves my mind for a moment."

"Then you will get something for me this week?"

"I'll try." Tannis sighed wearily and rubbed at a knot of tension in her neck. "Have you given any thought to how you're going to get me out of this when it's over?"

An evil-sounding chuckle came across the wire. "If this works out, maybe I'll just leave you there indefinitely."

At the sound of the abrupt click, Tannis slammed her own receiver down with a bang. "Sleazy weasel!"

Tannis would do anything to insure Meredith's welfare. But to stay indefinitely at Wizac Electronics? That would never work. Zachary Spencer was no fool. Sooner or later, he'd put it together. Probably sooner.

Now she had new expenses to consider. What if this neurosurgeon found some correctable condition and she didn't have the funds to pay for treatment? That would be almost as bad as giving up on Meredith completely.

By Friday of the second week at Wizac, Tannis's mind was brimming with ideas for the prealgebra project. In conference with Zachary that morning, she'd explained her objectives and been pleased that he'd seemed impressed with her thoughts. Despite the fact that she knew she wouldn't be around to finish the program, it was a matter of professional pride that she do a good job while she was there.

When the noon hour approached, Delilah's assistant, Karen, a young petite blonde, stopped at Tannis's desk. "A bunch of us usually have lunch at Kelsey's on Friday. It's just down the street. Want to join us?"

Not wishing to explain that she brought her lunch from home because the cost of eating out was not in her budget, Tannis smiled appreciatively. "Thanks, but I'm in the middle of something. I'll just eat a sandwich at my desk."

"Okay, but you don't have to do that. The Wizard isn't a slave driver."

"I know." Tannis found it amusing but apt that Zachary's employees referred to him as the Wizard. To most of them, she supposed he was part intellect, part mystic. "It's just that I don't want to lose my train of thought. Maybe next time."

Although it was a plausible-enough excuse, Tannis's intention was to seize the opportunity when the office was quiet to look through the papers on Zachary's desk. In his last phone call, Conway had increased the pressure, and Tannis knew she had to give him something.

When the office was empty, she waited a few minutes before embarking on her amateur espionage. Even those who brought their lunch with them went to the coffee room down the hall to eat, but she knew that someone could return at any moment. She had concocted an excuse in case that

happened while she was snooping. Cautiously she pushed
back her chair and went across the carpet to Zachary's desk,
dropping the piece of paper that was to be her protection on
the floor.

Affixed to his terminal were notes in Zachary's hand-
writing. *Brian's birthday Sunday,* one read, and *Pick up cat
food,* said another. Tannis felt a twinge of guilt as she
stepped behind the desk. Only Conway's malicious insistence urged her to disturb the papers. She knew Zachary
didn't want his work touched. She also knew he was likely
to notice if anything was moved even a fraction of an inch.

Carefully and thoroughly, Tannis went through the papers, wishing she could see the elevator doors from her position. The longer she stayed there, the faster her heart beat.
She didn't like it, didn't want to find anything, didn't want
to tell Conway if she did. But she had no choice. He was
getting anxious. If she didn't give him some morsel of information, no matter how trivial, he was likely to exert even
more pressure. She had to give him something to keep him
satisfied until she figured out another solution to this di-
lemma.

Finding nothing more exciting than sales reports and
marketing projections, she reached for a folder labeled
NASA. Just as she picked it up, a loud noise startled her,
causing her to drop the folder, spilling its contents on the
floor. She looked around the room, her heart in her throat,
then breathed a long sigh of relief when she realized it had
been the sound of the minirefrigerator's compressor kick-
ing on.

Paranoid! she blasted herself as she stooped to pick up the
papers. Glancing at them as she replaced them in the folder,
she quickly ascertained that Wizac had opted not to bid on
NASA's latest project. Her spirits lifted. That was information that Conway would relish, yet it wouldn't hurt
Zachary if she divulged it.

Conway Electronics had provided computers for several space projects. If Conway knew he didn't have to compete with Wizac on this tender, he'd feel better about his own bid. And since Zachary didn't want the government contract anyway, where was the harm?

Smiling to herself because she'd found at least a temporary reprieve, she reached for another stack of notes.

"What are you doing?"

Stunned, Tannis looked up and felt the blood draining from her face. Of all the people who could have walked in, why did it have to be her? "Delilah! You startled me. I thought everyone was gone."

"Obviously." The woman folded her arms across her chest and favored Tannis with an accusing stare. "I had a headache so I decided to come back. What are you doing at Zach's desk?"

Had Delilah come back to check on her? Tannis wondered. She'd certainly moved stealthily enough. Tannis made her voice sound casual. "I took notes when we were talking this morning. One page is missing. I thought it might have gotten mixed up with some of his papers."

"You'll just have to wait until he comes back. Nobody touches Zachary's desk."

"Oh, sure." Tannis moved around the corner of the desk. "Never mind. Here it is." She bent to retrieve the paper she'd planted earlier.

"What is it?" Delilah took the page from Tannis's hand.

"Really, Delilah, it's just a bunch of notes about the commutative, transitive and associative properties of positive and negative integers," Tannis explained lightly, certain the secretary would have no idea what she was talking about. "You'd think I was stealing plans for a spy satellite to sell to the Soviets."

Delilah handed the paper back. "Stay out of Zach's office."

Tannis fought down her quick temper. She knew she could not afford to further antagonize this woman, especially if she was already suspicious. She pasted on a friendly smile. "Sure."

Back at her desk, Tannis tried to ignore the nagging fear that she would be found out. Before long she was once again absorbed in her work.

Late in the afternoon, as she was sorting her papers into file folders, Zachary burst out of his office and sailed past her desk. "I have to go out for a minute," he announced without stopping. "Stay here until I get back." He stopped at the elevator and added, "Please."

Tannis had time only to nod her assent before the elevator doors closed and swallowed him, leaving her with the image of him standing tall and confident. Now what? she wondered as she remembered the way his emerald-green sweater had hugged his muscles as he moved. She busied herself with organizing her notes and tried not to think about him.

In about thirty minutes he was back, grinning. Everyone else on the floor had left. "Oh, good," he said. "You waited."

"You told me to wait," Tannis replied, trying to interpret the strange expression on his face. "Why?"

His gaze was locked on hers as he crossed the room. "I told you that I like surprises. I'm surprising you."

The cherry-tobacco scent assaulted her as he walked closer. "I thought I was going to surprise you."

"That's what you said." He stopped an arm's length away and studied her for a moment. "But I had the feeling that I would be waiting for quite a long time, so I took the initiative myself."

In the instant it took to calm her heart rate, Tannis lost herself in his eyes. Not dinner again, she hoped. She wasn't sure she would have the will to say no again. Dinner would lead to after dinner. And after dinner was a dangerous thought with this man, the man she had to betray in order to survive. She looked at him warily. "What's the surprise?"

"Ah, but that's the appeal of a surprise, isn't it? Let's go."

The inviting smile on his face pulled at her, but she resisted. "Dinner?"

"No, not dinner. It's business mostly."

"Mostly?"

"What are you afraid of, Tannis?"

He'd never called her by her first name before. She didn't want to like the sound of it in his deep masculine voice, but she did. She kept her eyes steady. "I don't want to get involved."

"Fair enough. I do have business in mind, but if you want to wait until Monday, that's fine. Never let it be said that the Wizard coerces his female employees into after-hours activities."

She couldn't help smiling. "You know that they call you the Wizard?"

He shrugged, as if the name made little difference to him. "Your choice. Now or Monday."

A small voice in the back of her mind whispered, "Go for it, Tannis." It was Meredith's message. Zachary noted the moment she ceased to struggle and led her toward the elevator.

"Wait a minute." He stopped suddenly. "I have to tell Avery where I am."

He moved to the nearest desk, picked up the phone and pushed some buttons. "Avery, I'll be in the garden for a while. Ms. Robbins is with me." He paused while the guard replied. From the look on Zachary's face, Tannis guessed that the comment was speculative at best, and graphic at worst. "In your dreams, Avery. Go back to your reading."

"You also know that your security guard reads magazines on the job?"

He dropped the phone to its cradle and came back to her. "Nothing goes on here that I don't know about." Taking her hand, he again steered her to the elevator. "Avery's mostly for show. There's nothing here worth taking except some expensive machines, and they're insured."

The pressure of his large hand around hers was doing extensive damage to her carefully composed reserve. In a rush of protectiveness, Tannis suddenly felt the urge to warn him. "Aren't you concerned that some rival company might try to steal your plans for upcoming projects?"

"Not really." He pushed the button to summon the car. "The terminals in my office and home are the only ones that have access to the R and D division. Anyone who gets in would be met by an intricate web of codes and passwords. If someone gets close enough and hits the wrong keys, the entire system shuts down and alerts me at home."

"That's fascinating," Tannis murmured, thinking she could forget about trying to hack.

"My R and D lab is on a floor that isn't accessible from the main lobby elevators. There's a computer guarding the door that requires a number code, fingerprint ID and voice verification."

Quietly impressed, Tannis compared that to the R and D division at Conway that required only a plastic ID card to gain entrance. "Sounds like something from a high-budget science-fiction film."

Zachary smiled. "Thank you. I'm not so naive as to believe the system is impenetrable. I did some hacking myself in my younger days, but I do think I've made it damned difficult."

When the doors opened, he ushered her into the car, pulled a large gold key from his pocket and inserted it into the control panel. Tannis stared in wide-eyed amazement, remembering he'd said something to Avery about a garden. "Where are we going?"

"Someplace very special," Zachary replied, smiling.

Alarms sounded in her mind. "Not your bachelor lair, I hope."

"Lair?" Thick blond eyebrows arched in surprise. "Do I have the reputation of a swinging playboy?"

Tannis considered that he had no reputation at all. Though Conway's dossier had described Zachary's career history in detail, there had been no information about his personal life. Suddenly she was aware of the motion of the car. "We're going up!"

"The only way to get to the roof."

Before she could react to that, the elevator stopped. Still holding her hand, Zachary led her down the hallway to a small unmarked door. He fished another key from his pocket and opened the door to reveal a dimly lit, narrow stairway. In complete faith, Tannis followed him to another door at the top of the stairs.

"For some reason I feel compelled to tell you that I've never brought another woman up here. Do you believe that?"

"I guess it depends on what's on the other side of the door."

"I guess it does." He twisted the knob and pushed open the portal.

Chapter Three

Whatever her hazy mind had imagined was nothing compared to the sights and scents that assailed her. It was a forest! Zachary beamed at the wonder on her face as she took small steps forward.

No, not a forest. Under closer scrutiny, she corrected her initial impression. A greenhouse. Through the jungle of leaves and blossoms, Tannis could make out windows, shaded a smoky gray to diffuse the sunlight on the more delicate plants.

Zachary urged her down a narrow aisle lined with rosé bushes, neanthe bella palms, dieffenbachia, ficus benjamina. A burst of colors came from potted begonias, geraniums and azaleas. At the end of the walk, they came to a wall of glass that looked out on the twinkling skyline of Boston.

Beside the window two chairs of natural rattan flanked a matching table set with fine china on a cloth of dusty rose. A bottle of wine stood on the table between two crystal goblets. A wicker basket of fruit and a variety of cheeses under a glass dome sat waiting. The table was framed by sculpted gardenia bushes, heavy with fragrant white blossoms. Tannis thought she must be in fairyland. It was like a breath of spring in the middle of winter.

Breaking free of Zachary's grasp, Tannis went near the glass and gazed out at the twilight. Below them a city bustled. Traffic moved. Lights flashed. People came and went. Here, in this tranquil arbor, the sounds, the smells, the demands of the city seemed a galaxy away. She understood why he needed this spot, understood why he didn't share it. What she didn't understand was why he had brought her here, and what she was going to do about it.

When she turned, her blue eyes sparkling, he held a long-stemmed rose of a blood-red color in his slender fingers. He extended the blossom. Barely managing to master the tremble in her hand, she accepted the gift. Lifting it to her face, she breathed in the bouquet.

The simple movement pleased Zachary immensely. In contrast to the strong, determined exterior that she presented, there was a soft, vulnerable woman just below the surface. He felt the tightening in his stomach again and made a silent vow to bring that woman to the forefront and keep her there.

Stepping behind the chair, he held it out for her. "Sit down."

Cautiously Tannis moved to the chair and took a seat. "You said it wasn't dinner."

"It isn't. At least *I* don't consider wine and cheese and fruit dinner."

She watched his long form fold into the chair opposite her. "But it isn't business, either."

"I said mostly." He lifted the uncorked wine bottle and filled both glasses. "Remember when I hired you, I said it was for a two-week trial period? I thought you might want to know that I'm satisfied with the arrangement if you are.

If we're going to work together on bigger projects, we should get to know each other better, don't you think?''

Tannis didn't want to get to know him better. She already liked what she saw far more than was comfortable. And she definitely didn't want him to know more about her. "I suppose."

"I have constant interruptions in the office, but here there's no phone and no terminal, so I thought this would be a pleasant place to talk." He lowered his glass to the table. "The rose, I'll confess, was entirely personal. Growing flowers is kind of a hobby of mine."

That surprised her. Somehow she couldn't picture the computer wizard knee-deep in mulch and fertilizer. Gripping her own goblet by its crystal stem, Tannis fought to keep from squirming under Zachary's penetrating gaze. This was a mistake. She couldn't play this role when his eyes were so uncommonly green, his lips so incredibly inviting, his expression so undeniably seductive. "Mr. Spencer..."

"Zachary," he corrected. "You don't call a man who has just given you a rose 'mister.'"

"I guess you don't," she said thoughtfully, staring at the flower that she still clutched in her hand. Mark had never given her roses or any other kind of flowers, for that matter. He'd termed it a waste of money to pay for something that was only going to wilt and die in a few days. At the time she'd thought it was practical. Now she saw it as cheap. But she knew Mark's true colors now, she thought with a wry smile.

"Tannis?"

Abruptly she raised her eyes back to Zachary's look of concern.

"Where did you go?"

"I'm sorry. I was just thinking that a man's never given me a rose before."

"Really? I'd have thought you have scores of suitors lined up outside your door, each with at least a dozen long-stemmed."

She gave a self-mocking laugh. "Hardly."

Zachary noted the way her hair caught the light, and he wanted to touch it. He noted the way her skin tightened across her throat when she tilted her chin, and he wanted to stroke it. He noted the way her mouth formed a perfect curve when she smiled, and he wanted to kiss it. "In that case, I'm glad I'm the first."

Unable to hold his gaze any longer, Tannis lowered her eyes to the wineglass and drank deeply. Zachary sensed her discomfort and turned his attention to the food before them. Picking up a small paring knife, he selected an apple from the basket and peeled and sliced it. Then he lifted the glass lid that covered the slices of cheese and offered it to her.

"I'll also confess that I find you a bit of a puzzle," he said.

Somehow she found the courage to meet his eyes again. "Is that good or bad?"

"Well," he said with a grin, "I'm working on it." He plucked another apple from the basket and began to peel it for himself. "You may have heard that I have a rather analytical mind."

"It's been rumored."

"That can be either a blessing or a curse, depending on the problem that's being analyzed. For the last two weeks, it's been a curse."

A slice of cheese halted halfway to Tannis's mouth. "Are you implying that I'm a problem?"

"Not an unpleasant one. But a problem just the same."

An icy finger of fear trailed up Tannis's spine. Had he found her out already? She lowered the cheese to her plate and swallowed against the dryness that closed her throat. "Why?"

"There it is right there. That trace of panic in your eyes. I've tried to reason it out for several nights. I don't understand why, but every now and then, I get the impression that you're afraid of me."

"I'm not afraid of you, Zachary." Anything but, she added to herself. "If I'm afraid of anything, it's myself." She took another deep drink of wine, hoping for its numbing warmth to speed through her system and deaden her response to those polished jade eyes.

"What's lurking inside Tannis to make her afraid of herself?" Zachary pressed gently.

"Secrets. Tannis is filled with secrets."

Zachary lifted the bottle and poured more of the rich red wine into her glass. "And is she going to reveal them?"

"No."

Round one to Tannis, he thought. He picked up a tangerine, peeled it and offered it to her. She took it, unavoidably brushing his fingers with hers. "I've never been able to walk away from an unfinished puzzle. Sooner or later, I'll solve the mystery."

She lifted her long dark lashes in surprise. "There's nothing mysterious about me."

"There's everything mysterious about you. You're a study in contrasts. You stiffen your shoulders as if they carry the weight of the world, yet your eyes at times reveal a fragile vulnerability. You're far more intelligent than most people, yet at times there's an appealing naïveté about you."

In a far softer tone, he continued. "You have a body that's made for flowing silk, but you shroud it in defeminizing career-woman clothes."

"How else should I dress in the office?" she said lightly, but his words struck her emotionally. There were times— dark, lonely times—when she longed for a few luxuries. But her undying devotion to Meredith kept her barely one step ahead of her creditors.

She discounted most of his observations and focused on the safest one. "How do you know that I'm intelligent?"

He slid his empty plate to the side and refilled both wineglasses. "Because I recognize it. And value it."

"Most of the men I meet like women a bit dumb."

New insight swept Zachary. Here was at least one of her secrets. A less intelligent man might feel his ego threatened by her. It was something Zachary had never considered because the situation was foreign to him. He'd never known a woman—or man, either—more intelligent than he. It wasn't something he flaunted. It was simply true. "Only an insecure man would prefer a less intelligent woman."

"I've always felt that way, but I haven't ever met a man who did." Her admiration for him grew by leaps and bounds. For a moment Tannis forgot her true reason for being there and concentrated on the intriguing man before her. "Tell me more of Zachary's secrets."

He caught the change from defensive to curious. His responsive smile was slow and easy. "Zachary has no secrets."

"Then tell me his dreams."

Lifting his wineglass, he sipped slowly, shifting his gaze to the window. What dreams? He'd always had goals and dreams, but lately it seemed he'd lost sight of them. Most of his personal projects had sat idle for months. The need to create, the inborn drive, the constant questioning were lacking.

He turned to face her, meeting her expectant, vibrant gaze. Something in her expression made him want to share. Considering for only a microsecond, he decided to reveal the private plan that only one other person had gleaned from him. "I'm working on artificial intelligence."

"AI?" Delicate brows arched over vivid blue eyes. "In what capacity?"

"I don't know yet. Right now I'm still debugging the language problems. I've refined a voice synthesizer, but many of the words are hard to define clearly."

"You talk to it?"

Zachary smiled, amused by the combination of admiration and amazement on her face. "And she talks to me."

"Something like C-3PO in *Star Wars*?"

"More like HAL in *2001.*"

Tannis was awed. Even as much as she knew about computers, what he had in mind was beyond comprehension. It was a formidable task that had been tackled by the best for decades. "Do you think it's possible?"

"Anything's possible." His eyes darkened as he lost himself in the dream. "Just as there's so much that we don't know about the human brain, there's an endless supply of possibilities for the computer that are yet to be tapped. It's more than an instrument for data processing. There's so much we're only beginning to discover."

It was impossible not to catch his enthusiasm. Although she might hate herself for asking, Tannis knew that the question was for herself and not for Conway. "Is that what you have locked away on the R and D floor? A talking computer?"

"No, it's just something I tinker with at home. R and D's working on a blockbuster toy for Christmas." But he smiled to himself because he knew there was nothing exciting on the drawing board. "A Sorceress to go with the Wizac Storyteller."

In spite of her admiration for the man, Tannis couldn't hide her dislike for the doll. It was a white-haired, kindly old man who wore a purple cape spangled with silver stars and crescent moons. Perched on his head was a pointed wizard's hat. In one hand he held a magic wand with which he gestured as he told a story by magnetic tape that synchronized his movements. Incredibly, the expression on his face changed as he spoke.

"Every wizard needs a beautiful sorceress at his side." Zachary noted the disapproval in her eyes and the slight wrinkling around her nose. "You don't like the Story-teller."

"Not especially."

"Tell me why." Sensing her hesitation, he added, "I can assure you I've heard every criticism."

"It strikes me as a trendy toy for status-conscious parents who don't want to be bothered with reading a story to their children. 'Here, honey,'" she mimicked, "'stick a tape in the Storyteller so little Zachary will leave us alone, and pass the tofu.'"

"Yes, I've heard that one." Zachary nodded. "What about the child whose parents aren't going to read him a story anyway? Consider the hours of entertainment he will derive from the Storyteller. Concede that it's an improvement over run-of-the mill cartoons."

"Not counting Disney?"

"Ah, Disney." His eyes took on a dreamy look. "The father of audio animatronics. My hero."

Tannis laughed. "Excluding Disney, I'll concede an edge over cartoons."

She'd not laughed—really laughed—in his presence before this. Zachary found it a delightful sound that reminded him of crystal wind chimes on a fresh spring zephyr. He wanted to hear it again and often.

"I like you, Tannis," he admitted spontaneously. "Because I do, I'll tell you why I created the Storyteller."

Again, Tannis felt an urge to warn him. "Zachary, are you sure you should be telling me these secrets?"

"What are you going to do? Run back to Conway and sell him my plans?"

Tannis froze at his words, although she realized he was joking. "Some people would."

"Perhaps, but I think I'll go with gut instinct and believe that you won't betray my confidence." A sparkle of humor lit his eyes. "Besides, if you told anyone about the AI project, he'd just shake his head and mumble about the Wizard going off the deep end. The reason I created the Storyteller is not a secret. I just haven't made it public knowledge because publicity can be harmful to children."

Children? Zachary had children? That wasn't in the dossier. A small frown puckered her brow. Who was their mother?

Relaxing, he settled back in his chair and crossed one leg over the other, ankle against knee, steepling his hands together at the fingertips. "I have two nephews. My brother is Pete Spencer."

"The baseball player?" Tannis leaned forward in anticipation. "The baseball in your office!"

"Pete pitched it in a World Series game." He smiled at the childlike enthusiasm on her face. "You're a fan?"

"My father was. In our house a person didn't have any choice. I could probably still recite Pete's stats from every season he played." The light faded from her eyes as she recalled the rest of it. Gambling debts, drug deals, a messy divorce, expulsion from the league. She thought there had been a jail term as well. "Where is he now?"

"I haven't seen or heard from him in over a year." Rising, he walked to the wall of glass and studied Boston. "He breezed into town, harassed his ex-wife, Sylvia, frightened the boys and asked me for ten thousand dollars to get him to Vegas. He had a surefire tip that couldn't lose."

Tannis watched him rake a large hand through his hair, then square his shoulders. She guessed that he hadn't intended to tell her this part, but it was something she could understand. He had a deep-rooted sense of obligation to his family. She knew that feeling well. She debated for a second, then moved to stand beside him, looking at the diamond brilliance of the city lights. "You gave it to him."

"He's my brother," Zachary said almost apologetically. "How could I not?"

She understood. Good Lord, how she understood! She slipped her small hand into his. "You take care of his ex-wife and sons."

"As much as Sylvia will let me." He brushed the back of her hand with his thumb, but still stared out the window. "She tries very hard to make it on her own."

Tannis turned to study the square, firm line of his jaw. This might be—quite possibly could be—a man who would understand her obligation to Meredith. And her sole purpose for being here, she realized with a painful twist of irony, was to cheat him. "You created the Wizac Storyteller for your nephews?"

"Brian and Justin. A few years ago, Brian had hepatitis. Sylvia was working full-time and trying to finish college. She had dropped out to marry Pete. Justin was about five then. He's a handful under the best conditions."

Finally he turned, and in his eyes she could see the depth of his love for his nephews. "Brian's medication kept him awake most of the night. Sylvia was about to collapse from the pressure and fatigue, so I made the Storyteller to keep him entertained while Sylvia slept."

Tannis smiled into his eyes. "I just raised my opinion of the Storyteller."

"You have some experience with children?"

"No, but I have some experience with pressure and fatigue. I'm for anything that relieves it."

Pressure and fatigue. He'd seen them both on her face, more at other times than tonight. Tonight—a few times—she'd dropped her guard and softened her eyes. Like now. Now, when she'd placed her hand voluntarily in his. Earlier, he'd had to take it. His fingers curled around hers. "What about Tannis?" he asked gently. "What are her dreams?"

She turned back to the window. Dreams. Before Meredith's illness, she'd had plenty of them. Marriage. Family. She'd thought those were still attainable until Mark's bitter words had dashed her hopes. Life's cruel awakening had forced her to make a more practical choice. Now her dream was singular and necessary. "Survival."

"That's all?" Zachary asked with surprise. "Just to survive? I'd have thought you'd at least say career success or financial gain."

"All means to the same end. Survival. Keeping the wolves away from the door."

She had the grace and carriage of good breeding. It didn't seem that she was the type who had ever worried about her next meal. Yet she had been anxious enough to get the job to take the risk of hacking into his system to get his attention. So far, she'd completed every task, no matter how trivial, without complaint. Zachary had the feeling that she would give her best to any chore.

Her eyes looked out on the nightscape, but he knew she didn't see it. She focused instead on some inner vision that haunted her. In a surge of protectiveness, he longed to take that sadness from her eyes. "I want to kiss you."

As Tannis turned to him, her eyes widened and darkened. Her breath suddenly seemed heavy. "No," she whispered.

"Yes."

Tannis saw his mouth move toward hers, but hadn't the will to dodge it. His thick blond lashes swept down as his lips touched hers.

It was a slow, gentle kiss. Not exploratory. Not demanding. Just a warm pressing of mouth against mouth. But it lit fires within Tannis that had needed only this touch for fuel. It had been a long time—a lonely time—since she'd allowed herself this pleasure. Instinctively her fingers tightened in his grasp.

With infinite subtlety he parted his lips and caressed her mouth. It was every bit as soft and giving as he'd imagined. Drawing in his breath, he drew in also the subtle scent of her. She wore no expensive perfume. She needed no feminine trappings to allure. Carefully, because he knew she was far more fragile than she permitted even herself to believe, he traced the inside of her lower lip with the tip of his tongue.

Shivers darted through her body. She drew his tongue into her mouth and entwined it with her own. He tasted of wine and, faintly, cherry tobacco. She drank her fill and gave back of herself. Somewhere on the edge of reason, she knew she could not, should not do this. Sanity took control, and she pulled her lips away. Just the clasp of hands remained to bind them.

"I shouldn't do this," she murmured.

Zachary raised his free hand to touch her hair. It was thick and silky, just as he'd guessed. "You should. You do it so well."

As his fingers slid beneath the bun of auburn tresses to cup her neck, she forced her thoughts to center on her assignment to deceive him. "I can't," she said forcefully.

His eyes were so intent, she felt as though she were being searched by a scanner. "Two words I wish you'd lose from your vocabulary: *shouldn't* and *can't*. You use them far too frequently."

"There are so many things you don't know about me."

"I listen well."

Not to the words she had to say. No man would listen well to a confession that she had been sent to destroy him, no matter how strong the obligations that had led her into it. "Maybe some other time." Her voice was soft with regret. "I think I should go home."

Making no attempt to mask his disappointment, Zachary pulled away the hand that caressed her neck, but kept a firm clasp on her with the other one. "There will be another time, Tannis. I haven't solved you yet."

"Maybe you never will."

"If I don't," he said with complete seriousness in his eyes, "it will be the first time I've left a puzzle undone."

Stepping to the table, he picked up the rose and gave it to her. Still holding her hand, he led her down the verdant aisle and the narrow stairs. In the elevator he inserted the key and pushed the button for the lobby. "I'll walk you to your car."

"You don't have to do that."

His eyes narrowed as he assessed her. "Why do you have such a hard time accepting kindness from me?"

Because it makes it that much harder to betray you, she thought. "I guess because I haven't had a lot of kindness in my life for a long time."

As the doors slid open on the lobby, Zachary decided that he intended to correct that situation immediately. They both smiled as they approached the guard station. A sleeping Avery leaned back in his chair, his magazine spread across his wide paunch. His snowy eyebrows jumped up and down as he snored.

"I hate to wake him," Zachary said, "but I left my keys to the front door in my office."

With a gentle hand he shook the old man's shoulder. "Avery, wake up. There's a band of ruthless marauders at the door."

Avery's feet hit the floor with a thud. He came up from his chair in an instant. "Zach! You startled me, boy! What in tarnation's going on?"

Zach? Boy? Tannis felt her eyes widen. What exactly was this all about?

"Unlock the door for me. I left my keys upstairs."

"Shoulda brought 'em with ya," Avery grumbled. Then his gaze fell on Tannis, and it was his eyes that widened. "Oh."

Avery pulled a set of keys from his pocket while the trio headed for the door. "Leave it open," Zachary instructed. "I'll be back in a minute."

"Yup," Avery acknowledged, then smiled at Tannis.

"What sort of electronics wizard lets his security guard call him boy?" Tannis asked as soon as they were outside.

"I've known Avery since I was in diapers." Zachary smiled affectionately. "He used to live next door to us. That's the guy who taught Pete Spencer how to throw a curve ball."

This man was full of surprises, Tannis thought. Every one of them more pleasant than the last. But every one of them was drawing her deeper and deeper into turmoil. "And what did he teach Pete's brother?"

A boyish grin brought the dimples to his cheeks. "How to kiss a girl."

They walked in silence across the asphalt parking lot, hands still laced together, while Tannis digested that last morsel of information. "Well," she said at last. "He did a good job."

When they reached her car, Tannis pulled the keys from the pocket of her coat and opened the door, then turned to him. "Good night, Zachary."

The moment their eyes met, she knew he wasn't letting her go that easily. His arms slid around her and drew her close to his chest.

Tilting his head, he found her mouth, seeking her warmth, exploiting her softness, drinking her moistness. Needs ripped through him, setting nerve endings on fire. The tightening in his stomach returned with immeasurable force. He wanted this woman, if only to discover her secrets.

Tannis knew she should back away even as she was drawn closer to him. As her hands clutched the thick knit of his sweater, she felt the rose petal brush against her cheek. A thorn pricked her thumb. She didn't feel it. She shivered, but not from February's chill.

Zachary drew his mouth away, but kept her locked in his embrace, searching her eyes, trying to find a way to get inside the dark secrets of her soul. He found no access. "Sunday is Brian's birthday. Go with me to the party."

Sunday. Any day but Sunday. Tannis would have given anything to go with him, to revel in the love of family that she missed so much, to see yet another side of this remarkable man. But not on Sunday. She had a meeting at Greenbriar with a brain specialist. "I can't."

His brow knotted in a frown. "I'm sorry. I realize that you must have reservations about socializing with the man who signs your paycheck, but I sense an uncommon attraction that I'd like to explore. Does that make you feel threatened?"

Tannis had to take a step back and examine the situation. She was playing one role for Zachary and another one for Conway, neither of which was real. She didn't want to get closer to Zachary because she knew there was no future in it, not because he was her employer. But she couldn't tell him that. Maybe it was easier to let him think his assumption was correct. "It's something to consider. I like this job, and I want to keep it, but not at the expense of professional ethics for you or for me."

He accepted that. Temporarily. But he promised himself that he'd find a way around the employment relationship because this woman had brought to life a part of him that had been too long dormant. "All right." Slowly he loosened his arms to release her. "I'll respect that, but I'll also work on a way to resolve it."

Tannis had to smile. Absolutely nothing thwarted the man once he had his mind set on an objective. Zachary stood near the car as she got in, watching her movements. After securing her seat belt across her lap, she looked back up at him. "How old is Brain going to be on Sunday?"

"Twelve." He looked at her curiously. "Why?"

Both understanding and amusement twinkled in her eyes. "Is he having some problems with prealgebra?"

An acknowledging grin eased across his face. "A bit."

"It will take months to finish the software. School will be out."

"I know. He isn't going to fail. I just want him to have a better grasp before he moves on."

"You're an unusual person, Zachary Spencer."

"Yeah." He shoved his hands into his pockets, still grinning. "That's what they've been telling me since kindergarten."

Without another word, Tannis slammed the door and drove away. Zachary stood watching her go, staring at the car as it disappeared. The combination of letters and numbers on her license plate were etched in his mind. It wasn't that he wanted to commit them to memory. It was just that having seen them, they would stay. He didn't question it. It just was.

Whistling, he walked back to the building. Though it was the end of February, though the temperature was near thirty, though he wore only a sweater, he glowed with warmth.

When Avery opened the lobby door, he grinned at Zachary. "That Tannis is one fine-looking woman."

"That she is." Zachary nodded, returning the grin.

"What are you gonna do about it?"

"I haven't decided yet." He punched the button beside the elevator. When the doors slid open, he stepped inside.

"You will."

"I know."

He still whistled all the way up to the seventh floor, through the outer office and across the carpet to his desk. Sitting in the brown leather chair, he put on his glasses and focused on the paperwork he hadn't been able to concentrate on earlier. He was no more ready for it now with the taste of Tannis still on his lips, but obligations pulled at him. Soon he was totally involved in his task. He didn't hear the hum of the elevator or soft footsteps in the outer office.

"Zach?"

He looked up at the sound of the sultry feminine voice. "Delilah, what are you doing here?"

"I was just driving by and I saw your car." She moved fluidly across the deep pile carpet and into a chair across from him. "I just..." She trailed off, skimming a fingertip with a perfectly lacquered nail across the edge of the desk.

Reaching for his pipe, Zachary dumped the ashes into a large glass ashtray. "Something bothering you?"

Lifting her long black lashes, she looked at him, chewing her bottom lip as if undecided. "Tannis bothers me."

Zachary paused in the act of dipping the pipe into the pouch of tobacco. "In what way?"

"How much do you know about her?"

Not a hell of a lot, he admitted to himself. He filled the pipe and struck a match, watching the smoke curl up from the bowl before answering. "She worked for five years at Conway under the supervision of a man I know well and trust. He gave her an excellent recommendation." He drew deeply on the pipe and expelled a stream of smoke. "Why?"

"Well, I..." She hesitated, studied her hands as if her manicure seemed intensely interesting, then looked back at Zachary. "I came back early from lunch today and found her snooping around your desk."

Zachary's eyes narrowed with suspicion. "Snooping?"

"Yes, she was going through your papers."

"Did you confront her?"

Delilah nodded. "She said she'd lost a page of her notes."

Zachary remembered Tannis scribbling furiously on a pad while they'd talked. "Did she find it?"

"Yes, it was on the floor by your desk."

"Well?" He lifted his brows inquiringly.

"I don't know." With a long-suffering sigh, Delilah stood up and walked to the large window that ran the length of the wall behind Zachary's desk. "She acted guilty."

Frowning, Zachary gave Delilah's theory deep consideration. He knew Conway wasn't above sending someone to infiltrate his office, but Tannis? Thinking of the delightfully sensuous woman he'd so recently held in his arms, he couldn't make it fit. Still, she'd told him herself that she had secrets. "What else?"

"That's all."

"This incident happened today, but you've been unfriendly to her since her first day."

Delilah turned sharply, her raven hair fanning over the soft knit of her sweater with the movement. Zachary saw the protest form on her lips and stopped it with a raised hand. "Come on, 'Lilah, admit it. You don't like her. Why not?"

"Why did you hire her?"

"You knew I wanted someone to help me. I've gotten bogged down with the mechanics of running the company. I don't have time for everything."

She lowered her gaze, staring at the floor, fighting tears. "I thought I had that job."

Jealousy? Zachary wondered in amazement. Job anxiety? Laying down his pipe, he went to her and lifted her chin with one hand. "You do have that job within the limits of your training. I needed someone to help me with my projects. Your computer expertise ends with the instruction manual." He let his hands settle on her shoulders. "Besides, I need you to keep doing the tasks you already perform. Don't you know that you're indispensable to me?"

Looking into his eyes, she placed her hands against his chest. "I was just trying to protect you."

Smiling, he thought what a beautiful woman she was. Why didn't he feel any stirrings when she touched him, the way he had with Tannis? Probably because they were too close. When he'd hired her at the outset of incorporating his business, he'd been too recently stung by Rebecca to even consider a woman, alluring though Delilah was. Now he thought of her with a familial affection.

"I don't need protection." He placed a brotherly kiss on her forehead. "But I appreciate the thought. Now go home. It's late."

Sighing, Delilah let her hands trail down his chest and drop to her sides. "All right," she said in a voice laden with disappointment. "Good night."

"Good night." Zachary watched her go, then returned to his desk. Tannis snooping? He just couldn't believe it. Turning to his computer terminal, he tapped the keys to log in. He knew that he could access personnel and get her Social Security number. With the nine simple digits, his resources were unlimited. He could attach a modem and in minutes review her IRS returns, bank accounts, credit cards or college transcripts. Pieces of information that the business world took for granted were literally at his fingertips. He could do it.

For a long silent time, he sat at the terminal staring at the empty screen, the amber cursor awaiting his instructions. As desperately as he wanted to solve the puzzle, he didn't want to cheat. It would be like looking up the answer in the back of the book. Every time he'd done that as a boy, he'd been disgusted with himself for not solving the puzzle on his own.

Tannis wasn't ready to reveal her secrets, but she would be. Hell, he'd only just begun to learn about her. She didn't know that she could trust him. Even though his gut instinct told him that he could trust her. Implicitly. But he couldn't ignore Delilah's warning. He'd be careful. Very careful.

Usually Tannis hated to sleep. There were so many other things to do. She loved the corny old movies that came on TV late at night in which the hero swept the woman away as if in a fairy tale. She loved to read—mystery, romance, science fiction, horror. Most of the time, if a book gripped her, she didn't put it down until she came to the end. Challenging puzzles and brain teasers captivated her. Many nights she'd sat up until two or three o'clock, following step after logical step to the solution of a sophisticated puzzle.

Sleep was usually an inconvenient waste of time, but to-night . . . tonight she yearned for sleep's escape so that she could stop thinking about those two searing kisses.

It was well after midnight when Tannis crawled into bed. With a last look at the rose in the vase on the small table beside her bed, she turned off the light and curled her body into a ball, clutching her pillow to her chest. Casting aside all of the problems, fears and obligations, she allowed herself a few moments to dwell on the pleasure of the evening. She relived both kisses from start to finish, dissecting, analyzing every move. She burned the feel of Zachary's lips into her memory because she knew she couldn't let it happen again.

Oh, sure, it was because she was hired to steal from him. She couldn't do anything to jeopardize her cover. But it was also the reason she insulated herself from emotional involvement. It was the hard truth she'd learned from Mark. No one wanted to be saddled with a wife who had financial obligations the size of hers.

Burrowing under her covers, she let her mind dwell on that Christmas Day when they'd had the showdown. After exchanging gifts, Tannis had asked Mark to go with her to visit Meredith. She'd been stunned by his violent explosion of temper.

"But it's Christmas, Mark," Tannis pleaded. "I want to visit my sister."

His eyes burned with anger and impatience as he stared at her. "Tannis, she won't know if you're there or not. I'm tired of giving up our time together to sit beside her bed. How much longer are you going to play this charade? She's not going to get any better. You're throwing your money away."

Horrified by the coldness of his words, she barely managed to whisper. "You're not suggesting that I put Meredith in a public institution and let her wither away?"

"I'm not only suggesting it, I'm insisting on it." His hands gripped her shoulders as his eyes blazed into hers. "I love you, Tannis, but I can't take this any longer. Meredith doesn't know where she is or who she's with. When you become my wife, I'll not allow you to squander your time and money on her. No sensible man would."

Squander? Allow? Her mind reeled as she saw illusions of marriage as a loving partnership dissolving before her eyes. When at last she spoke, her voice was quiet. "Then I will never be your wife."

In retrospect, she had to admit that she'd seen it coming. Mark had stood by her, solid as a rock, when Meredith first became ill. Then little by little, he'd begun to display resentment toward every choice she'd made that put Meredith's welfare before his.

It was the financial bind, true. But it was also the fact that he would never be first in Tannis's life. He loved her, she'd been sure of that, but he'd wanted more out of marriage than she was capable of giving.

Although she'd never seen him again, the ripples of that ill-fated relationship still touched her. Meredith was her first obligation. No man could change that.

And yet Zachary...? No. Keeping a watchful eye on his brother's family was not nearly the same as covering the almost insurmountable expenses that she laid out monthly for Meredith's care. Not to mention the emotional expense.

For the third time she wished she had met him under different circumstances. He was a unique individual. There was no other Zachary Spencer in the world, and she wanted him. What would she do if he asked her out again?

Pressing her fingertips to her lips, she traced the outline of her mouth, remembering the second, more passionate kiss. Zachary had ignited desires in her that she had no right to enjoy.

She felt her body begin to tremble, felt the tears backing up behind her eyes. It had been a long time since she'd cried, but tonight she gave in to sorrow and grief. Sometimes—quiet, anguished times—she wondered how much longer she could carry this burden without losing control. Because she needed her twin to make her feel whole, she rarely let her mind consider the possibility that Meredith might never wake up. But there were dark, lonely hours when she acknowledged it as her greatest fear.

Chapter Four

Early Saturday morning, Zachary got in his car to head out of town, but on impulse he turned in the direction of Tannis's apartment. He'd slept little all night, his constantly active mind stumbling over questions that had no answers. If it weren't problem enough that he was attracted to a woman who worked for him, Delilah's accusation had continually haunted him.

He wasn't sure what had prompted him to look up her address and drive by, but when he turned into the parking area, all of the unresolved questions fled his mind for newer ones.

This couldn't be the right address. Although it wasn't a slum, it was quite a few steps below what a woman of her means could afford. The one-story concrete building was in dire need of paint. Wood trim around the windows was rotted and sagging in many places. Snow had melted into sludge over the cracked cement of a walkway.

Could this be where she lived? Scanning the license plates of the vehicles pulled up to the crumbling curb, he spotted the one he'd seen last night. Again, he was struck with disbelief. He hadn't noticed in the darkness of night how old and battered her car was. Was this decrepit automobile dependable? Was it even safe?

He pulled into an empty space, looked around for another minute, then got out and approached her door.

Tannis was about to eat breakfast when she heard the knock. Crossing the compact living room, she paused with her hand on the knob to look through the peephole. Zachary! With his thumbs hooked through the belt loops of faded jeans, he looked at the fisheye as though he knew she was staring in shock.

She glanced down at her own too-tight, too-worn denims, remembered that she had on not a dab of makeup and couldn't clearly recall whether she'd brushed her hair all morning. She felt her heart slam wildly against her chest and drew a calming breath as she opened the door. "Good morning, Zachary."

He grinned unashamedly. "I know I should have called first, but you might have said no. I can't truthfully say I was just in the neighborhood, but here I am." As he watched, a crimson blush crept into her cheeks. He guessed that she was embarrassed by the disrepair of her home. "May I come in?"

"Of course," she mumbled and moved aside, hoping that he wouldn't ask the obvious questions about her living quarters.

As he stepped across the room, shedding his jacket, Zachary's discerning eye took in the apartment. Though clean, the interior was in need of repair as well. While he scanned the rust-colored love seat and matching chair, the long row of shelves overflowing with books and the small wooden desk that held her personal computer, he noticed that it wasn't much warmer inside than outside. The entire apartment would fit inside his bedroom, he observed. The kitchen was separated from the living room only by clever placement of furniture. There was one closed door that he assumed led to the bedroom and bath.

"You have a Conway," he said, approaching the terminal. His calculated avoidance of comment on her home was an attempt to put her at ease. "I'd be offended that you don't have a Wizac, but I worked on this model."

"I know." She stood in the middle of the room, watching him move around her living room with complete ease. Why was he here? Did he just want to see her, or was he checking her out?

"Yeah, I guess you do." Tilting his head, he sent an amused glance over his shoulder, then dismissed further discussion of his tenure at Conway. "Do I smell something burning?"

"Oh!" Tannis raced to the stove in time to pull two charred pieces of bread from under the broiler.

Zachary followed her and propped an elbow on the countertop as he watched her furiously trying to scrape the blackened crust away to salvage the toast. This scenario didn't fit. Why would a woman of her position appear so destitute? "Tannis, if that was your last piece of bread, I could run to the store and get you another loaf."

"No, of course not!" Embarrassed, she abruptly stopped her task, realizing the absurdity of it. Her reaction had been pure instinct. Although in the last two years she had learned to be frugal, it wouldn't put her checkbook in the red to lose two pieces of toast. But it helped to have something to do with her hands when Zachary was so close in the confining space of her apartment.

"I have more bread. See?" Jerking open a cupboard door, she held up half a loaf to prove it. "I just hate to throw away food. You know, all those starving children in Africa."

"Would you like to go out for breakfast?"

"No, thank you." She twisted the wire that already held the plastic wrapper securely closed. "I wasn't really hungry anyway."

Watching her fingers move nervously on the bread package, Zachary wondered whether she was just unsettled by his unexpected appearance. Or could it be that she'd spent as much of the night awake as he had? He hadn't been able to lose the image of her pleasure when he'd given her the rose. At that thought he scanned the tiny apartment for the flower. "What did you do with the rose I gave you last night?"

Her eyes shot to his defensively. He was getting too close, too personal. "It's in my bedroom," she admitted, and turned away to return the bread to the cupboard.

He liked that she'd kept a flower he'd cultivated himself in her room. Had she looked at it and thought of him as she lay in her bed? He'd certainly lain in his bed and thought of her. And wanted her. Most of the night. He moved behind her and touched her shoulders, turning her to face him. "What is it, Tannis? What are you so nervous about?"

Her heart pounded. She seemed to feel each individual drop of blood as it raced through her veins. His fingers burned into her shoulders. From somewhere in the depths of her soul, she called up control and met the polished jade in his eyes. "I told you I don't want to get involved."

"Too late." His fingers loosened and slid down her arms to her elbows. Uncommon patience calmed his response and softened his voice. "I'm the one who kissed you last night. You can't deny that you kissed back, that you enjoyed it, that you thought about it long after you got home."

"Okay!" Jerking her arms away, she stalked across the kitchen to stare out the window. "I enjoyed it! I thought about it! Does that please you? I thought about it so much that it nearly drove me mad!"

Zachary was silent, waiting for her to continue, hoping that admitting the attraction would help her accept it.

Finally she turned. His casual stance, his nonthreatening expression calmed her response. "You've awakened feelings in me that I have no right to acknowledge."

"Why not?"

She held his gaze in silence, unable to tell the truth, unable to lie. "I just can't."

He wanted to move closer to her, but he took one step backward instead, leaning against the counter again. Secrets! She'd told him last night she was full of them. Delilah's accusation rose up in his mind as it had for a good portion of the night. Was he walking blindly into a setup? He searched her eyes, looking for betrayal. She was upset and nervous about something, not at all the picture of sophisticated poise one would expect in an undercover agent. Was that part of an act to confuse him?

Oh, hell! He was letting Delilah's suspicious nature drive him crazy. The response he'd felt in Tannis last night when he'd kissed her was no act. Neither was the compassion when she'd slipped her hand in his as he'd talked about Pete. He wished he could analyze emotions as easily as he analyzed mathematical equations. "Did I assume too much by coming here uninvited?"

"No." Tannis watched as he stroked his chin in a gesture she'd come to recognize over the last two weeks. He didn't like a problem he couldn't solve, but she was one problem she had to make sure he never found the answers to. "I just wasn't expecting to see you today."

Now he took the steps that he hadn't felt she was ready for a moment ago and reached for her hand. "I told you I like surprises, but I don't like intrusions. If I'm out of line, I'll leave."

Staring at the strong fingers that clutched her hand, Tannis formed lies in her mind that would send him on his way. But when she lifted her eyes to his face, her heart betrayed her with the truth. "Actually, I was just trying to think of something interesting to do today."

"Good." With a lazy smile, he raised his other hand to lose his fingers in her hair. Tannis thought he was going to kiss her again. She would have welcomed it even as it frightened her, but instead he turned her to the window and pointed outside. "Look. It's a beautiful spring day out there."

"It's forty-five degrees at the most," she countered. "The vernal equinox is three weeks away."

"Use your imagination. At least the snow is gone." Wrapping his arms around her, he crossed them at her waist. "Perfect day for a drive in the country, wouldn't you say?"

Settling her back against his chest, she closed her eyes and surrendered to his warmth, his scent, his strength. "Perfect," she murmured.

"Then get your jacket and let's go."

Turning in the circle of his arms, she smiled. To hell with Richard Conway and his orders. She wanted this day with Zachary, and she was determined to take it. "Can I have five minutes to put on my boots and brush my hair?"

"Five minutes." He nodded, fingering her auburn locks. "Promise not to put it in that unbecoming bun that you wear to the office. It's so much prettier this way."

Astonished, Tannis slid from his arms and dashed to her bedroom, skillfully ignoring all the promises she'd made to herself last night about denying her emotional response to Zachary. She stuffed the bottoms of her jeans into brown leather boots and brushed her hair hurriedly, leaving it loose and flowing below her shoulders as he requested. When she returned in just under the allotted five minutes, Zachary smiled appreciatively and pulled open the door.

Walking beside him to the parking lot, she shook her head in disbelief when he steered her to a Jaguar of a deep turquoise color. Not a more sedate conservative model as she would have guessed, it was a low-slung, dangerous-looking sports coupé.

"Zachary, how decadent!" she exclaimed as she slid into the leather seat. "You should have a Porsche or a BMW."

"Boring." He slammed her door and walked around to the other side. "I like to do the unexpected."

I noticed, she thought and settled comfortably. "I bet you drive like a bat out of hell."

He gave her a curious look before turning cautiously onto the road. "Wrong again. I respect the machine's power and don't abuse it."

In a few minutes the metropolitan area rapidly diminished to less congested scenery. Traffic thinned. Trees began to dot the roadside—maples, birches, oaks with their branches still bared by winter's frost but on the verge of bursting forth new life.

Zachary drove in silence, content to have her by his side, glad she'd decided to trust him if only for the day. He could take it from there at an easy pace until he discovered a solution to their work-relationship problem, though he wasn't sure why it seemed so important.

Relaxing, Tannis shifted in her seat to study his profile—firm jaw, straight nose, unbelievable eyes. Why hasn't some gorgeous woman already snagged this man? The unexpected again?

He took his eyes from the road long enough to catch the curious expression on her face. "What?"

"Nothing." She shook her head and faced the rolling hills before them. "Where are we going?"

"Mystic Grove."

Tannis didn't think she'd ever heard of it, but the name seemed to suit a trip with a Wizard. "What's in Mystic Grove?"

"Not really in it. Just near it. My farm."

His farm? The unexpected? Try incredible. "Okay, I'll stop being surprised. An electronics wizard makes millions of dollars with an innovative computer design, so naturally, he buys a farm."

"Ah, Tannis, you try too hard," Zachary said with a chuckle. "It's much simpler than that. My grandfather left it to me."

"So every Saturday you drive out to milk the cow and feed the chickens."

"No. Every March I drive out to see if there was any damage from the winter snowstorms. I sold everything except the house and ten acres to raise the capital for the Wizac."

"Because you'd rather run an electronics empire than a farm?"

"Nope." He shook his head and grinned. "All I ever wanted to do was play in a lab for the rest of my life, but I had to eat and pay the rent. When I saw the opportunity to make a lot of money, I took it."

And he did make a lot of money, Tannis thought, if what she read in the finance magazines was true. According to the gossip she'd heard, he hadn't been happy at Conway. "There are people at Conway who say you knifed him in the back when you left."

Dark blond brows arched in consternation at her comment. "Richard Conway himself, no doubt. It was his father who hired me. It never set well with Richard to hear the old man praise my accomplishments. You've used Conway computers for years. After one week on a Wizac, you should be able to see that I stole nothing from him."

Tannis knew he was right. There was no comparison between the two systems. Zachary's machine was far superior to Conway's. And she'd learned it in a remarkably short time. "That was just an observation, Zachary. Not an accusation."

"I know, but I'll defend my position anyway. When Apple opened up the personal computer market, Conway wanted a piece of it. The original consumers of PCs were computer buffs, but there was an enormous untapped market that I thought we could reach.

"I walked around the college campuses and talked to people finding out what would make them buy a PC. The most common resistance stemmed from the fact that the average person didn't understand how the computer worked. I countered every time by pointing out that they didn't understand how their television worked. Or their microwave or telephone."

"And none of them did," Tannis injected, "but they all had one."

"Exactly." Zachary turned briefly and smiled. "I also realized that in many households, the finances are controlled by the woman."

"Hence the television commercials with the sexy blonde at the keyboard."

"Yeah." This time his grin indicated a trace of embarrassment. "That commercial appealed to men, too. But when I went to Conway with my ideas, he thought I was wrong. He doesn't have much respect for women."

"No kidding." Sarcasm dripped from her voice.

"Yeah, I guess you know that. Anyway, I pitched it to him for about six months, but he wouldn't buy it."

"So you set up shop in your garage," she finished for him, "developed it yourself, and the money is still pouring in."

Zachary chuckled. "More or less."

And Richard Conway never got over it, Tannis added to herself. Though far different from the story she'd heard at Conway, Zachary's version meshed with the man she'd come to know in the past two weeks. Her own experience with Richard Conway made it easy to imagine the resistance he'd given Zachary. His rise to success was phenomenal, but something was wrong. She considered it a moment before asking, "Then why aren't you happy?"

Startled green eyes shot to Tannis then turned back to the highway. He took a long time to answer, as if he were searching his soul for something that he hadn't allowed himself to acknowledge. "Because I find myself in the role of businessman," he said quietly, "when I want to be a scientist."

There was nothing unexpected in his statement. Tannis understood, and she sympathized, but he needed the financial independence if he truly wanted to spend all his time in the lab. "Couldn't you hire a CEO to run the company?"

"I could." He nodded, solemn for a moment, then changed the subject. "I didn't drag you to Mystic Grove to talk about myself. Tell me about Tannis. Have you ever been married?"

The bluntness of the question took her by surprise, but Tannis answered honestly. "No, but I came close once. Have you?"

"No." A sardonic smile curved his lips. "But I came close once."

So there had been a gorgeous woman to snag him. "What happened?"

His fingers tightened around the steering wheel. "She didn't really love me. What happened to you?"

Tannis turned her face to the window to hide the emotion that spilled from her heart despite her struggle to suppress it. "He didn't really love me."

He must have been a first-class jerk, Zachary thought. The wound was either very fresh or very deep. Without even being aware of it, she'd given him a key to the secret. "I'm infinitely delighted that you didn't marry him."

Tannis turned and stole a glance at him from beneath lowered lashes. His face was serene as he shifted in his seat. "Tell me about your family."

That subject appealed to her even less than the last one had, but she knew he would press. She answered woodenly, hoping that he would let it pass. "My parents are dead."

"Sisters and brothers?"

"One sister."

"Really?" Zachary smiled. "Is she as beautiful and in-telligent as you?"

Would you believe exactly? Tannis inwardly groaned. "I'd rather not talk about my sister."

Noticing her hands clenched into tight fists in her lap, Zachary dropped the subject for the time being and sought to draw her out. "How did you get interested in com-puters?"

Breathing a sigh of relief, Tannis stared at her hands for a moment, then tilted her head toward him. "Promise you won't laugh?"

"No."

"Then I won't tell you."

He reached across the car and patted her hand, grinning. "I promise to try not to laugh."

"Not good enough." She slid her hand from beneath his and folded her arms across her chest.

"All right, I won't laugh." His fingers played against her denim-clad thigh. "I promise."

Feeling the warmth of his palm through her jeans, Tan-nis struggled to ignore the contact. "When I was in the tenth grade, I had a crush on the president of the science club." She studied Zachary carefully for signs of a snicker, but he was stone-faced, though his eyes gleamed merrily. "I didn't know a bit from a byte, but he was eager to share his knowledge."

The muscles twitched in his jaw, but Zachary maintained his control. "He showed you his floppy disk?"

"No." Her voice was as sweet and innocent as a babe's. "He had a hard drive."

Zachary let his eyes meet hers—a fatal mistake—and they both exploded into giggles.

"You promised!" she accused.

"But you didn't play fair!" he defended.

"You asked for it."

He moved the hand on her thigh to capture her wrist, stroking the satiny skin as he sobered. "Thank you, Tannis. I needed to laugh. It's been a long time since I took a day off from the world."

"Me, too," she whispered. She needed more than a day off. She needed a way out of the entangling web that was drawing her deeper and deeper every moment she spent with him. The unmistakable attraction between them was steadily growing. The revulsion about stealing from him before she'd met him was nothing compared to the way she felt now that she knew his strength of character, his intelligence, his innate goodness. More than ever, she knew she couldn't do it.

They drove in a comfortable silence. Soon, Zachary turned onto a less-traveled road. The route took them through farmland, still barren from winter's shroud.

"My land begins there." Zachary gestured toward a stand of birch. A few yards past it, he turned onto a narrow blacktop road. In the distance a white two-story frame house rose from the bleak brown terrain. Behind it, as far as Tannis could see, stretched row after row of long narrow buildings.

Chicken coops? City born and bred, Tannis really wasn't sure. As they drew closer, she inspected more carefully. Not chicken coops, she realized. Greenhouses.

"Zachary!" Her eyes were wide and blue as the significance of the rooftop garden fell perfectly into place. "Your grandfather grew flowers!"

"Cultivated," he corrected, turning to smile at her excited reaction. "He had an emotional attachment to each bud."

Navigating slowly on the rough, weather-beaten road, Zachary maneuvered the car close to the house. When they got out, they both looked around. Tannis studied the homestead that was obviously an integral part of the man's past. Zachary's more critical eyes took in minute details.

Frowning, thoughtful, he pulled a set of keys from his pocket and opened the door.

Tannis followed him into a large living room. Furniture draped with protective cloths faced a stone fireplace. Yellowed Priscilla curtains, once a snowy white, were tied back at the windows. The hardwood floor was bare, but trailing across from the front door to the fireplace was an indistinct line of dried mud.

Zachary's frown deepened as he followed the trail, stooping at the hearth. He examined the charred remains of logs, then straightened and turned, his gaze sweeping the room.

Tannis picked up a framed photograph from a small table and smiled at the image of a teenage Zachary. He was thinner, rangier, but with the same impatience in his eyes. Because she'd spent a lifetime watching baseball with her father, she recognized the slightly older boy beside him as Pete Spencer. More muscular than Zachary, he shared the same coloring; his features, though similar, were arranged less attractively. The lines of his face were hard, but his eyes were exactly the same shade of green as his brother's.

When she shifted her gaze from the photograph to the man, Tannis caught the concern on his face. "Zachary, what's wrong?"

"Somebody's been here."

He crossed to the stairway and bounded up the stairs. Tannis followed as he looked in every room, quickly scanning for signs of disturbance. In the doorway of the fourth bedroom, Zachary stopped abruptly, causing Tannis to collide with his back.

With a murmured apology, he stepped aside, almost as if he had forgotten she was there. Once his massive frame was out of her way, Tannis saw what had halted him. A closet door stood ajar, with linens lying where they had fallen. The bed, a pine four-poster, was in disarray, its tangled sheets exposing one corner of the mattress. Zachary bent to pick up a rumpled patchwork quilt and folded it with care before he placed it back on the bed.

Zachary's shoulders sagged. Tannis knew just enough about Pete Spencer to guess that he was the uninvited houseguest, and just enough about Zachary to know how much it upset him.

At his side, she placed a comforting hand on his arm. "Have you got a washing machine?"

Slowly he turned, his eyes vacant. "Yes."

"Then let's get started." She moved to the bed and began to strip it.

Together they carried the soiled linens downstairs to the kitchen. The stench hit them before they entered the room. A garbage can near the back door overflowed with empty cans and decaying food. The sink and adjacent countertops were littered with stacks of dirty dishes. Everywhere they stepped, their boots found sticky goo on the linoleum.

Zachary flung the sheets down in disgust and swore. "I would have let him stay here. All he had to do was ask!" His hands clenched into fists at his sides. "He didn't have to leave it like a pigsty!"

Tannis understood completely the effect a sibling can have on a person's life. She wanted to comfort him, to let him know that she cared. "Well, at least you know where he spent the winter."

"But why couldn't he tell me he was here?" Zachary kicked the pile of sheets toward the basement door. "And where is he now?" And what is he up to? Zachary added to himself, hoping that Sylvia and the boys hadn't heard from him.

It took three hours. The bathroom was as much a disaster as the kitchen. Zachary and Tannis took turns going up and down the basement stairs to transfer the laundry from the washer to the dryer. Zachary stuffed plastic bags with garbage. Tannis washed dishes. She folded sheets and towels and straightened the linen closet. He scrubbed the kitchen floor.

Just as Tannis polished the last speck of grime from the kitchen faucets, Zachary entered from the bathroom where he'd tackled the mildew in the tile. He gave a low whistle as he looked around at the sparkling appliances. "For a woman who makes a living with her brain, you certainly threw your soul into this kitchen."

"Don't spread it around the office, all right?" Tannis turned, stifling a gasp at the sight of his bare chest. Obviously he'd removed his sweater while he scrubbed in the confining space. Her eyes were drawn to the curling, golden hair, following the natural narrowing growth down his hard flat abdomen until it tapered into the waist of his jeans, which were riding low on his narrow hips. Dragging her gaze back to his face, she smiled.

"I promise." As he tugged his sweater over his head, he moved closer. He hadn't missed the path of her eyes nor the hungry look before she disguised it. The fist of desire that he'd come to expect when he was with her punched him squarely in the stomach. It would have been the easiest thing in the world to take her right there against the kitchen counter.

Tannis looked up at his eyes, recognizing desire in them. "How could I refuse? You needed help. I was here. Why shouldn't I do it? You couldn't leave the place like this, and I wasn't going to sit around and watch you do the work."

"Thank you." He took the final step that separated them and bent his head to claim the kiss he'd been wanting all day.

The instant she tasted his lips, Tannis lost herself in the intimate touch. Her arms came up to circle his neck. He tilted his head and plundered with lips and tongue. No gentle, exploratory kiss of last night, this melding of flesh was urgent, demanding. Tannis accepted the challenge and gave back with all the hunger she'd spent the night trying to deny.

With a shuddering moan rumbling deep in his throat, Zachary wrapped his arms around her and tangled his hands in her hair. The fist that held his stomach in its grip exploded, sending desire coursing through his body. The need to have her was a searing pain. His hands slid down her back to slip under her sweater. They both gasped as one when his palms met flesh.

So soft, so silken, so warm. He couldn't believe the texture of her skin. He wanted all of it, naked against his. Leaving her mouth, he trailed his lips along the line of her jaw, down her slender neck to the hollow of her throat. She smelled of soap and fabric softener. His hands skimmed lightly around her back to the fine ridges of her ribs and up to cup her breasts.

Tannis was on fire. Zachary's touch was unlike any she'd ever experienced. Her blood was boiling through her veins. As her nipples hardened against his fingers, the rest of her body melted. Wrapping her hands around his face, she pulled his lips back to hers.

Primal need took control. Grasping her hips with his hands, Zachary sank to his knees, pulling her with him. Thigh met thigh. Masculine hard met feminine soft. Still assaulting her lips, he splayed one hand against her back and eased her to the floor.

Stretched out beside him, Tannis felt one leg slide between her thighs as one hand fingered the snap at the top of her jeans. Even in her surreal state, her mind raced to the logical result of that action.

"Zachary," she whispered, prying at his fingers, trying to untangle her legs. "Stop."

His fingers stilled, but his lips teased across her jaw to the lobe of one ear. "I want you, Tannis."

Her first impulse was to say yes to those breathless words, but somewhere in her thoughts, reason and control jogged forward. Making love with him now would put everything on the line. It was Conway's suggestion that she try to seduce him that stopped her. She pushed at his shoulders and tried to sit up. "Zachary, we're wallowing around on the kitchen floor."

"Mmm." He pulled her close to his chest and continued to nibble her ear. "When there's a perfectly good bed upstairs."

"That's not what I meant." His arms locked her in his embrace. She was helpless to break free. "Don't push me."

A ragged sigh escaped as his arms relaxed. "I've never taken a woman against her will."

Once freed, Tannis sat up and assumed as much dignity as she could by straightening her clothes. "I don't imagine you've ever had to," she snapped.

Deliberately not touching her, he sat beside her and shook his head to clear it. What had happened to cautious ease? Too much, too soon, too fast. He'd meant to be so careful with her, but once he'd tasted her, he'd wanted everything. "I'm sorry. I lost control."

When she faced him and saw the sincere apology in his eyes, the panic faded. "Don't blame yourself. I lost control, too."

Yes, but you fought it, Zachary thought. He wanted to ask why, but instead he stood and reached down to pull her up. "I'm going to check the grounds and outbuildings. Want to come?"

She looked from his outstretched hand to his easy smile and let him help her up. They picked up their jackets from the kitchen table and went out the back door.

The air was crisp and clear without a trace of the haze that clouded the city. Having always lived in the metropolitan area, Tannis delighted in the freshness of the country. There was a pungent smell that she realized was the thawing earth, something she missed in her world of concrete and steel.

Zachary circled the farmhouse, looking for signs of damage. When he came to the narrow basement window, he stopped and touched the lever that held it in place. "Here's where he got in."

Tannis knelt beside him as he tried the window. It opened easily. "Are you sure it was Pete?"

Leaning back on his heels, he ran a hand through his hair and sighed. "This window never closed properly. He knew that. There are no signs of forced entry anywhere. Who else could it have been?"

"Vagrants? Thieves? Kids?"

"No. I don't know how to explain this, but I wasn't surprised to find the house in a mess. I don't usually come out here to check on things until the end of March. I just had a feeling."

He rose and walked to the greenhouses. Tannis followed. She knew from personal experience not to question feelings. If Zachary thought the intruder was Pete, then it probably was. As they walked up and down each row between the buildings, they saw that nothing had been disturbed.

Finally satisfied that Pete's visit had been limited to the house, Zachary headed back. As they walked between the long metal buildings, Tannis was deep in thought. Each greenhouse was wired for electricity. Running water was provided from a well. The natural conclusion came easily. "It wouldn't take much to convert these buildings into a lab."

Zachary's eyes narrowed. He'd been thinking the same thing. Away from the city. No interruptions. No distractions. "No, it wouldn't."

"But?" she prompted.

He turned and faced her, grinning. "But who would run the company?"

"Someone with an MBA from Harvard?"

They reached the back door and tramped the mud from their boots before entering. "Why do you think I hired you?" Zachary asked as he gathered the bags of garbage.

"Since I have to run the company, my personal project is suffering from lack of attention. If I have someone to test run and debug the programs, I'll progress a lot more quickly."

Tannis's eyes were wide with disbelief and excitement. She didn't dare to hope. "You want me to help you perfect AI?"

"Maybe." Lugging the bags of garbage outside, he added, "I haven't decided yet."

Tannis stared at his retreating form as she rinsed the dishes she'd used to make instant coffee. An opportunity to assist the Wizard with his AI project? She'd kill for it! Anybody would. But with a deep sense of regret, she knew it would never happen.

"I put the garbage in the trunk of my car," Zachary said, reentering the kitchen. "There's a county dump about two miles down the road. Do you want to get something to eat?"

Drying her hands on a dish towel, Tannis suppressed a giggle. "I'm not sure. I've never eaten at a dump."

He laughed. "I have a tendency to run thoughts together. I guess my mind works faster than my mouth."

Oh, I don't know, Tannis thought, letting her eyes rest on his sensuous lips. I think your mouth works pretty fast. "I would love to eat at a quaint country inn where they bake their own bread and have a roaring fire in the fireplace."

"I know the perfect place."

Because it was well past the lunch hour, the white frame restaurant on a blacktop country road was almost empty. They were able to sit beside the fireplace. The homemade bread was warm enough to melt the butter as they spread it on the fresh loaves.

Tannis felt more at ease with Zachary than at any time since she'd met him. As he described his summers spent working with his grandfather, she let her guard down completely and forgot every emotional blockade that kept her natural responses in check.

They were comfortable and content on their way back to Boston. When he reached for her hand, she met him halfway. He settled her fingers on his thigh when he needed both hands to drive, and she left them there, enjoying the tactile link.

It was growing dark when they reached the city. Tannis felt reality capturing her. She didn't want the day to end, but she knew it had to.

"I could take you to my house," Zachary offered as he neared the intersection where he had to choose one direction or the other. "We could have dinner."

"We just ate."

"That was lunch."

"For you maybe." Tannis patted her full stomach. "I'm not eating again all day."

"Then you could stay for breakfast."

"No." She jerked away the hand that had lain on his leg, suddenly aware of the intimacy in that contact. As he took the turn that led to her apartment, she relaxed.

"I don't understand why you deny the attraction between us." Zachary tried to read her expression in the dim light, but the city traffic commanded his attention. "I'm not going to force you into anything just because you work for me." As soon as it was safe, he reached across to cover her hand with his. "But neither am I going to stop trying just because you work for me."

Yes, he would. Tannis was grateful for the shadows that allowed her to hide from his probing eyes. Sooner or later this budding courtship would come to an end. And it had nothing to do with who worked for whom. *Everything she looked for in a man.* That thought kept coming back to her again and again. He was intelligent and caring and resourceful. As he made all the turns that took them to her street, she began to wonder exactly how resourceful he was.

"Zachary." Her tone held a hint of accusation. Why hadn't she asked him this when he turned up on her doorstep? "How did you know where I live?"

"The Wizard always knows." He grinned wickedly and tapped a finger against his temple.

"This isn't Oz." He wasn't getting off that easily. "How did you know?"

The grin only widened, plunging the dimples into deeper creases. "Suppose you guess."

Streetlights pooled on aging brick buildings. Traffic lights passed in a blur of color. Brakes squealed behind them. Tannis stared unseeing out the windshield as she thought. "You accessed personnel and got the address from my employment records."

"That would have worked, but I didn't."

As oncoming headlights briefly illuminated his face, she saw that he still grinned. Undoubtedly, he loved these battles of wits.

"Okay." She bit her lip and thought again. "You have a photographic memory, right?"

"Right," he acknowledged with a chuckle. She was so far off, but he loved the way her mind worked.

"You memorized my license plate last night and hacked into the DMV."

"In the first place I didn't memorize it. It just stuck there whether I wanted it to or not." He glanced at her, meeting her confusion with amusement. "In the second place I haven't hacked into anything since I had an unpleasant conversation with an FBI agent when I was in college."

Before she could question him about his run-in with the G-men, he continued. "Try again. Only this time think of me as just a guy who wants a date with you."

Tannis thought about what she would do if she wanted a date with someone. When it came to her, it was so simple that she felt truly stupid. "You looked me up in the phone book."

"Congratulations!" Zachary beamed as he recited. "Robbins, T. L. Seventeen twenty-eight Cherry Laurel Lane. 555-8273. But I didn't see any cherry laurels. What's the *L* for?"

When she mumbled something under her breath, Zachary cocked his head to one side. "What was that?

"Lenore!" she blurted out. "My mother was a fan of Edgar Allan Poe."

"Just be glad it wasn't Longfellow. Your middle name might be Hiawatha."

"Thank God," Tannis groaned. "Who would burden a child with that name?"

He just stared straight ahead with that dopey grin in place, mocking her, mocking himself.

"Zachary Hiawatha Spencer?" she asked with incredulous amazement. "Why?"

"My mother was into genealogy at the time. She thought she'd discovered Indian blood in the family. By the time she found out she'd made a mistake, I'd already been christened. When I was older, she told me I could change it if I wanted to, but I kind of like it."

"The unexpected," Tannis murmured, nodding.

"Exactly. But I don't volunteer that information to just anyone."

He pulled into the parking lot of the apartment complex and cut the engine, then turned to face her. "Last chance to change your mind about dinner, breakfast or Brian's birthday party."

His eyes were intense, as green as the first shoots of life in the spring. His smile was pleasant, endearing. Her heart unfolded, then curled into a tight fist. She shook her head, but felt a twinge of regret. "Maybe another time."

With one hand he touched the ends of her hair, wrapping a curl around his fingers. "I appreciate your help at the farmhouse today. I can't picture any other woman I know up to her elbows in soap suds."

The dark quiet interior of the car lent an intimacy to the atmosphere. Tannis let her carefully constructed guard fall, if only for a moment. "The truth is, I can't imagine any other man I would have done it for."

Encouraged, his smile widened. "Well, that's a start."

Tugging gently on the strand of hair, he leaned closer, aiming his lips toward hers. She saw it coming. She wanted it. But she stopped it with a hand on his chest. "You would have done the same for me, wouldn't you? If my brother had created some kind of problem, would you have helped me?"

The unmistakable urgency in her eyes caused him to straighten and search her eyes. This was another piece of the puzzle. Gently, cautiously, he probed. "You don't have a brother."

"No, but I— Never mind."

As she turned her face away, Zachary reached with tender fingers to urge her back. "Tannis..." He hesitated. "Anytime you need me—for any reason—I'll help you."

"Thank you." She could only whisper. If only she had known that before she got involved in the deceit. But it was too late now. She had become a victim of her own lies.

This time when his mouth moved toward her, she accepted the kiss. No more than a delicate brush across her lips, it still had the power to make her quiver.

Easing back slowly, he opened his door and went around to open hers. With her hand in his, he walked her to the apartment and waited silently while she unlocked the door. Light spilled from inside, washing her in a pale yellow glow as she turned for a last look, a last touch, a last word.

When she would have gone inside, he kept her for another moment. When he wanted to show her his desire, he showed his tenderness instead. "I don't want to leave. You have some burden that needs to be shared."

There was no hint of seduction in his voice, only compassion. Gazing into his eyes, glittering green-gold in the pale light, she came close—so close—to leaning her head against that strong shoulder and letting everything pour out. But she couldn't be sure he'd be as understanding if he knew that she was attempting to steal from him. She shook her head in denial. "Not tonight."

"You can trust me, Tannis. And I can wait." Raising her hand to his lips, he turned it over and seared a kiss on the inside of her wrist. "Think about it." He dropped her hand and walked away.

For several minutes after Tannis had closed her door, Zachary sat in his car and stared at the apartment building. Why did she live in near squalor? And what, if anything, did it have to do with her refusal to talk about her sister?

Shrugging, he started the engine and drove away. Usually his mind worked quickly to make logical connections, but on this occasion he was drawing a blank. Maybe he was letting emotions shade his instincts, but when he was with Tannis, far more primitive instincts took over his mind and ruled his body.

Chapter Five

When Dr. Adam Warfield walked into Dr. Moore's office at Greenbriar, Tannis's first thought was that he couldn't possibly be old enough to have finished medical school yet. All of the doctors in her realm of experience were wizened men with graying hair. Deep lines etched their faces, signifying years of practicing medicine.

But when Dr. Moore made the introductions and the young man grasped her hand, she felt strength and confidence in the firmness of his grip. He sat down in a chair beside Tannis and flipped through Meredith's medical file. As he studied the data, Tannis studied him. His face was thin. Unruly brown hair fell across his high forehead. From the impatient way he brushed it aside, Tannis guessed that he wore it long not as a deference to style, but as a testimony to the fact that he stayed too busy to sit in a barber's chair.

After some minutes of silent study, he raised his head. "I'm going to be totally frank."

Tannis sucked in her breath and waited in trembling anxiety.

"First the positives—her EEG continues to show brain activity. Her condition is not worsening. She doesn't require life-support machines, so we know that some portions of her brain are functioning."

He looked again at the file as if the facts could magically change, then shook his head. "But when I was with her a few minutes ago, she didn't respond to any aspect of the clinical examination. No pupillary reaction to light. No extremity motor response. No spontaneous eye movement."

Tannis responded with impatience. She'd heard this same report numerous times in the last two years. "What are her chances for recovery?"

The young doctor paused for a moment during which the only sound was the click of passing footsteps in the hall. "Almost nonexistent."

"Almost?" Tannis grasped hope where there was none. "There's a chance?"

"Tannis—"

"Ms. Robbins." Dr. Warfield cut off Dr. Moore's gentle tone with a more stern one. "You're listening with your heart instead of your mind. I understand that, but please be realistic. Even if she should open her eyes—which is unlikely—the possibility of complete recovery is remote."

"What about partial recovery?"

"Tannis, you're torturing yourself with infinite possibilities," the older doctor cautioned. "We've been over this before."

"I have to know." She cast a desperate look at him, then turned back to the neurosurgeon. "What about partial recovery?" she repeated.

He brushed his hair back with long, skilled fingers—fingers delicate enough to perform intricate surgery, yet strong enough to offer comfort. "I would guess the most likely outcome would be a vegetative state, awake, but not aware of anything, no response to any stimuli."

"You would guess?"

His eyes filled with compassion. "I really wish I could give you cold hard facts, but so much about the brain remains a mystery to medical science. She could be in what we call a locked-in state. Her eyes open, aware, but totally paralyzed, unable to communicate except by eye movement."

Tannis paled at the thought of her vibrant, energy-filled twin lying helplessly still forever. But wouldn't that at least be better than what she was like now? Tears filled her eyes at the grim image. "What about the telepathy?"

He glanced toward Dr. Moore, as if for help, then reached across and took one of Tannis's hands. "If you did receive a telepathic message from your sister—and I'm not disputing that you might have—what does it indicate? That there's brain activity? We already know that. It doesn't indicate that she'll regain consciousness or that her recovery would be anything other than marginal."

The tears that had been pooling in her eyes began to drift silently down her cheeks. "It's so damn frustrating," she whispered.

"I know." He closed his other hand over their joined ones. "I wish I could give you better news. More hope. But it just isn't possible. It isn't like a broken bone that you can set and wait for it to heal. The brain does not regenerate new cells for damaged ones."

She stared, realizing that she'd hoped for some miracle cure to be offered and that it wasn't going to happen. "What . . ." She stopped and swallowed against the tremble in her voice. "What can I do?"

Again, he flicked his gaze to Dr. Moore for support.

"Exactly what you have been doing, Tannis," the older man offered gently. "Know that she's receiving the best possible care, that she's in no pain and that apparently she feels and returns your love."

"There might be one other thing that you could do for her and for yourself," Dr. Warfield said in a soft tone. "You could stop concentrating all of your energy on her and get on with your life."

Tannis wrenched her hand from his grasp, fueled by anger. "Forget about her? Stop hoping? Give up as if she had died?"

"No, of course not. But accept that her condition probably will not change. You're a beautiful, intelligent young woman. Don't lose that. You might grow to resent her, and that would make you feel worse. You've done everything possible, more than most families would. You don't need to add guilt and resentment to your emotional state."

Tannis knew he truly wanted to help her, but he wasn't in the business of dispensing miracles. "I understand. Thank you." She stood. "I'm going to see her now."

Tannis sat by Meredith's bed for hours, pondering everything both doctors had said. The situation was all but hopeless, yet she could not give up. For two years she'd existed through this nightmare by maintaining, at least subconsciously, that Meredith would one day wake up completely normal. Was that unrealistically optimistic?

"Oh, Meredith," she whispered, curling her fingers around her sister's pale, still hand, "What should I do? What would you do?"

That was a new thought. What would Meredith do if their roles were reversed? Tannis had no doubt that her twin would sacrifice anything for her care. But would she let it rule her life? Tannis's active imagination conjured a picture of Meredith sitting beside her own bed ad infinitum as the years slipped silently away.

I wouldn't want that for her, Tannis thought. I'd want her to live her life to the fullest, excel in her career, devote herself to a family. "Is that what you want for me, Merrie?"

Tannis asked, surprising herself with the use of the childhood nickname.

But there was no way for Meredith's injured mind to form an answer.

Tannis spent a tortured week pouring her energy into the prealgebra program, holding Conway at bay with lame excuses and doing her best to avoid Zachary—no easy task since he pursued with the energy of a man whose system was on overload.

Her own system was running at a relatively high level as well. It only took a whiff of the scent of cherry tobacco or a glimpse of seductive green eyes to thrust her thoughts back to the kitchen floor at the farmhouse. God, how could she forget the feel of that masculine body pressed against hers? That hungering mouth that ravished her beyond reason? Those deceptively gentle hands that stroked her to levels of passion she'd never before attained?

He'd asked her to lunch, to dinner, for drinks, and every time she'd turned him down, hoping he would give up. But every time he'd patiently insisted that he understood her reluctance to become involved with her boss and said he would wait until she felt more comfortable. He'd added that he realized she had other things on her mind and reiterated his willingness to help.

Now, as she wheeled into the guest parking lot at Greenbriar for her ritual Sunday afternoon visit, she wondered how he would take it if she did open up to him. "You, Mr. Sexual Wizard, are the problem," she could say. "You see, I can't make hot, passionate love to you. Not that I don't want to, you understand. I just think it would be kind of tacky to catch you at your weakest moment."

Or would that be his strongest moment? The mental image of Zachary making love to her caused her to stumble on the front steps. Straighten up, Tannis! she cautioned herself, pulling open the heavy glass door. Meredith will not be amused if you walk in flustered by carnal fantasies.

Yes, she would! some inner voice argued. She'd think it was hysterical, and she'd demand every gritty detail.

Pausing in the hall outside Meredith's room, Tannis let new awareness fill her. All of their lives, they'd discussed in descriptive terms their first dates, first kisses, first sexual experiences. "One person, two bodies," they'd always joked about themselves. Now, Tannis realized, she was treating Meredith as if she'd been canonized. That wasn't fair to either of them.

"Okay," she said aloud, and pushed open the door. "No more Ms. Nice Guy."

She looked at the bed as if she expected Meredith to sit up and laugh at her.

"I've either come to my senses or lost my mind, take your pick," she announced, hopping up on the edge of the bed and swinging her legs over the side. She was about to continue when the door opened, admitting the portly frame of Dr. Moore.

"Tannis," he greeted her, "I thought I saw you come in. How are you doing?"

"I've had one of the worst weeks of my life. But I'm surviving."

"I knew you would." He eased into the vinyl-covered chair beside the bed. "I hope you've thought about Dr. Warfield's advice. About living your life, I mean."

"I have." Turning, she picked up Meredith's hand and cradled it against her thigh. "I've spent the last two years taking one day at a time. Waiting to get Meredith back to Boston. Fighting the disease. Tests, tests and more tests. Always expecting to walk in here one day and find her wide awake and screaming at me for not dressing her in a more attractive nightgown."

Her fingers had tightened around her sister's hand. Deliberately she eased the pressure. "Now we're coming up on the second anniversary, and even I have to admit that if she were going to wake up, she probably would have by now."

Dropping her gaze to their joined identical hands, she drew a long breath and let her words flow out in a husky whisper. "But it hurts so badly to give up."

Dr. Moore leaned forward, covering Tannis's free hand with his older, wrinkled one. "You don't have to give up, Tannis. Just take your life off of hold. Meredith is the one in the coma. Not you."

She looked up, ready to protest loudly, but there was so much concern on his face, she let her words die unspoken.

"When was the last time you had a date?" he challenged. "Went to a party? Did something frivolous? About two years ago?"

Tannis smiled despite her turmoil. "About that."

"Long enough," Dr. Moore proclaimed, and stood, giving Tannis a pat on the head, as if she were his child. "Plenty long enough."

Tannis stared after him as he left the room. "Long enough," she muttered quietly, and let her gaze drift to her twin. "What do you think, Merrie? Should I shove you to the back of my mind and do something frivolous?"

I told you to go for it, Tannis.

This time the message didn't make her blink an eye. And this time she didn't doubt that it had come from her sister through some mysterious means that defied medical or scientific methods.

"I know you did. And I guess I would say the same to you if our positions were reversed. I also know that you won't blame me if I grab for some excitement in my life."

Then, for over an hour, she talked to her twin about Conway's disgusting threats and the outrageous thrills she experienced just thinking about Zachary.

Emotionally exhausted after the hours at Greenbriar, Tannis couldn't remember when she'd last had a regular meal. But as she opened the refrigerator door, the telephone rang. She was in no mood to talk to anyone, but rather than let the shrill sound continue, she picked it up.

"What do you have for me?"

He didn't bother to identify himself. Tannis decided that saying your name over the telephone must be a no-no in the cloak-and-dagger business. "How nice to hear from you, Mr. Conway," she said in her sweetest voice.

"Cut the crap. Do you have anything?"

Tannis hesitated. She'd run out of excuses. Should she tell him about the Sorceress? Surely anyone with good business sense would expect it, so it probably couldn't hurt Zachary for her to tell it. "He's got a female version of the Wizac Storyteller in the works. He calls it the Sorceress."

"No, that's not what I'm after unless it's vastly improved. Have you seen it?"

"No."

Conway uttered an explicit oath. "My information is that he's got something phenomenal in the experimental stages. What is it?"

"I don't know!" Could he mean the AI project? She would die before she'd tell him that, though she really didn't know anything worthwhile about it. "All I've heard about is the Sorceress."

"I don't think that could be it, but find a way to get a look at it. Better yet, get me the plans."

"I can't do that! I don't even have access to R and D. It requires a voiceprint and fingerprint ID."

"Then you better find some way to get in there. You aren't shifting your allegiance to Spencer, are you?" Conway asked suspiciously. "Believe me, I can arrange for him to find out that you're a spy."

Alarmed, Tannis calmed herself with logical thought. "You can't do that without implicating yourself."

"Don't count on it," Conway threatened. "I always leave myself an out. A person with my resources can do anything."

The sound of a harsh click marked the end of the conversation. Filled with frustration, Tannis glared at the receiver before she hung up.

Conway, she knew, probably could arrange to have her caught and come out of it unscathed himself. And before long, he'd have good reason, because she wasn't going to reveal Zachary's secrets, at least not any that could hurt him. So where did that leave her?

Sighing, she folded her arms across her chest and closed her eyes, remembering the pressure of Zachary's lips on hers. If she weren't on a mission to destroy him, she could easily fall in love with him. At the office she could discipline her mind to think of him in professional terms. At home, desires intruded. She remembered the way his presence had almost overwhelmed her tiny apartment. She recalled the sincerity in his eyes when he'd told her he'd always be willing to help her. Could she believe it? Maybe she should take her chances with telling Zachary herself before Conway could.

Desperately she longed for someone to talk to about her overpowering obligations. Most of her friends had long since deserted her. Who wanted a friend who could never afford to go out? Besides, Meredith had always been her best friend. They understood each other so completely that they'd never needed anyone else.

Hovering on the edge of indecision, she gave serious thought to going to Zachary and telling him everything. It was the right thing to do. It was the smart thing to do. It was the only thing to do.

Quickly, before she lost her nerve, she dived into a kitchen drawer for the phone book. Her enthusiasm waned when she found he was not listed, but that only stopped her for a minute. Using ingrained problem-solving skills, she went to her computer terminal, still attached to the modem she'd used to access Conway systems when she'd worked at home. Within minutes, she had Zachary's address and unlisted phone number from the Wizac personnel files.

Zachary wadded up a computer printout and tossed it near the wastepaper basket in a corner of the lab he'd built in the basement of his home.

"Damn!" he muttered, and snapped a pencil in two. For the first time in weeks, he'd felt the inclination to work on his personal project, and nothing was running right. Thoughts of Tannis had inundated him all week long—rampant, sensuous thoughts—so he'd sought sanctuary in the lab to get her out of his mind. With considerable effort, he forced her image away now and concentrated on debugging his program.

Before long he was absorbed in his work, almost to the point of ignoring the security system as it alerted him that someone was ringing his doorbell. Finally he looked up, grumbled and flipped on the video monitor to see who it was.

His mind must be playing tricks on him, he thought as the image came into focus. Sure looked like Tannis. The picture sharpened, and he peered at the screen. It was Tannis. What was she doing here?

By the time he climbed the stairs from the basement and walked the length of the house to open the front door, she was halfway to her car, but she turned when he called her name. Leaning casually against the door frame, he watched her move toward him with the late afternoon sun turning her auburn hair to molten copper. That old familiar fist punched him in the stomach at the sight of her.

One glance at his long, lean form and Tannis felt her pulse race. She was doing the right thing, she was sure. Crossing the yard to the house, she swept her gaze from his head to his feet, taking in the dark chocolate cords that molded to his thighs and the ivory fisherman's knit sweater that hugged his broad shoulders. She'd never known a more attractive man, certainly not one who had intelligence, too.

She wanted him. Even as she acknowledged it to herself, the fear of becoming involved forced her to cool her response. She had to tell him everything—Conway and Meredith—before she could examine that feeling. But as she smiled in answer to his wide grin, she admitted that it might be too late. He was already under her skin.

"Hi," she said, suddenly timid beneath his boldly assessing gaze. "You said you like surprises."

"Absolutely love them." He nodded, still grinning, and stepped back a few paces. "Come in."

Zachary took her coat and hung it in a closet beside the door as Tannis surveyed the house. It had to be a hundred years old, but appeared to be lovingly preserved. And big. The polished wood floors seemed to stretch interminably. High ceilings and wide arched entryways added to the feeling of spaciousness. Peeking from the hall into the formal living room, she saw furniture from the turn of the century. Authentic, she was sure.

As he turned from the closet, Zachary saw from her expression that she liked his house, and he was immensely pleased. "I find the library more comfortable." He gestured with his arm. "Over here."

One corner of her brain registered cozy overstuffed furniture in muted shades of brown, but she was drawn almost magnetically to the books. Shelves lined the walls, broken only by the window on the front and the fireplace at the back. Lured to the titles, Tannis found every book she'd ever read in every English class. Shakespeare to Salinger; bestsellers to cult classics. One long wall held mystery; Sherlock Holmes side by side with Travis McGee.

"Zachary!" Her eyes shone as she turned to him. "You're a one-man library!"

"A man's entitled to a few vices. I can't walk past a bookstore." He propped one arm on a shoulder-high shelf, letting his glance wander appraisingly over her body. "I'm glad you came."

"But I interrupted you, didn't I? You were working."

"It's all right. How did you know?"

"Elementary." Intensely aware of the boldness of his gaze, she smiled. "You aren't the only one who's read Sherlock Holmes. You only wear your glasses when you're at your terminal."

Zachary's hand shot to his face. In his surprise and delight, he'd completely forgotten. He removed them now and toyed with one stem in his hand. "Well done, Watson. I was working in my lab. That's why it took me so long to answer the door. It's in the basement."

"Sequestered in the dungeon, Wizard?"

"Yeah. Something like that." Considering adverse consequences for only a second, he acted on impulse. "I'll take you down there if you like."

Eagerness lit her eyes. She desperately wanted to see his lab—for herself, not for Conway. "Yes, I'd like that."

"Come on." He extended his hand to her. "The entrance is in the kitchen."

Damp, dark, musty. Tannis expected Zachary's basement lab to be as foreboding and unpleasant as any basement she'd ever been in. "Dungeon" was an apt description of the cold, spooky room at her childhood home. Even as Zachary led her down the wooden stairs, she expected to see spiders, the occasional mouse, maybe even a bat.

Her eyes grew round in wonder as she took it in. More sophisticated than the R and D floor at Conway, she noted as she dropped his hand and wandered among the high-tech instruments. Bright fluorescent bulbs bathed the huge room in stark white light. Six terminals dotted the work area.

Hooked into what? she wondered. The mainframe at the Wizac offices? An internal system? Both?

She ran her hands over cold metal and high-impact plastic, listening to the familiar hum of machines standing ready to carry out instructions. An electronic playground. "Zachary!" Her exuberance shone in the lilting tone of her voice. "It's wonderful!"

When she turned to him, his eyes glistened with pleasure. He'd known she would love it and had used it to lure her. The wide smile slashing across his face was triumphant.

Deep in her soul, warnings sounded. He's drawing you in. Don't let him do it. He doesn't know the truth yet. But she ignored them all. What harm could there be in examining his machines? she asked the sentinels that guarded her heart.

"Come over here," Zachary called.

As she approached, she saw him fiddling with switches at another computer. At first glance, it was a Wizac, but it wasn't. There were subtle differences an untrained eye probably wouldn't pick up. Even with her knowledge, she wasn't sure what the changes meant.

"Sit down," he offered. He removed a pile of green-and-white printouts from a folding chair and dragged it to a position beside his at the terminal. He tapped some more keys while she settled, then angled his head toward her. "Ready?"

Ready for what? Tannis tried to interpret the strange look in his eyes. Excitement was there. A little pride. And maybe just a trace of apprehension.

"I guess so."

Grinning broadly, he faced the computer, but did not touch it. Instead, he spoke. "Pandora, wake up."

"Good evening, Zachary."

Tannis stared, her mouth dropping open, her eyes wide in response to the sultry feminine voice. "Zachary? She talks!"

He only smiled, crossing his arms over his chest.

"Is someone with you, Zachary?" Pandora asked.

"Yes."

"Who is it?"

"This is my friend, Tannis."

"Good evening, Tannis."

Amazed, in awe, dumbstruck, Tannis couldn't answer right away. She drew a breath and managed a mumbly, "Hello, Pandora."

"Should I store his voiceprint?" Pandora asked.

Both Tannis and Zachary laughed. "I'm still working on teaching her to identify gender," he explained. "Pandora, Tannis is female."

"Should I store her voiceprint?"

Zachary looked thoughtfully at Tannis for a moment, then smiled. "Yes. Now she'll respond to your instructions and questions."

Tannis was impressed. Though she'd seen computers with voice synthesization before, Pandora had the most enticing voice she'd heard. She didn't have the mechanical, robotic sound of other machines. "How does she know whether you're talking to me or to her?"

"She doesn't. This is her first three-way conversation. If she doesn't understand a question, she won't say anything, but if I were to say to you, for example, 'What is the capital of California?'"

"Sacramento," Pandora answered immediately.

"That's right, Pandora." A teasing twinkle lit his eyes. "What's the capital of South Dakota?"

"Pierre. Or is it Bismarck? I get those two mixed up."

What had been wide-eyed wonder on Tannis's face now amplified to disbelief. How did he program a personality? But, of course, he didn't. She would answer exactly the same way, no matter how many times times she was asked. Wouldn't she? "Ask her again."

Chuckling, Zachary guessed the direction of her thoughts. "Pandora, what is the capital of South Dakota?"

"Pierre. I think. Maybe it's Bismarck."

"Okay," Tannis conceded to his expertise. "You gave her several answers to choose from on that question. She's programmed to pick out operant words and give standard responses."

"Well." Zachary smiled mysteriously. "Not exactly." He altered his voice to a melancholy tone. "Don't you think the Wizard could have tossed a little magic into the circuits?"

"What's wrong, Zachary?" Pandora asked. "Are you upset?"

"No, it's all right, Pandora. I was just a little disappointed because Tannis wasn't properly impressed." He turned to Tannis, grinning. "I've been working on explaining emotions to her."

"Terrific," Tannis observed dryly. "When you finish programming Pandora, maybe you could take a stab at explaining them to me."

Oh, yes, Zachary thought. There are dozens of emotions I'd like to explore with you. He raised a hand to stroke her cheek, but halted when Pandora spoke.

"Zachary, are you in love with Tannis?"

Two pairs of eyebrows shot up in shock. Two heads turned to stare at the computer. "Guess I explained it a little better than I thought," Zachary mumbled. "Pandora, go to sleep."

One of the lights went out, but the machine still hummed in readiness. Sleeping, Tannis thought. Waiting for the Wizard to wake her up again. Turning to face him, she spoke in a voice full of admiration and respect. "You were wrong. I *am* properly impressed."

"I hope so." His eyes softened, searching hers. "One other person knows about her, but you're the only person who has met her."

In all honesty, Tannis surmised that there must be significance in the fact that she was the only woman he'd taken to the rooftop garden and the only person who had spoken to Pandora. But that knowledge only frightened her. She couldn't encourage anything between them—physical or emotional—until he knew all her secrets. "You place too much faith in me."

"I don't think so."

He leaned closer—to kiss her, she thought. And she had to escape before he lured her again, because she knew that resisting that hard male body would be more and more difficult every time she had to do it. She stood, his reaching hands skimming the length of her as she moved. "I . . . uh, I really like your lab."

"Thank you." Zachary tried to interpret the sudden change in her attitude. "Actually, I was thinking about you just before you rang the doorbell. I spend so much time with the routine things that there isn't much time left for refining the equipment. I want you to help."

Amazed, Tannis's breath caught in her throat. She had to gasp. "You want me to help you work on Pandora?"

A low chuckle rose in his throat. "Don't you think you can do it?"

"Of course I can do it," she assured him. "I just... How do you know you can trust me?"

"I don't, do I?" As his eyes probed into hers, seeking the secrets of her soul, he considered the pieces of the puzzle that he hadn't yet fit together. Perhaps he should be more cautious, but emotions were pulling him. He felt that he could trust her. Especially now with her unbound hair spilling around her shoulders and her subtle scent filling his senses.

He lifted his hands to her shoulders and rubbed lazy circles with his palms against the silky fabric of her blouse. "Are you going to betray me?"

She wanted to melt into the floor, vanish into thin air, transport her body to another place in time. But she couldn't even take her gaze away. How could she answer that question? With honesty—pure and simple. "Never."

The motion of his hands slowed. His fingers tightened against her as the sincerity in her tone overwhelmed him. His voice was low, as smooth as satin. "Seal that promise with a kiss."

Her mind formed a protest, but before it reached her lips, Zachary did. His mouth moved over hers with amazing softness, eliciting her response. She raised her hands to dive into the thick shaggy locks at the back of his neck, her hunger as great as his.

Heat slithered through his veins. Zachary slid his hands down to the small of her back and pulled her closer. She came fluidly against him, increasing his urges that were too long unsated. Gentle became hard. Caress became knead. Exploration became demand.

Trembling, Tannis traced the outline of his wide shoulders. When he tilted his head to taste more deeply, a soft moan fluttered across her lips to be swallowed in his mouth. Tearing his lips away, he ravaged the length of her neck and sank into the silken juncture where shoulder met throat.

Desire was a tangible thing. She could feel it when his lips branded her delicate skin, when the swollen tips of her breasts strained against the silken texture of her blouse into the rough weave of his sweater.

His hands moved. Up. Down. Back to front. He filled his palms with her breasts, stroked her nipples with his thumbs. She shivered and gasped for breath. He took her lips again, his fingers driving her beyond reason.

Talk, she thought somewhere in her mind. She was supposed to talk. How could she when she couldn't even breathe? She didn't want to. This was madness, and she was drowning in it. Happily, readily, joyfully drowning with no regret.

Then he moved his lips to tease the lobe of one ear. She felt his breath, warm and moist against her skin. "Tannis . . ." His voice was a hot whisper. "Sleep with me."

Oh, yes! His words darted down the length of her neck, teasing her skin with the promise of complete fulfillment. Her body was aching, throbbing for more of his touch. She wanted to give him everything he asked for, take everything he offered.

Everything! Panic shot through her like a jolt of electricity. Not yet! She couldn't do this yet. She stiffened against him, then struggled for escape. But this time he did not let her go. With one arm hooked securely around her waist, he placed a hand against her cheek and tilted her head to meet his gaze.

"I want you, Tannis. As I've never wanted any other woman." He read desire in the depths of her eyes, even as she fought to deny it. "Don't make me spend another night without you."

"No." Lost in the polished jade eyes, she tried to find words. Her mind was a swirling confusion of emotions. Rational thought seemed a foggy entity, not easily embraced. "Please..."

Impatience warred with the need to understand. He loosened his grip, but still held her against him. "I know you want me. What's wrong?"

Tannis's heart pounded wildly against her chest. She wanted to tell him everything as much as she wanted to forget everything and fall wantonly into his bed. Logic and reason were impossible when she was crushed in his embrace. "Please... I have to tell you..."

The shrill alarm of the security system made her jump. Instinctively, protectively, Zachary tightened his arms around her. Glancing over her head at the video monitor, which was still turned on, he cursed quietly.

"It's Sylvia," he informed her. "I just left her about an hour ago. Something must be wrong. Will you wait while I go see what she wants?"

Unable to trust her voice, Tannis nodded slowly. Zachary gave her shoulders a reassuring squeeze as he smiled. "Be right back."

He flipped the switch to turn off the monitor before he hurried up the stairs. Alone in the lab, Tannis thought that Conway would smack his lips in devilish delight if he knew where she was right now. But she would never tell him. If circumstances necessitated, she might give him some small crumb of information about Wizac projects, but she would never hint that she'd seen Pandora.

In Zachary's absence, she wandered around the lab, but her mind absorbed nothing. The still-glowing embers of passion flamed through her system. She knew she had to either tell him immediately or get out. She would not sleep with him with secrets between them. And if she stayed, she admitted to herself, she *would* sleep with him. On the drive to his house, she'd thought she was ready to bare her soul. Now she couldn't think clearly.

At the sound of the kitchen door opening, Tannis turned toward the stairs to see Zachary coming back with a frown on his face. "I'm sorry," he said as he approached. "Sylvia's had an unpleasant visit from Pete. She's very upset, and I need to talk with her."

When he stopped in front of her, he touched her arm, letting his hand trail down it until he took her hand. "I'd like you to wait."

Seizing the opportunity to escape, Tannis shook her head. "I think I should go. If Sylvia needs you, I don't want her to feel hurried knowing that I'm waiting for you."

"Damn it!" Barely curbing his anger and frustration, Zachary turned away, dragging a hand through his hair. "I've run out of patience with my brother's intrusion into my life. If he does one more thing to threaten Sylvia or the boys, I'm going to have him thrown in jail!"

Shock waves reverberated through Tannis's body. My God! If he'd have his own brother arrested—admittedly with good reason—what would he do to her if he knew she'd been sent to destroy him? And she'd very nearly told him!

"I understand that you're upset." She marveled that her voice was capable of such a convincing tone. "It was time for me to leave anyway."

"Wait a minute." He turned back, the pain his brother caused him evident on his face. "You wanted to tell me something."

"Another time." She managed a smile. "It's all right."

Disappointed, Zachary walked with Tannis up the stairs and to the front door, bypassing the library where his distraught ex-sister-in-law sat waiting for him. Pulling Tannis's coat from the closet, he held it for her while she slid her arms into the sleeves. When she turned around, his hands lit on her shoulders.

"I don't want you to leave with unanswered questions between us." Gently he freed her hair that was trapped inside the collar of her coat, letting the silky strands slide through his fingers. "We'll finish our conversation later."

The suggestiveness of his soft tone caused her heart to pound again. Avoiding his eyes, she nodded slowly. "We will."

Chapter Six

Tannis scrambled into her car and resisted the urge to peel out of Zachary's driveway at breakneck speed. She felt she'd just escaped near disaster. Her knuckles were white from the strength of her grip on the steering wheel. An iron will forced every conscious thought from her mind as she robotically took the roads to her apartment and parked the car.

Once inside, with the door firmly shut behind her, she lost control. Her limbs started to shake, no longer willing to support her. With her back braced against the wall, she slithered down the length of it to crumple on the floor in a ball. She shook with fear, with grief and with regret.

He didn't mean it! He wouldn't really have his brother put in jail. And even if he did mean it, that didn't necessarily indicate he would do the same to her. After all, she hadn't really done anything illegal yet. But could she afford to take the chance? She'd based her decision to tell him the truth on the devotion he displayed toward his brother's family. She'd thought because of that, he would understand why she'd had no choice but to accept Conway's ultimatum.

Oh, God! She'd almost slept with him! She'd wanted it just as desperately as he had. But not like that. Not with this between them. Wrapping her arms around her drawn-up legs, she buried her face against her knees. She was tired. So tired of deceit, so tired of frustration, so tired of denying her emotions. When? When would she ever be free?

Hours later, Zachary sat alone in the lab, lost in his thoughts. In an attempt to give Pandora some semblance of a personality, he had tried to instruct her to recognize the subtle differences in voice tones. He had also programmed her to associate the voices with a wide range of emotions. But tonight was the first time she had ever made the comparison on her own. He hadn't even been sure that she could do it. As a scientist, an inventor, a computer wizard, he knew he should be overjoyed by the development. Instead, he was damn close to petrified. In love with Tannis? Impossible. He'd been in love before. He would know if that strange and elusive emotion had caught him again. Wouldn't he?

Laughing derisively at himself, he had a strong urge to dump the emotions from Pandora's memory. His hand even hovered over the keyboard for a moment. Then he sighed and let the hand fall to the table instead to rest on a stack of printouts. Tannis had become an obsession with him. He had to either slake this nearly unbearable craving for her or forget about it and get on with his business.

"Ah, Pandora," he said, running his hand across the grainy plastic that encased the computer. "What box of evil did we open tonight?"

Monday morning's sunlight was streaming across her pillow when Tannis awoke. The instant she opened her eyes, she knew that there was too much light. "Oh, hellfire!" she exclaimed, looking at the clock. In exactly five minutes, she should be sitting at her desk.

Bolting from her bed, she took the quickest shower in the history of running water. Anxious fingers fumbled with buttons and zippers, but she managed to smear concealing makeup across the dark smudges beneath her eyes. What time must it have been when she'd finally fallen asleep? Nearly dawn, she guessed, or she'd never have slept through the alarm.

Who cares? she grumbled, fighting rush-hour traffic. It wasn't as if she were in a hurry to see Zachary. Besides, she doubted that he had slept too well himself. Why, he was probably still asleep right now. In fact, he might not come in all day.

That optimistic theory crumbled when the elevator doors slid open on the seventh floor. He was leaning over Delilah's shoulder at her desk, watching something on her terminal. The sleeves of his dress shirt were rolled up to the elbow. His tie was loosened at the neck. His glasses were perched low on the bridge of his nose.

As she walked toward her desk, across the aisle from Delilah's, he looked up. The polished jade eyes registered no emotion. He studied her briefly, then turned and walked into his office without a word.

Aware of Delilah's stare, Tannis sat down, stuffed her purse in a bottom drawer and tried to remember what she'd been working on last Friday. She reached for her notes, but the coolness she'd seen in Zachary pulled at her. Swiveling in her chair, she looked through his open office door. He was hunched over his terminal, his fingers tap dancing on the keyboard. As if he sensed her eyes on him, he paused and angled his head toward her.

She held his gaze for long silent seconds. His expression remained stony as he looked at her, but gradually his eyes softened. After a moment, he turned back to his terminal.

As one level of his mind watched figures scroll across the screen, another dwelled on Tannis. He'd been frantic during the hour and thirty-seven minutes that she'd been late. His ever-active mind had thrown ominous possibilities at him. Her relic of a car hadn't made it home. She was sick and hadn't the strength to call. He'd pushed her too hard and she'd decided to seek other employment.

He'd sensed her presence the minute she'd stepped off the elevator. It had taken all the control he could summon not to rush to her and take her in his arms. She'd looked gorgeous with her cheeks flushed from the chilling wind and her auburn hair flying around her face. Had she worn it loose because he'd said he preferred it that way? Probably not. He shook his head to clear it and concentrate on his work. It was going to be a long day.

Tannis tried to ignore Delilah's scowl. Clearly, the woman had missed none of the silent exchange that had passed between Zachary and Tannis, and it was eating at her.

From the rumor mill, Tannis had learned that Delilah had been with Zachary since the beginning when her secretary's desk had been a card table in a corner of his apartment. According to the gossip, everyone knew that Delilah was in love with Zachary—everyone except Zachary. For some reason, he missed it. Why would such an astute man not notice something like that? Tannis wondered. She had picked up on it the first day.

Her thoughts were interrupted when Delilah moved across the aisle to stand beside her desk. "Zachary doesn't like anyone to be late."

Keeping her eyes on the paper before her, Tannis answered sweetly. "I'm sure Zachary will tell me if he's displeased."

Delilah glanced into Zachary's office, where he was bent over his keyboard, and leaned closer, resting one hip on the corner of Tannis's desk. "Don't think for a moment that I don't know what's going on. If you want to keep this job, you'd better be on time whether you're sleeping with him or not."

With deliberate, cautious movements, Tannis laid down her pencil and took a deep breath to keep from slapping Delilah off her desk. She raised her head and met the dark, accusing eyes before speaking in a controlled, even voice. "Whom I do or do not sleep with is none of your business. Whether or not I keep my job is entirely up to Zachary. Take care of your own job."

"Taking care of Zachary *is* my job. I've done it for seven years. I won't let you or anyone hurt him."

What did that mean? Tannis wondered with a trace of panic. Did Delilah know something about her true reason for being there? Was it just feminine jealousy? Thinking that she didn't need this aggravation on top of everything else, Tannis drew another long breath. "Get off my desk, Delilah. I have work to do. *That's* why I'm here."

Delilah finally moved back to her own desk, but before Tannis had time to pick up her pencil, Zachary summoned her in a booming, impatient voice. Her frazzled control at an end, she burst from her chair and stomped into his office. It wasn't enough that she'd overslept, she'd had to listen to Delilah's accusations, and now Zachary was angry with her for God knows what. She tossed her hair over her shoulder with a shake of her head and sighed. Some days it just didn't pay to get out of bed.

"Close the door and sit down," Zachary said in a more controlled tone.

Silently she closed the door, but didn't sit. Instead she stood before him with her tightened fists braced at her hips in defiance. But he stared at her for so long that she shifted her gaze to the window behind him.

Good Lord! The fire in her eyes could make a man tremble. Did she know how that challenging stance made her breasts jut out against the thin material of her blouse? He stifled his frustration and spoke gently. "You were late this morning."

Surprised, Tannis said, "So dock my pay."

"I'd rather you told me why."

"It's none of your business."

All night, Zachary had tried—really tried—to forget how badly he'd wanted her. Now the frustrated desire came back to fuel his anger. "At precisely eight o'clock every workday morning, your life becomes my business!"

Fury flashed deep in the blue of her eyes. How could she tell him that she'd hardly slept all night, vacillating between wanting to make long, furious love to him and plotting out a way to avoid stealing from him? "Are you the same man who promised our personal and professional relationships wouldn't conflict?"

Zachary took off his glasses and flung them down on his desk. "I was worried about you."

God, she couldn't stand it when he treated her as if he really cared. Why couldn't he just leave her alone so that nobody got hurt? "Worry about Delilah!" she snapped. "I very nearly killed her."

He suppressed the smile that tugged at his mouth. "Why?"

It infuriated Tannis that he found this encounter amusing. She braced her palms on his desk and leveled him with a look of sapphire ice. "She just insinuated that I have this job because I'm sleeping with you." The surprise that registered on his face gave her an obstinate twist of pleasure. "Since you and I both know that isn't true, why don't you set her straight so I don't have to listen to her jealous accusations?"

"Delilah? Jealous? That's ridiculous!"

Sighing, Tannis rolled her eyes to the ceiling. Oh, Wizard! For one so smart, how can you be so dumb? "Can't you see what's going on right outside your door?"

His patience snapped. "Damn it, Tannis! I don't want to talk about Delilah!"

Now it was Tannis's turn to be amused at his emotional display. "A bit testy this morning, aren't you, Wizard?"

Because he had to do something with his hands, Zachary picked up his pipe and ran his fingers over the smooth surface of the stem. "I didn't get a lot of sleep last night. From the shadows on your face, I'd say you didn't, either."

The quiet concern in his voice soothed her irritation. She sank into the chair opposite him. "I'm sorry. You were worried about your brother, weren't you?"

"Among other things." Taking his time, Zachary raised the pipe to his lips and lit it, leaning back in his chair as he studied her carefully. "Pete's an old problem. I've been dealing with it for years. What kept me awake most of the night was the unfinished conversation between us when you left. What did you want to tell me?"

Tannis's pulse leapt, but she couldn't allow herself to dwell on the whispers of passion when her survival was at stake. The cherry-sweet aroma wafted to her. How in the world did he keep dragging her into these emotional situations? "I don't want to talk about this right now."

The intercom on his desk buzzed loudly. "Damn! Apparently no one else wants us to talk about it, either." He flipped a switch on the small box and answered impatiently. "Yes?"

"R and D wants to know if you're on line yet," Delilah informed him.

"I forgot. Tell them just a minute." Switching off the intercom, he turned back to Tannis. "I'm sorry. I told AI I'd look at something on the terminal. Let's hold this conversation until we can go someplace where we won't be interrupted midsentence."

"Sure." Tannis smiled easily, relieved to be off the hook again, but she knew eventually he would pin her down.

"I have a business dinner tonight, but I'm free tomorrow evening. We could go to the roof. I have the only key."

The roof. It was tranquil and nonthreatening. And there was no bed. Between now and then, she could reinforce her defenses. "I'd like that," she said with complete honesty.

"Good. Tomorrow night then." Shifting to his role of corporate executive, Zachary put on his glasses and turned his chair from the terminal at which he usually worked to the other one that was hooked up to his Research and Development system.

Rising slowly, Tannis watched him log in, hating herself for stealing the opportunity to ascertain his access code. His fingers flew over the keyboard. As he'd explained, the system required more than one password. When the computer asked for a third one, he paused and looked up at her. "Something else, Tannis?"

"Uh, no." Flustered, she felt a hot rise of color singe her cheeks. "I was just watching how fast your fingers move. It's fascinating."

Zachary grinned. "Only an overworked programmer would recognize the value of that talent."

"True." Tannis mustered a smile before leaving his office.

Back at her desk, she sat down to concentrate on the math project, but her thoughts continually strayed to the amber words she'd seen printed on the screen. Add to that the knowledge that Zachary would be at a meeting tonight, and she didn't see how she could pass up the opportunity to get into the system. She didn't know how many passwords she needed beyond what she'd seen, but at least it was a start. She had to try. She had to do something to hold off an increasingly demanding Conway.

The tension built in Tannis all day. By outward appearance she worked on the math project, but in her mind, she weighed the wisdom of trying to break into Zachary's computer. She'd already convinced herself that hacking was the only way to get some shred of information that would hold Conway off until a better idea came along.

Occasionally, she let herself wonder about getting caught. A little fear was probably good for a thief, she decided. But she was far from being professional about this. If she didn't stop worrying, her fingers would tremble too much to hit the proper keys.

Tannis made a point of leaving at five o'clock, riding down in the elevator with several members of the staff, including Delilah, who hadn't stopped glaring all day. When they passed the guard station in the lobby, she smiled and nodded to Avery.

In her car she drove a few blocks down the street, knowing that the front door would remain unlocked for about an hour to let the stragglers out. That was her only hope for getting back in unnoticed. Coming to a small restaurant, she pulled into the parking lot behind the building.

After locking her purse in the trunk of the car, Tannis walked back up the street toward the Wizac building. The frosty chill in the air belied the fact that spring was only a few weeks away. As she burrowed her hands into the pockets of her coat, she watched her breath stream out of her mouth in white clouds. The rhythmic click of her shoes on the sidewalk matched the loud thud of her heart.

Drawing closer to the building, she slowed her pace and cautiously scanned the parking lot. Only a handful of cars remained, but the turquoise Jaguar was one of them. Hellfire! He should have been gone by now. She stepped into the shadow of one of the bare-limbed maple trees that lined the sidewalk and waited.

Shivering—from cold or from fright, she wasn't sure which—she watched the front door. Finally Zachary emerged from the building.

Watching him until he drove away, Tannis steeled her emotions, reminding herself of Meredith's plight and Conway's hold over her. She *had* to do it. Gathering courage, she approached the building.

Through the glass doors, she saw Avery standing by the waterfall, talking to a man she recognized as someone from accounting who had been in Zachary's office the previous week. From their exaggerated arm movements, the two appeared to be replaying a ball game. Good! As long as they didn't turn around, she could make it across the lobby to the stairs. The sound of the cascading water would drown out the sound of the door opening.

With her eyes constantly on Avery, she pushed open the front door and moved quietly to the stairwell. As soon as the heavy metal door closed behind her, she leaned against the wall and paused a moment to catch her breath. Calming her nerves and her heart rate, she slipped off her shoes to make the seven flight ascent up the echoing stairwell on stockinged feet.

With only a portion of his mind on driving, Zachary's thoughts raced. The problem with AI's project still plagued him. If only there were some way to—the proverbial light bulb in his head clicked on. How dumb! he marveled as soon as the solution occurred to him. He couldn't believe neither of them had seen it. But would it work?

Glancing at his watch, he looked for a place to turn around. If he hurried, he could go back to R and D, try out his theory and still make it to the dinner meeting on time. He didn't care for the B.S. session at the cocktail hour anyway.

Tannis sat at Zachary's desk with her hands on the terminal. Dim light from the outer office slanted through the open door, providing just enough illumination to read the letters on the keyboard.

Password? the computer asked.

Tannis typed, *Wizard*.

Password?

Zach.

Password?

Now what? she wondered, her fingers trembling slightly. Wizard. Zach. Pretty obvious choices. What else would he use? She tried to put herself in his mind. What other code could there be? The unexpected, she decided, and typed *Hiawatha.*

Password?

Another one? How many more could there be? Tannis knew she only had one chance to get it right. She'd better give it a lot of thought.

Zachary stopped in front of the door that opened to R and D. After punching a number code into a small panel, he passed his left hand across a laser scanner and said, "Zachary Spencer." The door slid sideways with an automatic *whoosh.* As soon as he crossed the threshold, the opening closed quickly.

At the closest terminal, he sat down, then frowned when he noticed the disk drive light blinking, indicating activity at another terminal. He was alone in the lab. The only options were his terminals at his home or in his office.

Must be a malfunction, he thought. Couldn't be anyone at his home. His office? When he pressed keys that would allow him to tap into that channel to monitor the activity, he froze in disbelief as the code unraveled before him.

Acting quickly, he picked up the phone and called the guard station. "Avery, lock the doors, front and back. No one goes out. No one!"

"Zach! What's wrong?" the old man asked, but Zachary had already headed for the door.

The only elevator accessible from the R and D floor opened on the seventh floor at the opposite end of the hall from the main elevators. Zachary knew that anyone in his office would not hear it. When the doors slid open, he moved stealthily down the hall. Whoever it was, he wanted to catch him in the act.

Tannis let her shoulders slump as she dropped her head into her hands. She couldn't do it. She'd correctly guessed her way to the menu, and the cursor was blinking, awaiting her choice. But in her mind she saw Zachary's eyes when he'd promised to help her, whatever her problem. She couldn't invade his system. Why couldn't he be as mean and ruthless as Conway?

"What's wrong, Tannis? Didn't you see enough of the code this morning?"

With a gasp of fright, she dropped her hands. His voice was cool, but there was a raging fury in his eyes. Her worst fear had been realized. Zachary had caught her red-handed. Oddly, all she felt was relief. She squared her shoulders. "All I got this morning was Wizard and Zach, but I'm in."

"I don't believe it." The fury faded for a moment, replaced by astonishment. He flicked the switch beside the door, pouring bright light over her. Circling the desk, he looked over her shoulder, remembering precisely the point in the code where she'd left his office earlier. By God! She *was* in! But how was not the question. More pertinent was why.

Straightening, he grabbed the back of her chair and spun her around to face him. "Conway?"

Tannis ventured to meet his eyes and found a frosty ice that chilled her straight to her heart. She thought she much preferred the fiery rage. "Yes."

"What have you given him?"

"Not much." She wasn't surprised that his first concern was whether Conway had any information that could damage his company. "I told him that you weren't bidding on the NASA project, and I told him about the Sorceress."

Stuffing his hands in his pockets, Zachary walked to the window and stared out. "Neither of those facts is surprising. Couldn't you find anything else?"

"Well, I . . . I didn't really want to find anything else."

It struck him that if she'd really wanted to get close to him, she could have slept with him the first week. Why hadn't she tried that? Turning, he studied her, thinking how small and frightened she looked. He remembered every time that he'd seen panic or fear in her eyes. Now he knew why. "What's he bribing you with?"

Tannis looked away. "Does it matter?"

"Not really." All the way up in the elevator, he'd told himself that it was probably some kid from any one of the various schools in the area, answering the challenge of classmates. He'd been ready to admonish him severely and send him on his way. He hadn't expected it to be Tannis, despite Delilah's warning. And he hadn't been prepared for it to hurt so badly. "Maybe I'd feel just a little better if I thought it was something worthwhile. Not just money or nude centerfold photos. Maybe a child who needs a heart transplant or an alcoholic mother. Something like that."

"Yes." Her voice trembled, and she fought back tears. "It's something like that."

"You could have told me. I would have helped you."

Now she looked at him, and she couldn't stand the hurt on his face. She wished he would yell at her, throw something, shake her. "I know that now, but I didn't at the beginning. By the time I realized how kind you were, I was in too deep."

She stood up, walked around the desk to stand beside him and looked into his eyes that were as cold as green ice. "Zachary, I couldn't hurt you. Conway said that you were onto something phenomenal. The first time you told me about Pandora, I knew that was it, but I didn't tell him. Even after I saw Pandora, I didn't tell him."

He lifted his eyebrows cynically. "Do you expect me to thank you for that?"

"No, I..." She lowered her eyes, staring at her hands, linked together in front of her. "I'm sorry."

"So am I." When she looked up, startled, he raised a hand and traced a line down her cheek with his fingertips. "We could have been good together."

That, she realized, was her biggest regret. Tannis turned away from him again. "I'll just get my personal things out of my desk." She started to move away. "At least this solves the problem of our employer-employee relationship."

"No."

Though he didn't touch her, the command in his voice stopped her as effectively as a viselike grip. When she turned back, his eyes were focused on her, moving rapidly, the way she'd come to expect when he was forming ideas. She didn't speak, just waited for him to fight his way to the logical conclusion.

"You'll stay," he said at last.

Tannis's eyes widened in disbelief. How could he want her to stay? She knew he'd never trust her again. "Why?"

A slight smile turned his lips, bringing the twin creases into view, but his eyes remained cold. It was a spontaneous notion, not well thought out, but he went with it. "You're going to help me catch Conway."

Disbelief gave way to shock. "You're crazy!"

"Could be."

"What do you want me to do?"

"I haven't decided yet." Stepping around the desk, he turned off the terminal. "When do you have to check in with Conway?"

"I don't." Tannis followed his movements with her eyes still wide. "He calls me."

"Good. Tell him you were about to get in, but you almost got caught. Stall him for a few days until I get the plan together."

Tannis agreed with a nod. Zachary came back to her and gripped one arm in his hand. "Let's go. I'm late for my meeting and you can't get out. I told Avery to secure the building."

When the elevator doors enclosed them in the intimate space, Tannis moved to the far corner, but Zachary followed. Gripping her chin in one large hand, he ran his thumb across her lips. "All of those times that I kissed you, Tannis, when you kissed me, was that part of the deceit?"

Without conscious thought, she lifted her hands to rest on his arms, feeling the tension in his bunched muscles. Her heart was in her throat as she looked into his eyes. "Never," she whispered. "That was always for me."

Zachary dropped his hand abruptly just as the doors opened on the lobby and stepped aside for Tannis to precede him out. "You can call off the red alert, Avery," he called to the guard who was pacing nervously beside the door. "I forgot that I asked Tannis to come back. We're leaving now."

Relieved, Avery fished keys from his pocket and unlocked the door. "Not like you to forget anything."

"I'm not allowed to make a mistake?"

Whatever Avery answered was lost when the door closed. The Jaguar was parked next to the entrance. Zachary scanned the parking lot. "Where's your car?"

"Down the street."

"Come on." He unlocked the passenger door and held it open. "I'll take you there."

"No, I . . ." Taking a step backward, she shook her head. She couldn't sit in that confining space with him for even a few seconds. Her mind was still reeling from the overwhelming turn of events. In light of what she'd done to him—or almost done—she couldn't stand his solicitude, strained though it was. "I'll walk."

"It's freezing, Tannis. You're already shivering." He gripped her arm and impatiently tugged her toward the door. "Get in the car."

She did, though her shivers had little to do with the temperature. They drove in thick silence until she pointed out the restaurant where she'd parked. When he pulled into the space beside her car, she intended to get out quickly, but with her fingers wrapped around the cold metal of the door handle, she turned to face him.

Staring into his glittering green gaze, she saw the impatience, the intelligence and the slight shadows of pain. She couldn't stand the knowledge that she'd hurt him. If there was the slightest chance that he might understand, she had to take it. "Zachary, when I went to your office, I fully intended to break into your system and get something to appease Conway. Figuring out the code seemed like a game to me. I forgot the danger and deceit and just concentrated on the task. But when I got in..."

She paused, choking back emotion, struggling for control. "I couldn't do it."

He watched the anxiety in her eyes. Her hands trembled. Her chest rose and fell with shaky breaths. She looked so frightened and so alone. Damn her to hell, he wanted to kiss her. She'd lied to him, tricked him and tried to steal from him. If it had been any other person, he'd have immediately called the police. Instead, he wanted to pull her into his arms and hold her until he'd soothed her fears. But he couldn't allow those feelings to reign. "Good night, Tannis."

A mist of tears clouded her eyes. She turned her head quickly and got out of the car.

Zachary stayed in the parking space until Tannis had started her car and driven away. His photographic mind wouldn't lose the image of Tannis sitting at his terminal, her face in her hands, her shoulders drooping in defeat. God, he wanted to believe that she wouldn't have taken anything.

The emotional pull was dangerous. He had to shove it away and resort to logic.

But nothing about the way Tannis made him feel was logical.

Tannis was at her desk at eight o'clock the next day after another sleepless night. All morning, she wrestled with the prealgebra programs, feeling guilty, certain that everyone in the office knew what she'd done. Paranoid, she told herself. She just wasn't cut out for a life of crime.

It was nearly noon before Zachary came in, looking a bit rumpled, as if he'd not had a very good night, either. When he stopped beside her desk, Tannis looked up and confirmed that suspicion from the haggard lines around his eyes.

"On the roof," he said, leaning close so that no one else heard. "At five. We won't discuss this matter in the office."

"Fine," she managed to whisper. But he'd already walked into his office. And although he was alone, he closed the door.

As the rest of the staff started leaving at five o'clock, Tannis stayed at her desk, waiting for Zachary and their rendezvous on the roof. When he finally came out, she rose and walked beside him to the elevator. Neither spoke while they waited for the car or after they stepped inside. The last time she'd watched Zachary insert the special key, Tannis remembered, he'd held her hand.

His words of last night echoed in her head. "We could have been good together." There had been so much regret in his voice. But she couldn't dwell on that now.

Zachary's thoughts centered on the plans that were still forming. Yet as he walked through the rooftop garden, he couldn't help memories of the other time he'd brought Tannis there. He'd thought that night he'd finally found a truly special woman, one who could understand him and challenge him.

Only when they reached the chairs did he look at her. "Sit down, Tannis."

She chose the same large rattan chair that she'd used the other night and watched Zachary settle across the table from her. Trying to appear calm, Tannis let her hands rest on the arms of the chair, fingering the rough texture of the straw. The fragrance of blossoms and rich earth enticed her as she turned her eyes to the foliage near the window against a backdrop of already darkening sky.

As Zachary gazed at her—the soft lines of her lovely face, the copper-toned wealth of hair, the sensuous curves beneath the sweater and skirt—he wondered how such a delicate-looking woman could become involved in deceit with a man as ruthless as Conway. That was only one of the questions that had kept him awake last night. And he'd have the answer before they left this garden, he vowed.

"Tannis." He spoke softly. "I talked with a friend in the police department and our corporate attorney. Unless I have substantial proof that Conway's out to steal my plans, they can't do much."

"My word—"

"Against his," Zachary interrupted. "A standoff."

True enough, Tannis conceded. And Conway was resourceful enough to stack the deck against her. They needed more proof. "What are you going to do?"

"Set a trap."

"How?"

"I don't know yet, but I have a few ideas." He reached into his shirt pocket for his pipe, found it wasn't there and let his hands fall to the arms of the chair. His fingers curled into fists. "In the meantime, to keep Conway off your back, you're going to tell him that you're very close to finding out what my big project is, but you have to be careful. You'll tell him that I'm falling in love with you and that you're leading me on. Imply that it's just a matter of time before I ask you to marry me, and you'll be able to find out everything."

Tannis's eyes had grown wider and wider as he unfolded the plan. It was ridiculous! "He'll never believe that!"

"We're going to make him believe it."

"How?"

"Simple. I'm invited to a party Saturday night. Conway will be there. You'll go with me. Before the night is over, every person there will be convinced that you and I are lovers."

"Just because we go to a party together?"

"No." His lashes lowered in a seductive gesture, and a small smile played about his lips. "Because we're going to act as though we're lovers."

Color flooded her cheeks. She couldn't play a charade like that! It was entirely too close to the fantasies that had plagued her since the first time she'd looked at his photograph in the file. "I can't do it!"

Abruptly she pushed back the chair and stood near the window, her arms folded across her chest, her mind running wild.

Zachary was beside her in a second, gripping her arm to turn her toward him. His eyes were intense, the line of his mouth grim. "You can and you will. You have no choice."

She wrenched her arm from his grasp. "How do you know I won't tell Conway what you're planning?"

"Would you prefer to tell him I caught you?"

Defeat was never easy for her to take, but he was right. She had no choice. "Of course not."

"What did he do to you, Tannis? How did he force you into this bizarre charade?"

Tannis sighed. Might as well tell him, she decided. There was certainly no reason not to. "I have a sister, a twin. She's very sick. Her care requires a lot of money. But money wasn't the entire issue."

She moved to stand beside the chair, her hands resting on the woven straw edge, her face turned away from Zachary. "Our parents were rather old when we were born. They thought they couldn't have children, so they'd never planned for them. It was a financial bind to have two at once, but we made out until it was time to go to college. Meredith won a scholarship from a service organization, and I..."

She paused, her fingers running absently over the edge of the chair, her thoughts focused on events of ten years ago. "Conway sometimes recruits promising high school seniors. He offered to pay my tuition in exchange for my agreement to work for him for five years after graduation. I was young and naive, and I saw it as a way to keep my parents from worrying."

Watching her, seeing the way she stiffened her spine as she spoke, Zachary had no doubt that what she said was true. "You've been out of college for more than five years."

"I know. But before my time was up, Meredith got sick. The initial expenses wiped out my savings. I had to ask Conway for a personal loan. A huge one."

That explained the run-down apartment, the barely running car and the less-than-fashionable wardrobe. It angered Zachary and made him more determined than ever to catch Conway. "What's wrong with your sister?"

"She's in a coma."

"Why?"

"She was working on an island in the South Pacific. She caught a rare tropical disease. There were no doctors, no antibiotics. By the time I got her back to Boston, it was too late. Her fever was too high for too long."

"No insurance?"

Tannis shook her head. "She'd just started a new job. There was a sixty-day waiting period."

Zachary pulled his hands out of his pockets and dragged them through his hair in frustration. "You should have told me. Especially after I told you about Pete. You should have known that I'd understand.''

"I went to your house on Sunday to tell you, but…" She shrugged and turned away from him. "We got side-tracked."

That was the thing that she'd wanted to tell him before Sylvia came? That she was a spy? Never had he wanted more to take her in his arms and solve all her problems for her, but he was still stinging from the shock of finding her at his terminal. He'd been upset that someone had broken into his system, but he'd been more upset that it was she. Still, he couldn't stop himself from stepping forward and laying a hand on her shoulder. "We're going to stop him, Tannis. You don't have to worry about Conway any longer."

No, now she had to worry about Zachary. His kindness was almost too much to take. They had been on the verge of discovering something wonderful, and she had ruined it before it even had a chance to take root. And now she had to pretend to be his lover. "This party on Saturday, who's giving it?"

"Jack Hunter. It's his birthday."

The name was familiar. She tried to place it. When it hit her, she couldn't suppress a childlike excitement. "Dr. Jackson Hunter? The computer pioneer? You know him? Well, of course, you do," she answered herself. "You must have worked with him at MIT."

"I did." Zachary gave her a sincere smile for the first time all day. "You'll like him, he'll like you."

As they started to walk back through the forest of flowers and plants, Tannis decided that she should be extremely grateful. Things could have turned out far worse than they had. Could she put on a convincing act as his lover? It would be easy, she thought, sneaking a glance at his long, lean form. Too, too easy.

Chapter Seven

Kneeling on the floor beside her bedroom closet, Tannis scattered empty shoe boxes. Where were the shoes she wanted? Her makeup was perfect. Her hair was clean and shining. Her dress hung ready to be slipped over her head. But where were the shoes?

She spied a heel sticking out from under a sweater that had fallen from its hanger and dived for it. She grabbed both shoes, backed out of the closet and took the dress off the rack.

It was beautiful—a clinging knit in a vibrant shade of royal blue with a full skirt and long tapering sleeves. It was elegant. And it belonged to Meredith. It hurt Tannis that she'd gone into the crate of clothes she'd steadfastly kept for her twin. But she'd had to do it.

This dinner party was to celebrate Dr. Jackson Hunter's seventieth birthday. It was being held in one of Boston's grand old hotels. And she was going as the date of Zachary

Spencer. Nothing in her closet met the requirements of such a splendid occasion.

As she gently slipped the dress from its hanger, she heard a knock at the door. On stockinged feet she ran to look through the peephole.

"Zachary!" she called through the door. "You're early! I'm not dressed yet!"

She saw him grin as if he liked that image. "Need any help?"

If the door weren't between them, she might have punched him in the stomach. "I'm going to unlock the door. You count to ten before you open it."

When he heard the slide of the chain and the click of the bolt, he put his hand on the knob, said "Ten" and opened the door. She was fast, but not fast enough. He caught a glimpse of satin and lace before she disappeared into the bedroom. Cursing himself for still being affected by her, he sat down to wait.

In a few minutes she emerged, breathless but confident. Zachary turned his head at the sound and rose slowly.

Her dress was breathtaking, accenting her eyes, which shone like jewels. But his memory of the fleeting glimpse of delicate undergarments was more intriguing. Playing the role of her lover was going to be immensely pleasant. If it didn't drive him insane. Though he'd fought to suppress it all week, he still wanted her.

She broke the spell and took a step closer. Remembering the rose he held in his hand, Zachary also took a step and offered the flower.

"Thank you," she whispered, bringing the bud to her nose.

"Going to put this one in your bedroom?"

She looked at him thoughtfully for a moment and shook her head. "I have a better idea."

Curiously he followed her into the kitchen and watched as she rummaged in a drawer. With a small pair of scissors, she snipped off most of the stem. Turning, she smoothed the fabric of his jacket and pinned the rose to his lapel.

Touched by the gesture, Zachary circled her hand as it rested against his chest, but quickly released it, fighting desires that would not be ignored. "Let's go."

A combination of excitement and apprehension seized Tannis as they crossed the hotel lobby. Following orders, she had told Conway that Zachary was in love with her, a prospect that gave the vile man perverse delight. Tonight she had vowed to play her part for all it was worth. And she was determined to make the best of it.

They had barely walked in and checked their coats when Tannis saw Dr. Jackson Hunter making his way through a crowd of people toward them. His unruly mane of white hair flew wildly about him as he moved.

"Zach!" The elderly man threw his arms around Zachary and embraced him like a son. "I'm so glad you came. It's been far too long since I've seen you."

As Zachary returned the greeting, his mentor's eyes fell on Tannis and gleamed wolfishly. "Don't tell me." He released Zachary to take Tannis's hand. "This exquisite creature is my birthday present."

Chuckling, Zachary made the introduction, slipping easily into his role. "Sorry, Jack, Tannis is mine, but I might let you dance with her later."

"I'm honored to meet you, Dr. Hunter." Tannis smiled as the guest of honor kissed her hand.

"Jack," he corrected, giving her hand back to Zachary. "I've been telling you for years that you need a good woman," he said to his former student. "Ever since you let Rebecca get away."

"Nobody 'let' Rebecca do anything," Zachary returned smoothly. If the reference to the woman had an emotional effect on Zachary, Tannis couldn't read it in his expression.

"Anyway—" Zachary tightened his hold on her hand and looked into her eyes "—I like this one better."

Jack turned back to Tannis. "I must circulate, but I'll hold you to that dance." He winked at Zachary and melted into the crowd.

With a possessive arm around her waist, Zachary led Tannis through the crowd to the bar. She looked around, awed by the company in which she mingled. The most brilliant minds in all of New England were present. Some people she had met; some she recognized from their photographs. Some she had worked with at Conway.

Just as Zachary handed her a goblet of wine, her eyes lit with pleasure. "Charlie!"

Zachary turned, following her gaze and saw Charlie Haskell, the man who had replaced him as head of R and D at Conway.

"Tannis! Zach!" The man beamed at the couple. "Why didn't I think of this?"

Tannis eyed him warily. "Think of what?"

"Well, you two are together, right? I've known both of you for a long time. I should have seen that it was a perfect match."

"Charlie!" Tannis exclaimed with a blush. "I can make my own matches, thank you!"

Charlie grinned. "Doesn't look like you need any help. What's the Wizard got you doing? Top-secret stuff?"

"No." She turned to Zachary and gave him what she hoped was an intimate look. "Actually, I'm tinkering with some personal projects for him."

"She's the best, Zach." Charlie shook his head. "Don't waste her talents."

Zachary drew Tannis closer to his side. "I'm well acquainted with all of her talents."

Charlie's brows shot up at the suggestive remark. "Say, I heard your brother's in town."

Zachary's eyes narrowed. His hand stiffened on Tannis's shoulder. "Where did you hear that?"

"Can't remember. Seems like someone told me that he'd been hanging out at some bar in Southey, hustling pool in the back room."

Just then one of the hotel's hostesses announced that dinner was served, and the trio moved to take their seats. Settling beside Zachary, Tannis noticed Richard Conway standing close enough to have overheard the conversation. She wondered if any of it was the cause for the wicked smile on his face.

All through the meal, Zachary was attentive to Tannis's every need, making sure that her wineglass stayed full and that she was included in any conversation that involved him. Between courses, he held her hand and gazed into her eyes.

"Don't overdo it," she whispered in his ear when he used his napkin to wipe whipped cream from the corner of her mouth during dessert.

"Overdo what, love?" he returned innocently.

It was all she could do not to roll her eyes.

While white-coated waiters cleared the last dishes, an orchestra began to play easy, contemporary ballads. Tannis made her way to the ladies' room. As she stood before the gilt-edged mirror, tugging a brush through her hair, she felt exuberant from the wine and the fellowship. Everyone seemed to know Zachary. Everyone loved him. She'd even seen a few pairs of envious female eyes surveying her. She stared at her reflection in the mirror, subdued by the glow of the amber lamps. Studying the sparkle in her eyes and the flush of color in her cheeks, she thought she indeed looked like a woman in love. Or a woman who'd had too much wine. Or both.

Love! She put the brush away and touched lip gloss to her mouth then headed back to the ballroom. The emotion was both exhilarating and frightening. Too bad it was only make-believe.

"You work very quickly, Ms. Robbins."

Startled, Tannis spun to find Richard Conway lurking in a doorway near the entrance to the ballroom. "Are you sleeping with him yet?"

"I don't think our arrangement requires that information, Mr. Conway."

She started away, but he shot out a hand to stop her. "The sooner you get in his bed, the sooner he'll tell you what I want to know."

Tannis tried to jerk her arm free, but his grip only tightened. "Let me go!"

Zachary stood only a few yards away, obscured by the shadow of a large potted palm. The moment Tannis started to struggle, he stepped forward. "Take your hand off my woman, Conway."

"Well, Spencer." Conway's eyes were cold gray steel, but his fingers loosened. "You wasted no time."

Fighting the urge to smash his fist in Conway's face, Zachary put his arm around Tannis. "You made a big mistake letting Ms. Robbins leave your employ. But you never were one to recognize the value in your people."

Without giving Conway a chance to reply, he turned Tannis back toward the ballroom.

"You heard everything!" Tannis accused when her breath had returned to normal. "Did you follow me to see if I'd planned to consort with the enemy?"

"When you're a double agent, everyone's the enemy." He led her toward a group of people that included Jack Hunter. "Stop scowling at me, sweetheart. We're supposed to be in love."

She painted a lovestruck expression on her face and said through clenched teeth, "Lucky for you I'm a good actress."

"Ah, Tannis." Jack smiled when he saw her approach. "Couldn't wait to dance with me, could you?"

"I've been counting the minutes." Placing her hand in his, she let him lead her to the dance floor.

Jack swept her into his arms as the music began. "You've known our Wizard very long?"

Tannis hesitated. It seemed that she'd known him forever. "A few weeks."

"Smart boy," Jack commented, moving lithely for a man of seventy. "I taught him everything he knows."

"I'll bet you did," Tannis agreed.

"You're a computer whiz kid, too?"

"I worked in R and D at Conway for five years. Now I work for Zachary."

"Ahh..." Jack leaned his head back to study her as if he'd just remembered something. "You're the one."

"Which one?"

"Hacked into Zachary's system to get his attention."

"Guilty," she said with a grin.

"I'll bet that made Zach mad."

Her grin widened. If only he knew the rest of it. "You can't imagine."

"Oh, yes I can." His eyes twinkled merrily as if he enjoyed someone getting the best of Zachary. "How are you getting along with Delilah?"

Tannis's eyebrows rose at the question. He was either very perceptive or an atrocious gossip. "She hates me."

"She would. She thinks Zachary belongs to her. He doesn't, of course, but she's very protective."

That was an understatement. "Zachary seems to be surrounded by protective people."

"Zachary's a special person." The expression on his face grew serious. "His intelligence sets him apart from the rest of the world. He's been alone for a long time. Not that he's been in seclusion, there just hasn't been a woman who understood him." Jack paused for a moment before correcting himself. "Well, there was one, but...never mind."

The movement of the dance brought Zachary into Tannis's line of sight. He stood with his feet wide apart, his hands in his pockets, watching her. When their eyes met, he smiled, and her heart dived, fluttered, leapt and dived again. What was that, Tannis? This is only a game!

"Yes, he's special," she murmured.

"And fiercely loyal to the people he cares about. Perhaps that's why we're all so protective of him. When my wife died four years ago, I was a raging, drunken fool for three months. Zachary moved in with me and stayed for ten days to dry me out. He said he didn't know the love for a woman could do that to a man. I told him he hadn't found the right woman yet."

Tannis drew back to study him. "Why are you telling me this?"

The music ended, but Jack still held her. "Thought you'd want to know. You did, didn't you?"

Moving her gaze back to Zachary, she saw that he was approaching. Her heart did that curious little flip again. She looked back at Jack and she nodded. "Thank you."

"My pleasure." He kissed the back of her hand and placed it in Zachary's outstretched palm.

As the orchestra started another song, Zachary drew her into his arms. "What was he telling you?"

Gazing into the polished jade eyes, she studied the man before her. She'd seen him as an expert in his field and admired him. She'd seen him as a victim of Conway's greed and hurt for him. Now for the first time, she let herself examine the finer qualities that she'd tried to deny. Compassion, loyalty, tenderness and magnetic sexuality. Tonight—for the duration of the party—she was determined to enjoy those qualities. "Later," she whispered, and settled her head on his shoulder, letting the music move her.

Zachary tightened the arm that held her and marveled at the way she fit against him. Resting his cheek against the silken softness of her hair, he felt desire stirring within him.

How could he be so easily ignited when he knew she was faking her actions? If the song didn't end soon, he was sure he would embarrass both of them.

Unsettled, he released her as soon as the music stopped. "Let's get another glass of wine."

For over an hour they talked with his friends. Tannis danced with Charlie Haskell and with Jack again. Zachary danced with Charlie's wife and watched Tannis, wishing that they were alone. And that the intimate facade was real.

Finally they met in the middle of the dance floor. The orchestra started a slow, sexy ballad. Their gazes locked, and she glided into his arms. He stared at her for a long moment before he moved. "You never told me what Jack said to you."

Laying one hand against his cheek, she stroked lightly. "He told me that you were special. I already knew that."

Zachary curled his fingers around the hand on his cheek and pulled her to his chest. Tannis closed her eyes and absorbed him—his hard strength pressing against her, his powerful arm circling her gently, the strength pressing against her, his powerful arm circling her gently, the bouquet of the rose still pinned to his lapel. She couldn't remember when she'd felt so peaceful. And so alive. She wanted the dance to last forever.

His fingers moved across her back, and she shivered. She felt his heat when his hips brushed against her as they moved. She was conscious of her nipples hardening when they pressed against him.

Zachary missed none of her reactions, his blood heating with wants and needs. She played her part well. Too well. He wanted her, and there was no pretense involved. When she moved her hand to let the fingers sift through his hair at the back of his neck, a low moan shuddered through him. Tannis felt the reverberations and lifted her face to look at him inquisitively.

Her eyes were too large and too blue. A man could easily drown in them. "You're a hell of an actress, love."

Sighing, Tannis nestled her head against his shoulder and decided there was no point in trying to deny it, to herself or to him. "I'm not acting."

Zachary's pulse leapt at the quiet admission. His arms tightened around her. No longer aware of the music, he stood still in the middle of the dance floor. Brushing her hair aside, he kissed her softly on the neck. "Let's go home."

Looking up, she searched his eyes. She saw desire burning in them and knew what he was asking. She couldn't answer. Her breath came heavily through parted lips. Her heart pounded—she thought loudly enough for him to hear. Her stomach twisted inside out.

He raised her hand to his lips and kissed her fingers, then placed her palm against his chest. The rampant rhythm of his heartbeat matched her own. "My home. Let's go."

To speak would be to shatter the spell weaving them together. Never taking her gaze away, she nodded.

Quickly, before either of them could realize the folly of their action, Zachary led her across the ballroom and collected their coats. Neither spoke as they walked with fingers interlaced to the hotel's entrance.

As Tannis stood on the steps with her hand tightly clasped by Zachary's, she let the cold, crisp evening air rush into her lungs. The night was clear. There would be stars and a sliver of moon, but skyscrapers and city lights disguised them. She felt the subtle brush of Zachary's thumb across the back of her hand and smiled. No secrets remained. She wanted him. He wanted her. If there could be no tomorrow, she didn't care. Tonight she was going to lose herself—her problems and her fears—in this incredible man.

Vaguely aware that Zachary spoke, she turned and saw that the valet had brought the Jaguar. Without conscious thought she felt Zachary usher her into the car, heard the door latch, knew that he slid into the seat beside her.

Once underway, he reached for her hand and gripped it tightly. Neither spoke as he drove, communicating instead with the touch. Tannis's hand was small inside his—yielding, clinging. Zachary's larger hand surrounded hers—protecting, enclosing. The first time he had to let go to downshift, she moved to rest her hand on his leg just above his knee. She felt the taut muscles of his thigh flex beneath her fingers when he moved from accelerator to brake and back again.

Tannis could not have told how long the drive took them. She remembered no street or building on the way. She heard no sounds above the pounding of her own heart. All her thoughts centered on the man beside her and their mutual desire.

After he'd unlocked the front door and ushered her inside, he raised both hands to frame her face, his eyes searching, probing, scanning. "No more secrets, love."

Bared by the boldness of his gaze, she shook her head. "None."

Slowly, easily, he settled a light kiss on her lips, pulling back almost as soon as he touched. "Would you like some wine?"

Shaking her head, Tannis knew the kisses, the touches, the scents were intoxication enough.

Taking her hand, he led her down the long hallway to the stairs, their shoes clicking in harmony on the polished wood floor. His bedroom was dark but for a swatch of moonlight beaming through the window. He stopped her there and turned her to face him. Raising his hands to his lapel, he unpinned the rose and brushed the velvety petals against her cheek. "Do you understand that this is not part of the charade?"

Tannis stroked her fingers over the back of his hand and took the rose from his grasp. "Nothing in my life has ever felt more real."

Unhurried, he moved his hands to her shoulders as he probed the sapphire depths of her eyes. He saw the truth of her words reflected in her expression. He lowered his head slowly, cautiously to the first kiss of assent. In those few seconds hearts pounded, pulses leapt, breath caught and held.

The first brush of lips touched off electric charges. Tannis locked her hands behind his neck and pulled him deeper into the kiss, parting her lips to allow him entrance. Zachary moved his hands to frame her face, tilting her head as his mouth took everything she offered. His thumbs stroked the lines of her jaw. His tongue delved into the dewy softness of her mouth. Her taste filled him, her scent enticed—feminine, sweet.

Lifting his head, he waited for her eyes to open. When they did, he found them crystal clear, not clouded by any fears or indecision. "I want you, Tannis," he whispered.

Afraid to speak, she nodded, watching the desire that kindled in his eyes.

With strong-muscled arms, he lifted her from her feet, carried her to the bed and laid her gently, then stretched beside her, gathering her into his arms.

Mouth found mouth, and passion exploded. Simple desire? Zachary wondered. This was need—primal, encompassing, necessary for his existence. Insatiable hunger, unquenchable thirst. To hurry would diffuse the wonder of it; to linger would drive him mad. No man had ever made love to a woman with such intensity.

No woman had ever responded with such fire. Tannis was raging heat. Writhing, spiraling, consumed by sensations too brilliant to name. No touch had ever made her feel this way, weak with want, strong with passion. Her hands moved, unguided, exploring the planes and contours of the man beside her, the man she had wanted from the moment she'd seen him.

Passion reigned. Patience waned. Hands tore at clothing. Shirt, trousers, dress, satin and lace were tossed from the bed. Mouths bathed flesh. Fingers stroked. Hearts pounded out of control. Neither could change their destiny now. As Zachary moved above her, she felt the press of his unrestrained desire. Of their own will, her thighs parted to receive him.

Engulfed now by the flames of desire, he no longer controlled his actions. Thrusting, shuddering, the heat built and built until it consumed him. He cried out and plunged again, exploding inside her. Shivering with exquisite pleasure, he buried his face in her hair.

Tannis plummeted, one step short of the pinnacle she'd almost reached. It didn't matter. She'd never been that close, never known it was possible to experience more. She knew now that no one had ever made love to her before this. These sensations that still tingled across her flesh were as foreign to her as they were to a virgin.

Turning his head, Zachary kissed her neck. "I don't think I can move," he mumbled.

"That's all right." Her fingers twined in his hair, stroking. "You don't have to."

"I'm sorry. I lost control. It was too quick for you, wasn't it?"

"Don't worry." She pulled his face to hers and kissed him. "It was fine. I never...I mean, I don't usually... It was the best it's ever been."

Raising his head, he searched her eyes. Incomprehensible in a woman this passionate.

"I guess there's something...wrong with me."

"Not a chance, love. There's nothing wrong with you. I'll show you."

She felt him stirring inside her, and her eyes widened. "Again? So soon?"

"Again." He smiled. "For you. Relax. This is not a contest."

As Zachary moved against her with long, smooth strokes, she closed her eyes. The sensations returned. The heat, the hunger enveloped her. He wrapped his arms around her, rocking his body against hers slowly, taking his time.

Tannis met each thrust, flowing with the motions. She felt the desire coiling inside her, spiraling upward and upward. Gradually he quickened the pace, feeling her tremble beneath him. Sensing that she drew closer and closer, he checked his own response, concentrating on bringing this precious woman to the ultimate release no man had ever shown her.

He felt the first tremors begin deep within her. Her breath came in shallow gasps. Her fingers tightened on his shoulders. Now he let his own needs run free, plunging again and again.

Tannis moaned as an unbelievable force moved through her. Wave after wave of sensation washed over her, and still he moved inside her. "No more!" she cried out. "I can't take it!"

"Yes, more," he gasped against her ear. "You can."

She crested and dived and crested again, writhing beneath him. When he plunged for the final time, spilling his life into her, she thought she would die. And happily.

Her hands fell from his shoulders, her thighs quivered. She hadn't the will to breathe.

Zachary lifted his head to look at her. So beautiful. Completely sated. No lines of tension on her face. *I gave this to her,* he thought with wonder. *For these precious moments, I gave her peace.* Trembling, he felt an indefinable emotion move through him.

Feeling his warm breath on her face, Tannis opened her eyes. "Thank you," she murmured.

He smiled and dipped his head to kiss her. "My pleasure." He wrapped his arms around her, rolled to his side and cradled her against his chest. "Sleep," he whispered.

She was on the verge of it. She felt it pulling her into its comforting darkness. Only his presence remained on the edge of her consciousness. "Zach...?" She moved one hand on his chest.

"I'm here, love."

Sleep pulled her deeper and deeper. Did she speak or did she dream it? "I never wanted to hurt you."

He captured her hand and kissed her fingers. "I know."

Drifting, she felt the strength of his arms around her, felt the beating of his heart beside her. Problems and questions might come tomorrow. Tonight she sought shelter in this amazing man's arms.

Long after Tannis slept securely in his embrace, Zachary lay awake, examining the unexpected turn of events. He'd wanted her. God knows, he'd never wanted any woman so desperately. He'd known from the beginning that she had secrets, but never would he have guessed her to be a spy.

So many times he'd watched her guard her emotions, curb her reactions. Tonight, in his bed, she'd opened for him, given herself completely, let him show her the mysteries of her own body. Just playing it over in his mind made him shiver. And yet... and yet, he'd be a fool to ignore caution. Instincts urged him to trust her. But experience and intelligence told him to hold back.

Pandora was important to him. Only Jack Hunter knew how close he was to a technological breakthrough. So far, Tannis hadn't seen enough to do any real damage. And anyone who knew him was aware of his interest in AI. Even if she told Conway what she'd seen, he wouldn't be able to duplicate it.

Although he wanted to trust Tannis, he knew he had to remain wary. He trusted his intellect, but emotions... Once, he'd let emotions hurt him. Before he would allow simple desire to deepen into something more substantial, he had to be sure he knew exactly what was in her heart and soul.

Tannis woke early as she did every morning. Her body seemed foreign to her, her limbs lethargic, almost as if she'd been drugged. But, oh, what a marvelous drug it was, she thought as she turned to study Zachary, still asleep beside her.

His hair spilled in unruly locks over his forehead. A faint shadow of beard darkened his face. Beneath his closed lids, she saw the rapid eye movement of dreams. Even in sleep, his brilliant mind never stilled. How easy it would be to love this man. But how hopeless.

Again, she told herself he didn't trust her. Hadn't she had proof of that when he'd watched from the shadows while she talked to Conway? And again, she couldn't blame him. He had a fortune at stake, an empire. Only a fool would trust a woman just because he and she had been good together in bed. Zachary was no fool.

Even if she gained his trust, there was still Meredith to consider. As long as she had that obligation, Tannis would not be free to give her full attention to any man. Mark's bitter lesson rang true. No man would play second to her invalid sister.

Quietly, with far-reaching regret that this one magical night was all she could allow, Tannis slipped from the bed and dressed. She saw on the carpet the blood-red rose that had dropped from her hand when passion exploded. Raising the blossom to her face, she closed her eyes and stroked it across her cheek as Zachary had done the night before. Some indistinguishable emotion shuddered through her, but she shoved it aside. Stepping carefully to the edge of the bed, she laid the rose on the pillow beside Zachary.

In the kitchen, she located the telephone and called a taxi. As she replaced the receiver, a tawny-coated Siamese cat leapt onto the counter to regard her indignantly. "Good morning, kitty," she murmured gently, and reached a hand to stroke the fur.

The cat hissed and bared her claws, swiping one paw at the unknown intruder. Tannis jerked her hand back just in time to avoid an angry scratch. "Oooh," she chided softly. "You must be a friend of Delilah's."

Her spine arched, the cat eyed Tannis venomously. Only a Wizard would be guarded by an attack cat, Tannis thought wryly as she backed slowly away. She grabbed her coat, then went outside to wait beside the road for the cab.

In a dreamlike state, Zachary sensed movement next to him in the bed. Mmm, Tannis, he thought, hoping she was still asleep. He wanted to watch her in the morning light before she had a chance to throw up defenses. Then make long sweet love to her with sunshine streaming across her body. With his eyes still closed, he savored the scent of her, sweet, enticing, like a rose. Her gentle breathing hummed in his ears like the purr of a cat. Reaching one hand, he touched softness, but not, he realized, the silkiness of her hair.

His consciousness snapped to full alert. His eyes flew open. It *was* the damn cat! What the hell? He sat up, the sheets tangled around his waist. A quick glance around the room told him that her clothes were gone, she was gone, his waking fantasies were gone.

Amber stretched, digging her front paws into the sheets. "Down!" Zachary ordered, and when the cat only tilted her head, he scooped her up with one hand and dumped her on the floor.

Then he saw the rose.

Picking it up, he twirled the stem between thumb and forefinger. Why did she leave? His eyes scanned the room, looking for a sign, a clue. Regrets? he wondered. Bringing the blossom to his face, he inhaled the delicate scent. No, she wouldn't have regrets. She'd had plenty of time to change her mind on the drive from the party.

She was probably just playing it safe. They'd shared a pleasurable night, satisfying mutual need, but neither of them could afford to read anything else into it. There were problems to be solved and a crook to be caught. She was smart to leave, and he should be glad she had.

Then why did he feel so empty?

Tannis woke up at five o'clock on Monday morning. She knew as soon as she opened her eyes that she wouldn't go back to sleep, but she didn't mind. She usually got by on only a little sleep. She preferred it that way.

Breathing in the steaming mists of a hot shower, she let her mind wander to the image of Zachary sleeping in his bed as she left him. It was the right thing to do, she told herself. She was already more deeply involved than was practical, and she'd be foolish to think a relationship between them could flourish. But what would he say when she saw him at the office? Would he ask her why she'd left? Would he even care? Maybe he was glad she'd relieved him from the morning-after protocol. The awkwardness, the hesitance, the uncertainty. Some of the very reasons she'd always avoided one-night stands. Only this one-night stand was her boss. Temporarily, she amended. To prove herself professionally, just on the off chance that Zachary might keep her employed after they caught Conway, she decided to go to the office early to work on the math project.

At just after six-thirty, she pulled into the parking lot of the Wizac building. When she saw the turquoise Jag by the front door, she was stunned. Not really eager to see Zachary yet, she considered going somewhere for breakfast and coming back at eight, but through the glass doors, she saw Avery pacing nervously in the lobby.

Something was wrong. Avery should have been sleeping. Or at least reading a magazine. She parked and walked quickly to the entrance. When Avery let her in, she asked, "What's wrong? Is Zachary all right?"

"Burglary. His office. Yes, he's all right." Avery laid a reassuring hand on her arm. "Go on up. I'm sure he can use your help."

Burglary! The elevator seemed to take an eternity to move. Conway? Finally the doors slid open on the seventh floor. She hurried across the outer office and halted in Zachary's open doorway.

He was on his knees in the middle of the room. His hair was rumpled, falling in his eyes, reminding her of the way he'd looked when she'd left him. He must have gotten out of bed to come here.

All around him was destruction. Every book was off the shelves. Every cabinet was open, every drawer emptied. The entire contents of Zachary's office lay in chaotic heaps on the floor.

He looked angry and sad and vulnerable. Her heart ached for him. "Zach? What happened?"

Sinking back on his heels, he gestured around the room. "Somebody wanted something."

"What?"

He shook his head slowly. "I don't know."

She crossed the room, carefully stepping over files and printouts, and knelt beside him. One hand on his arm, she worried with a fingertip at the raveled edge of a tear in his knit sweater. "What can I do to help you?"

Again, he shook his head, staring at the pile of papers he'd been stacking. "Nothing."

Her sweet fragrance came to him, and he realized how much it helped to see her. His entire day after waking without her had been spent wrestling with feelings that had surfaced. She was becoming more important to him than he'd allowed himself to admit. And here she was, quietly offering comfort. Wrapping an arm around her, he pulled her to his chest and just held her there, drawing her strength into him.

Snuggled against the well-worn yarn of his sweater, Tannis thought only of protecting him, of easing the hurt this invasion had caused him. She knew he was sensitive, knew that he would feel violated by the burglar's lack of respect for his personal and business possessions.

With his fingers in her silky hair, he realized how glad he was that she was the first one to arrive. The others would be arriving soon, and his office would be crowded as everyone came in to look, to speculate. At least they'd had these few private moments. Who knew when they'd have another?

He glanced at his watch, thinking that it must be nearly eight. Quarter of seven? He looked again. What was she doing here so early? As his mind ran through possibilities with lightning speed, he began to feel a chilling tremor creep over him. With stiffened muscles, he pushed her to arm's length, gripping her shoulders. "Why are you here?"

"I work here." She was confused by the look in his eyes.

"Now." His fingers tightened. "Why are you here now?"

"I couldn't sleep. I came to work on the prealgebra programs."

"At six-thirty?"

"I said I couldn't sleep. Zachary, what are you getting at?"

He released her so abruptly she fell to the side, catching herself with a palm against the carpet.

"Even an amateur spy should know better than to return to the scene of the crime so soon."

Tannis glared at him. He couldn't possibly think that she... Apparently he did. The look aimed at her was fire and ice. Tannis knew she couldn't hold her temper much longer. Only because she knew he was upset did she even try. "How can you think that I would do this to you after the night we shared?"

"A night. That's all. Now I see why we didn't share the morning as well." His eyes glittered the way they did when he'd just solved a problem. His mouth formed an ugly smirk. ''Were you hoping I might talk in my sleep?''

''You son of a bitch!'' Her hand streaked out to slap him so swiftly that she didn't realize it herself until she felt the sting on her palm. ''How dare you suggest that I slept with you for ulterior motives? Do you think I'm so heartless that I could destroy everything you hold dear? Don't you know I care about you?''

Slowly Zachary raised a hand to run across his reddened cheek. Tannis stared at the harsh print of her fingers on his face, horrified by what she had done and said. She saw the play of emotion on his face and couldn't bear to watch it any longer. With carefully controlled motions, she rose and went to the window, staring at the waking city below her.

She huddled against the pane and waited for Zachary to order her out of his office.

Chapter Eight

Zachary stood behind her, his hands hooked into his back pockets to keep from touching her. Emotion ran through him like an electric current. He took a deep breath, urging his body to relax. "Turn around, Tannis."

She closed her eyes, hesitating, then opened them. She faced him and found, remarkably, that his eyes were anxious, not angry as she'd suspected they would be.

"You're right," he said softly, pinning her with that gaze that she could never escape. "I should have known it wasn't you. If you were coldheartedly plotting against me, you could have gotten what you wanted and been gone by now. The only explanation I can offer is that I'm disturbed by this incident and you were the first person available for me to dump on. I'm very sorry."

That's all? Tannis's eyes widened in disbelief. He was apologizing to her? "You aren't angry with me for slapping you?"

"Well, I'd rather you didn't do it again, but I guess I deserved it."

Embarrassed, she twined her hands together and looked away. "I agree that you deserved it, but I still shouldn't have done it." She ventured to peek at him from beneath lowered lashes. "I'm sorry."

"I guess neither one of us handles our emotions very well." He took his hands out of his pockets, almost reached for her, then retreated, as if he'd thought better of it. "I have an important appointment at nine. I have to take a shower. Would you mind putting the books back on the shelves?"

"No."

Watching him take clothes from the closet and head for the small bathroom beside the kitchen, she noticed that his usual exuberance was missing from his movements. He wasn't just upset, he was tired. "Zachary, how long have you been here?"

He turned in the doorway, brushing the hair out of his eyes. "Avery called me shortly after three."

"Would you like me to make some coffee for you?"

A slow smile eased some of the tension from his expression. "I'd love it."

The minikitchen had been vandalized as well, but Tannis managed to salvage most of the sugar and all the coffee. As she filled the pot, she listened to the sound of water running in the shower. She laid one hand against the wall, knowing that he was on the other side. She imagined him standing nude, the hot spray hitting him, streaming down his body in glistening rivulets. No! She jerked her hand away as if it had been burned. That image was far too dangerous.

Instead, she centered her concentration on arranging the books on the shelves. Something about the disarray of Zachary's office reminded her of the farmhouse. Pete? she wondered. Could Pete have done this? Should she mention that thought to Zachary?

No, she decided. If it were a possibility, then Zachary would have thought of it already. Had he called the police? It didn't seem likely.

While she moved about the office, the running-water sound moved from the shower to the sink, and she knew he was shaving. A little while later, she heard the electric hum of the hair dryer and imagined his fingers raking through his thick blond locks. Wish it were my fingers, she thought absently, and straightened with a jolt, dropping the stack of books in her arms.

She had just retrieved them when she heard the bathroom door open.

"Tannis, what were you planning to do today?"

"Whatever the Wizard wants."

"You came in early to work on the math project?"

"Yes."

"Would you work in here instead? I don't know what the burglar thought he was going to find, but I don't think I want anyone else going through this stuff."

"Are you sure you want me to do it?"

"Yes." He watched as she stretched to reach for a book just beyond her fingertips. Determined, he thought. Stubborn. And proud. "Why won't you look at me?"

Because she'd almost walked into the shower with him, and that thought scared the hell out of her. "No reason." She stood, balancing a stack of books, and placed them on the shelf. The friendly smile she'd meant to give him wavered when she saw him. He had on the pants of a navy suit, but he was just slipping his arms into the shirt when she turned. It hung unbuttoned, stark white against the golden tone of his chest. "The coffee's ready."

The obstacles that littered the floor allowed her to keep a wide distance from him as she moved to the coffee maker. She poured the fresh brew into a cup and added the sugar.

"Aren't you having any?" he asked when he'd stepped over a mound of papers to reach for the cup.

"Sure."

Since the chairs were either overturned or piled high with papers, Zachary cleared a spot on the floor and sat down. Leaning against the wall, he bent one leg and dangled an arm over his knee, taking a long drink.

"Sit down," he offered when she had her own coffee. "I'm trying to figure this out."

She settled on the floor beside him, drawing her legs up beneath her and smoothing her skirt. "Is anything missing?"

"Not that I can tell. That's what I don't understand. A few of the books are first editions. That lithograph on the wall is a numbered print. Even the terminal is worth something, but I don't think it was touched. There's a good chance the intruder was here just to shake things up."

"How did you deduce that, Sherlock?"

"Well . . ." He drained the coffee, then set the cup beside him, toying with the handle, his brows drawn together. "Conway's after something, but he doesn't know what. He's got you on the inside, but we must have looked pretty cozy to him Saturday night. Maybe he's hedging his bets."

Tannis always enjoyed watching him think. She could almost feel the energy emanating from him. "He's just reminding both of us that he's capable of destruction in case I've decided to jump ship?"

His eyes narrowed. "Or maybe I just made him mad."

"Or maybe it has nothing to do with Conway."

Nodding slowly, he leaned his head back against the wall and sighed, his gaze settling on the baseball that had rolled under a chair. "Sure looks a lot like the farmhouse, doesn't it?"

From the weary slouch of his shoulders, Tannis knew how much the idea pained him. Neither of them had voiced the possibility that Pete was acting for Conway, though both thought it. It was one thing to give his brother money to get him out of trouble and quite another to accept that Pete might be aiding the enemy. Setting her coffee mug on the floor, she leaned closer, taking Zachary's hand in hers. "Should I mention this to Conway the next time he calls? Maybe he'll tell me something."

"Yeah, I guess so. If he is behind it, it will look suspicious if you don't tell him." He curled his fingers around her hand and cradled it to his chest. "I had no reason to doubt you, Tannis. I'm really sorry."

"Forget it. We both overreacted from the emotional strain." His shirt had fallen open, exposing the wide expanse of his chest. Her fingers trailed against his skin and felt it heat beneath her touch. She lowered her eyes, unable to meet that probing emerald gaze.

"Tannis?" With strong fingers he lifted her chin, forcing her to look at him. "You do care, don't you? More than you want to. Is that why you left before I woke up?"

She bit her lip in hesitation, then admitted, "Yes."

His eyes, reddened from the lack of sleep, gazed into hers as his heart thudded against her fingers. His voice was whisper soft. "I care, too." His hand moved with a slow touch to her cheek. "And I didn't want to, either."

Even as her mind told her to back off, she leaned closer to meet the kiss he offered. The moment that lips touched lips, his arms wrapped around her, pressing her against him. Her hand on his chest slid down to rest against the ridge of muscle just above the waistband of his slacks.

Shivering from her touch, he assaulted with a demanding kiss. His tongue swept hungrily over her lips. He took and took, having wanted this from the moment he'd awakened to find her gone. Desire ignited in him and raged out of control.

Tannis flamed. Want and need were combustible entities within her breast. She touched him, her fingers stiffened and dug into his flesh. She tasted him, the lingering mint of toothpaste. She breathed him, the scent of soap and shampoo assailed her, then gave way to more intimate, masculine fragrances. She hadn't known that it was possible to smell passion, to taste it, to touch it.

He felt before he heard the small cry of desire that issued from her throat. His arms tightened, moving her, easing her back. Was it possible to want her even more? If he'd thought one night could satisfy his craving, he'd been wrong. Totally, thoroughly wrong. The hunger was greater, knowing how sweet the taste. One hand found a length of stockinged thigh and reached beneath the soft wool fabric of her skirt.

"What the hell is going on?"

Two bodies convulsed in shock. Zachary straightened, bringing Tannis up with him, still holding an arm around her shoulders. "What the hell does it look like, Delilah?"

Tugging at the hem of her skirt, Tannis met the disgust in Delilah's eyes and smiled sweetly. "Good morning, Delilah."

Ignoring her, Delilah returned her accusing glare to Zachary. "How can you do this with her?"

"Get out, Delilah, and close the door behind you." His patience hung on a very thin wire, evident from his voice. "Don't ever enter my office again without knocking."

"Zachary—"

"*Now*, Delilah!"

With a last frosty glare at each of them, she spun and flounced from the room, slamming the door hard enough to rattle the hinges.

"Well, thanks a lot, Zachary." Tannis turned her face to his. "I'm sure I'll have a much easier time getting along with her now."

"Women!" he muttered, shaking his head.

"What's the matter, Wizard?" A teasing twinkle danced in her blue eyes. "Something about the feminine mystique that does not compute?"

With a quickening of muscle, he dragged her back against his chest, tangling a hand in her hair. "If I didn't have a meeting that I cannot miss, I'd show you exactly how I feel about feminine mystique." He crushed her mouth with his in a blazing kiss, then tore his lips away. "I've unlocked your passion, Tannis." The harsh edge of his voice held more than a promise. "You can't deny it, and neither can I."

Taking his hands from her quickly, he got up and strode to the closet. Tannis felt tremors shaking inside her and was helpless not to watch. As he stood with his back to her, he unzipped his pants with no modesty and stuffed in his shirttails, then zipped back up. He pulled out the vest and matching jacket, draped a tie around his neck and went into the bathroom to stand before the mirror.

Tannis rose on shaky legs and bent to pick up the coffee cups, glancing at her watch. Something wasn't right. What was it? "Zach...?" She moved to the doorway and met his eyes reflected in the mirror. "It's only seven forty-five."

"I know, but I'm going to Cambridge, and the traffic is bad this time of morning." His long fingers worked to form the knot in his tie.

"No, that isn't what I mean. I usually get here about quarter of eight. Delilah is never here before eight."

"So she couldn't sleep." He frowned at the lopsided knot and pulled it out to start over.

"Point well taken." Leaning a shoulder on the door frame, she crossed one ankle over the other. "But she didn't say a word about the mess in your office. Like she wasn't surprised?"

"I don't think you're on to anything, Watson, but I'll keep it in mind."

"Watch your arrogance, Sherlock. Does she have a key to the building?"

"Yes. So do a dozen other people."

"Oh." She worked on that thought for a moment, frowning, while he looped the ends of the tie. "Where are you going in Cambridge?"

An enigmatic smile curved his lips. "Secret." He glared at the tie in the mirror, swore and yanked the knot out again.

"Calm down!" Stepping in front of him, she took the silk material in her hands, straightened it and tied the knot. "Who usually ties your ties for you?"

"I don't usually have a cagey female staring at me with tempestuous eyes while I'm doing it."

"Oh?" The knot was perfect. She smoothed the tie and buttoned his vest over it. "What kind of eyes do they usually have?"

"Feline." Reaching, he hooked the jacket with an index finger and slung it over his shoulder. "I might not be back today. Sure you don't mind working on this mess?"

"Not at all." She smiled up at him, her hands still resting on the fabric of his vest. "Do you want me to try to put things back where they go, or just stack them in categories?"

"Use your own judgment. I trust you." Kissing her lightly, he grazed her cheek with his knuckles. "I could get used to having you around when I get dressed every morning."

Her insides liquefied, but her shaky smile remained in place. "I think that would make your cat jealous."

"Amber would just have to learn to live with it."

He scooped up his keys and wallet and strode across the office. Before he left, he turned back to her. "Try not to get into a fistfight with Delilah."

Grinning, he stepped out and closed the door behind him.

During the early part of the morning, various people poked their heads into the office to gawk. Tannis said little, keeping to the task of creating order out of chaos. When she uncovered a radio, she turned it on, found it tuned to a jazz station and left it there at a low volume while she worked.

She tackled the books first, until she had the massive shelves filled. The spines of each volume stood in precise alignment on the long rows. Next she took on the kitchen and the bathroom. The contents of the files and cabinets were the most difficult to reorganize. Though some file folders had remained intact, others had been scattered to the four corners of the room. Printouts, letters, legal pads and notebooks were strewn randomly. It was easy to determine where some things belonged, but with others, it was pure guesswork.

Tannis couldn't remember when she'd worked her muscles so strenuously, and she relished the thought of a long hot bath. As she gathered her purse and coat to go home, she turned and found Avery standing in the doorway, a look of dismay on his face.

"Well, you've had a busy day," he commented, running the rim of his gray guard's hat around in his hands.

"There's still a lot left to do." Her gaze settled on the old man's haggard face. "Avery, you look tired."

"I'm all right." He waved a hand at her, but perched on the edge of the sofa. "I hated to call him and tell him about it, but I had to. He was so upset."

"I know he was."

"I let him down."

"Avery, no." She crossed to the sofa and sat beside him. "I'm sure Zachary doesn't feel that way."

"No, he wouldn't, but I do. I'm supposed to take care of things."

"You do," she assured him.

Again he shook his head, his eyes fixed somewhere before him. "Me and my wife, we didn't have any kids. We loved those two boys—Pete and Zach. Watched 'em grow up. They were always comin' to the house. Treated 'em just like they were my own." His hands trailed down the black stripe on his gray uniform pants. "'Course, their dad, he wasn't around much. Always comin' and goin'. Like Pete does now."

He turned to her, his soft blue eyes filled with love. "Yeah, I let him down."

"I'm sure Zach doesn't blame you."

"I was the one who started calling him the Wizard. He was always runnin' across the yard to show me some new contraption he'd thought up. 'Here comes the Wizard with some new gizmo,' I'd say to my wife."

Tannis smiled at the image of Zachary as a little boy, though surely he'd never had a little boy's mind. "Are his parents still living?"

"Mother is. Not the old man. He died while Pete was playing in the big league. Sadie—that's their mother—she remarried a few years ago. Lives in Florida now. Zach bought 'em a condo on the beach. Takes care of his own, that boy does."

His eyes narrowed and hardened. "Now Pete, that's another story. Bright boy. Threw one hell of a curve ball. He was a hell-raiser. Can't tell you how many times I drove Sadie downtown to get him out of one scrape or another. Drinkin', carousin', stealin' hubcaps. Guess he just has too much of the old man in him."

"Avery, have you seen Pete recently?"

"No. Can't remember when I saw him last. Zach asked me the same thing." He tilted his head to look at Tannis. "You know Pete?"

"Only from Fenway Park. My dad was a great Sox fan."

"No kiddin'?" Avery gave her a wrinkled grin. "Not too many girls take an interest in baseball."

"They do if their dad wanted a son and only got daughters."

"No wonder Zach likes you." Avery stood and put his hat on. "A man couldn't ask for a better woman than one who likes baseball. Guess I better get back downstairs. You coming?"

"Yes." Smiling, she picked up her coat and purse and rode to the lobby with Avery.

It was almost ten when Zachary returned to the Wizac building. With a bottle of Scotch clutched in one hand, he approached the well-lit lobby. A nervous Avery paced the inside, as serious as the guards at Buckingham Palace. When he saw Zachary coming, he hurried to the door and unlocked it for him.

"Any excitement tonight?" Zachary asked as he headed for the elevator.

"Quiet as a tomb."

Reading the worry and the remorse on the old man's face, he beckoned to him, raising the bottle in the air. "Come on up with me."

A relieved smile broke out on Avery's face as he started toward the elevator.

"Uhh, Avery." Zachary was helpless to suppress an affectionate grin. "Don't you think you should lock the front door?"

Embarrassed, Avery went to the door as fast as his aching legs would carry him, then hurried back to the elevator. When they reached the seventh floor office, he could no longer contain his emotions. "I feel real bad about what happened last night."

"Don't. It wasn't your fault." Zachary took two glasses out of the cabinet by the sink and splashed a shot of Scotch in each. As he handed one to Avery, he laid a hand on his shoulder. "Somebody wanted to get in here last night. There was nothing you or anybody else could have done to stop it. It could have been someone with a key. Maybe somebody on the cleaning crew left one of the doors propped open. Hell, someone could have gotten to the roof and come in through the garden. The point is, if someone wants to get in, he'll find a way even if there are a dozen guards."

"You know who it was?" Avery asked, fortified by the Scotch he'd downed in one gulp.

"I have a few thoughts."

"Pete?"

"Maybe."

Zachary moved to the wide window, swirling the Scotch with a circular motion of his wrist. The glass felt cold against his skin. He took a drink and felt it burning all the way down until it hit the pit of his stomach and ricocheted around. "I've been with the president of Starfire Electronics all day."

"That's an impressive company."

"Right." He took another sip of Scotch and turned around. "Wants to buy me out."

Avery bristled with indignation. "You told him 'no way' didn't you, boy?"

"No, I listened to him. It's a hell of a good offer. More money than I'll need in a lifetime."

"You're gonna take it."

"Just thinking about it." Zachary grinned. "I could throw away all my three-piece suits."

"Well, that's worth something." Crossing to the mini-kitchen, Avery placed his empty glass in the sink. "You think about it, Zach. You'll come to the right answer."

"I hope so."

Avery left him alone with his thoughts. Looking around, Zachary saw how very hard Tannis had worked all day. She'd even cleaned the bathroom, he thought as he passed the half-open door. Glancing inside, he saw the towel he'd used draped across the shower rod to dry, the drips and puddles mopped up, even his jeans and sweater neatly folded. Reaching for the more comfortable clothes, he shed the businessman's suit and headed for his rooftop refuge.

As he stood before the wall of glass, looking out on the city, he felt a sense of direction seize him. Enough money to last a lifetime. Wasn't that why he'd built the company in the first place? He could take a few months to remodel the farmhouse, convert the greenhouses into labs, spend the next forty or fifty years in the quiet solitude of the country.

If Pandora never came to anything, there were always other ideas lurking in the back of his mind. And what a great place to raise children.

Children? He'd never before seen children in his future, but there they were. Auburn-haired children with sapphire eyes. Good Lord! He couldn't let his thoughts run in that direction. He cared about Tannis, wanted her, but he certainly wasn't in love with her. Was he?

He'd felt so close to her this morning as she'd straightened his tie. So comfortable. Sparring, making each other angry, matching wits. But always with that underlying spark of sexuality.

No, he wasn't in love with her. He had too much at risk right now to let emotions muck up his thought processes. Too many decisions to make.

But maybe when all of this was over...

Maybe.

Late that night, as Tannis sat at her personal computer working on the algebra project, her telephone rang. She stood up slowly, stretching cramped muscles and went to the kitchen to answer it.

"Anything to report?"

Tannis sighed. She truly hated this man. "I didn't have much of a chance to play cloak-and-dagger since I spent the entire day putting Zachary's office back together." She decided to force the issue. "You should have thought of that when you trashed it."

He chuckled. "You should know I never get my own hands dirty."

Tannis pictured a cartoon villain twirling a length of black mustache in bony fingers. "Who did you hire for the job?" she asked casually.

"You don't need to know," Conway snapped. "How did he take it?"

"He was angry. What did you expect?"

"Does he suspect me?"

"He has a list. You're on it." His casual attitude toward the vicious act angered her. "What was the point? There's nothing classified in his office. The big project is in his private lab in his home."

"I wanted you to be aware that I have unlimited capabilities. You made a pretty convincing picture of a woman in love Saturday night."

Tannis shivered. That came damn close to the truth. "You want me to win his confidence, don't you? Haven't you ever heard 'you can catch more flies with honey'?"

"You know, Ms. Robbins, you'd do better teamed with me than with Spencer. I could keep you quite comfortable if you'd dance with me the way you danced with him."

The thought turned her stomach. The tone of his voice chilled her. He couldn't be serious! It wasn't enough that he was jealous of Zachary's business accomplishments, was he jealous of the attention she'd given him as well? "All I want is to finish with this disgusting ordeal, square my debt and get as far away from both of you as possible."

Conway chuckled again—a low, evil sound. "Get the information I want. Then we'll discuss what you want."

With a resounding click, the connection was broken. Tannis slammed her receiver on its hook, more determined than ever to do whatever Zachary asked to see this vile man stopped.

At seven o'clock the next morning, Tannis took the elevator to the seventh floor and stopped at her desk to drop a folder of notes. Using her modem, she'd worked on the math project at her home terminal until after midnight.

Peeking into Zachary's office, she decided not to do any further straightening in there until he returned. Most of the papers and files that were left were things he needed to sort through. But it wouldn't hurt to have the coffee ready. She knew he'd probably been out late last night.

As she crossed to the minikitchen, she stopped when she noticed his clothes slung across a chair. Her hand moved of its own volition to pick up the wrinkled shirt and clutch it to her chest. His distinctly masculine scent still clung to the fabric. Vivid sensations of the night she'd spent in his bed raced through her mind. Oh, what a mistake that had been! She'd thought she could satisfy her longings and blithely walk away. Knowing what pleasures he could give her, she wanted him more than ever. In fact, if she let herself, she could imagine a lifetime of working by his side. But she knew it could never be. They'd been thrown together by circumstances. Once their mission was accomplished, the relationship would be over. Forcing herself to stop entertaining such ridiculous fantasies, she dropped the shirt on the chair and went to the minikitchen to prepare the coffee maker.

When the machine was ready to be switched on, she moved to the corner of the office to pull back the vertical blinds across the long window.

"I think there's an organization that treats workaholics, Ms. Robbins."

"Then you should probably join," she countered, smiling at the sound of Zachary's voice.

Standing just inside the doorway, he wore wool slacks and a bulky sweater, both black-and-white. One hand was planted against his hip, and in the other he carried a bouquet of roses. No green tissue paper enveloped them. No fern, no baby's breath. Just bare, long stems gathered into his fist. She felt her heart fluttering and worked at ignoring it. "Coffee maker's ready to go. Just punch the button."

"You expect me to make my own coffee?" he teased with mock horror.

"Oh, sorry." She started to the minikitchen. "Too complex. I'll make a flow chart for you."

With quick strides he intersected her path, clamping a hand around her wrist. "Flow chart *this*." His mouth claimed hers swiftly with possessive greed, then relinquished her.

"A kiss like that only flows in one direction." Tannis paused to catch her breath. "I'd rather not be rolling around on the floor again when Delilah comes in."

"Want to roll around somewhere else?"

"Oh, Zachary." She spoke with exaggerated emphasis and fluttered her eyelashes. "You're so romantic."

"You make fun of a man who's brought you thirteen roses?" He lifted the bouquet and placed it in her hands.

"Thirteen?" She buried her face in the buds, breathing in the fragrance. "Why not a dozen?"

"Boring. You would have expected a dozen."

"I didn't expect any, but thank you."

"Just a small show of appreciation for your hard work and your loyalty." He moved to the kitchen and started the coffee maker.

Wondering if he truly thought her loyal, she followed him and looked for something to hold the roses. The best she could do was a plastic half-gallon pitcher.

"You got a lot done yesterday," Zachary commented as he got the coffee cups, sugar and a spoon. "I think I can finish today. How late did you work on the math project last night?"

"About midnight." She answered automatically, then realized what he'd said. "How did you know I worked on it?"

"Elementary, my dear Watson." He turned to her, grinning. "You didn't work on it yesterday, but there's a folder of notes on your desk."

While they stood by the sink, waiting for the coffee to brew, Tannis arranged the roses in the pitcher. "Conway called me last night. He is responsible for this mess, though he wouldn't tell me who did it. We convinced him Saturday night. He's a little worried that I've gone over to the other side."

"But you assured him that you hadn't."

"Of course."

He leaned on the edge of the sink, watching her thoughtfully. "Tannis," he began casually, "have you ever been to San Francisco?"

"No, but I've always thought I'd like to some day."

"How about Thursday?" He smiled at the startled surprise in her eyes. "With me."

San Francisco? Thursday? With Zachary? Suddenly it made sense. "The electronics show?"

"Yeah. Want to go?"

She turned back to the roses, rearranging the long stems although they didn't need it. "Doesn't marketing usually handle those things for you?"

"Usually. But I've been asked to speak at the dinner Saturday night. We'll leave Thursday and come back Sunday." He watched her fingers nervously playing with the roses and reached for one hand. "It would be a good opportunity to get away from . . . everything."

Thursday to Sunday, she thought, feeling the soothing stroke of his fingers on the back of her hand. Four days alone with Zachary in San Francisco? Away from the pressures and the dangers of espionage? An exciting city, an elegant hotel, just the two of them. Uh-uh. No way. "I don't think so."

His fingers curled around her hand, holding it still. "Then I have to insist."

She turned sharply, alarmed. "Why?"

"Two reasons. If Conway buys that we're getting close enough for me to reveal my secrets, he'll expect you to go with me. And I know he isn't going, so I don't feel really comfortable about leaving you in Boston when I'm on the other side of the continent. Call it macho protective instinct if you want to."

Tannis hated being dominated. Despite everything she'd been through in the last two years, she prided herself on the fact that she'd maintained control of her life. Until now. Temper flared. "Why don't you call it what it really is? You don't want me free to snoop around while you're gone."

Zachary's fingers loosened, dropping her hand. His eyes narrowed dangerously. "I didn't say that, Tannis."

"But you were thinking it."

He considered her words. Had that been in the back of his mind? He struggled to keep emotions from clouding his thinking. "Maybe just a little, but the first two reasons are true. I can't afford to trust anyone right now. You should be able to understand that."

She did, but it still hurt. He wanted to trust her, she was sure, but knowing what was at stake, she couldn't blame him for being cautious. "You're right," she said with a defeated sigh. "I'll go."

"Thank you." He looked genuinely pleased. "I'll call the hotel and the airline."

Airline! Oh, hellfire! She hadn't thought of that. An uneasy feeling shivered through her, upsetting her equilibrium for a second. "Uh...Zachary..."

"What?"

"I don't fly very well."

He smiled. "That's all right. I do. I'll take care of you. How bad is it?"

"Can you give me Pentothal and wake me up when we get there?"

"Oh, dear." Zachary grimaced. "That is serious."

Chapter Nine

Tannis adjusted her seat belt for the third time, clenched her hands into tight fists in her lap and closed her eyes. She felt a cold sweat beading on her forehead and upper lip.

"Uh, Tannis."

She opened one eye, just a fraction, and peered at Zachary, who sat in the window seat beside her.

"We haven't left the terminal yet."

Both her eyes flew open, and she straightened her spine. "I know that!"

He pulled a handkerchief from his pocket and gave it to her, watching with concern as she pressed it to her lips "You aren't going to throw up, are you?"

"I have acrophobia, not motion sickness."

He gave her a smile that he hoped was reassuring while, typically, his mind put data together. "You weren't afraid when we were in the garden on the roof."

"You didn't notice that I never stood near the edge." Taking a long deep breath, she wrestled with anxiety. "Besides, I had a strong, solid building under me."

"Relax, Tannis. Air travel is safer than—"

"Driving a car," she interrupted. "I know that. But if something happens to my car, I pull over to the side of the road. What do we do if something happens to the airplane? Park on a cloud and wait for the skyway patrol?"

"Maybe I should have brought the Pentothal," Zachary muttered helplessly.

Almost imperceptibly, the plane began to roll away from the gate. Tannis swallowed hard and ventured a glance around the cabin. First class. She'd never flown first class, but Zachary had thought she might be more comfortable. She really didn't see how moving forward a few rows could make a difference. The only seat that could possibly be more comfortable was one on the ground somewhere. Still, she had to admit that he was taking her phobia well.

Across the aisle Tannis saw a little girl of three or four in a navy-blue dress with a wide white collar. She was clutching a Wizac Storyteller, looking around with wide eyes as brilliant as copper pennies and asking her mother an endless stream of questions. The woman answered patiently and smoothed the hem of her daughter's skirt.

If that little child can do this, I can do this, Tannis thought, shoring up her courage. She shifted her gaze to Zachary and found him looking out the window. Oh, God! We're almost at the end of the runway. A flight attendant droned safety instructions and pointed out emergency exits.

"Zachary, I've changed my mind. I want to get off!"

He lifted her rigid arm, uncurled her fingers and laced them through his. "Would I let anything happen to you?"

"You aren't flying the plane."

Glancing around, he saw the flight attendants sit down and buckle their straps. He heard the subtle change in the whine of the engines. He felt the tightening of Tannis's fingers. Once she got past takeoff, he guessed she would be all right. Considering carefully, he decided that distraction was the best method. "How old were you when you lost your virginity?"

As she snapped her head toward him, her eyes were wide, but blazing with fury, he noted, not fear or panic. She tried to jerk her hand away, but found it clamped firmly in his grip. "You really work at being obnoxious to me, don't you?"

"You give me too much credit." His wide smile was its most calculatedly charming. "Actually, it takes very little effort." The jet slanted upward as it left the earth. "So how old? In college, I bet. Nineteen? Twenty?"

As they heard the clunk of the landing gear being locked away, he asked, "Was it the president of the science club?"

"You're disgusting!"

"I agree, but look." He leaned back against his chair to give her a clear view. "It kept you from noticing that we're in the air."

Paling, she leaned closer to the window and saw clouds. "Oh."

"Now, unless you have a parachute under your jacket, I have you captive for the duration of the flight." He shifted in his chair again, blocking her view of the window. "What shall we talk about that will keep your mind occupied?"

A long breath eased out of her, and the lines of tension on her face gradually relaxed. She met his eyes and managed a weak smile. "You're too good to me."

A smile of amusement tugged his mouth. "I thought I was disgusting."

"You are. It was a cheap trick."

"But it worked."

"It worked." She nodded, her smile gaining strength. "Takeoff is the worst part."

In a few minutes the flight attendant offered drinks. Tannis took a glass of white wine. As she sipped slowly, she felt herself relaxing further. Zachary kept up a steady stream of conversation that almost made her forget that she was flying. Almost. One part of her mind remained constantly attuned to every change of altitude, every sound of the engines.

Somewhere over the midwest, conversation turned to the office, and inevitably Delilah's name came up.

"I can't do anything to please her," Tannis complained. "She glares at me all day long. If I speak to her, she's snippy."

"It's not that bad," Zachary returned. "You're exaggerating."

Exaggerating! Tannis turned her face to stare at the seat back in front of her. The woman had him completely fooled. Whenever he was around, honey dripped from her voice. As soon as he went back into his office, she was the Ice Princess. It was time the Wizard was enlightened. "I'm not exaggerating. Why do you suppose she's so jealous of me?" She turned to pierce him with a crystal sapphire gaze. "Zachary, she's in love with you."

He stared in stunned silence for a split second, then shook his head. "That's ridiculous."

Angry again, Tannis shifted her gaze to the little girl across the aisle who was sleeping now with her thumb in her mouth. Smart girl, Tannis thought dryly. "For a man with a genius IQ, you certainly can be dense sometimes. Can't you tell when a woman is in love with you?"

It flitted across his mind to wonder exactly what woman she meant. But she had a valid point. He didn't handle emotions well, probably because they weren't logical, not easily catalogued. Maybe he couldn't program Pandora's emotions correctly because he didn't understand them himself. Delilah in love with him? He gave it serious consideration, thinking aloud.

"Delilah has been with me since before I was incorporated. At the beginning—when there was no building, no lab, no factory—she did everything from answering the telephone to picking up Brian and Justin at day care. Now, she delegates most of the secretarial jobs to Karen and just takes care of me. Makes sure I remember appointments, decides which people on the phone or at the door are worth interrupting me, keeps a clean suit in my closet."

"Sounds like a wife," Tannis muttered.

"Maybe, but there's nothing romantic between us. We've never had anything that remotely resembles a date. Occasionally in the early days, she would whip up an omelet or grilled cheese sandwiches in my apartment if we were working late. That's the closest we've come to having dinner together. When I kissed her once at a Christmas party, she wiped her mouth and made a face."

"Maybe she was embarrassed."

"Maybe. I'll concede that she might care for me more than I realize, but I've never done anything to encourage it." Taking one of her hands in his, he stroked the back of it with his thumb. "It would mean a lot to me if you could get along with her."

"Zachary, I am not the problem," Tannis protested. "She tries to sabotage everything I do."

"Invite her to lunch."

"What!"

"Ask her to go somewhere with you and talk to her," he insisted. "She really is a fine woman. Invaluable to me. Fiercely loyal and protective. If you got to know each other, you could be friends." He leaned closer, running his fingertips down the side of her face. "It would probably also help if you assure her that you aren't going to hurt me. You aren't, are you?"

Before she could answer, the jet hit some turbulence. Tannis clutched his arm in fright.

Smiling, Zachary put an arm around her shoulders and drew her close to his side. "Want me to explain to you how the plane stays in the air?"

"No!"

As soon as the plane's landing gear touched the tarmac, Tannis relaxed completely. The release of tension made her giddy as she hurried, almost skipping through the terminal.

Matching her pace with his long-legged stride, Zachary smiled, drawing his joy from hers. It had been a good idea, a great idea, to bring her. He'd never seen her so animated, so free, so completely unencumbered.

Having retrieved their luggage, they hailed a taxi to take them to their hotel in the downtown area. Once inside, Tannis wandered the opulent lobby while Zachary checked in at the desk.

Amazing, she thought, moving across the plush carpet of a pearl-gray color. I am in San Francisco on a corporate-paid weekend with Zachary Spencer, the computer wizard.

How quickly her life had changed! Her job had changed. Her acceptance of Meredith's condition had changed. Even her nonexistent love life had changed.

Zachary. An amazing man, creating amazing ripples in her life. If she weren't extremely careful, she could find herself in love with him. As an undergraduate, she'd heard of him and speculated on how interesting he would be. But the man in person outshone the legend. She'd admired his intelligence and his wizardry. Now, remembering how painstakingly he'd worked to calm her on the plane, she knew that his genius was only a fraction of the appeal.

Sensual. Good Lord, she'd never known a man who could shoot through her carefully constructed defenses with just a look. Those eyes were deadly. The memory of lying in his arms sent shivers racing through her. If he even hinted at seduction, she knew she would not resist despite her staunch determination not to let it happen again.

Oh, no! she thought suddenly. He did get *two* rooms, didn't he? Even as she wondered, she saw the desk clerk pass two keys to the bellman. Was that disappointment or relief that flooded her as she closed the distance between them?

When they arrived at Tannis's room first, Zachary took her luggage from the bellman's cart. "Take my bags next door." He handed the young man a folded bill. "I'll assist Ms. Robbins with hers."

"Adjoining rooms?" Tannis asked when they were inside.

"Not adjoining. Just next door." In response to her lifted brow, he continued, "In case you need anything, you can just knock on the wall."

"Or call the front desk."

"In case you need anything the front desk doesn't provide," he countered.

Breaking from the unspoken offer in the polished jade eyes, she studied the room, decorated in midnight blue with accents of dusty rose.

"It's beautiful. Elegant." She turned and found him watching her, smiling.

He moved across the room to stand inches from her, his eyes never leaving hers. "You were very good on the plane. I didn't even need the Valium in my pocket."

With his hands, he framed her face, tipping it up so that his mouth hovered a breath away from hers. "I'm glad you came with me."

His words fluttered against her skin as he lowered his lips in a soft, caressing kiss. His magic touch coaxed passion from her depths, unfolding inside of her like the opening petals of a rosebud. No, she would not resist again. That knowledge frightened her as much as it excited.

Lifting his head, he read the conflicting emotions in her eyes and battled the urge to lead her to the bed. Watching, waiting, he searched her expression in the hope that desire would reign over the other feelings. No, not yet, he thought, deciding not to push.

"I know it's only five o'clock here," he said and dropped his hands. "But in Boston it's eight. My appetite doesn't understand the difference."

"Mine, either. I skipped lunch."

"You'll want some time to freshen up. How much? Half hour? Hour?"

Her eyes sparked with mischief. "Why don't I just knock on the wall when I'm ready?"

Alone in her room, Tannis contemplated the way he'd pulled back from the kiss. Clearly, he wanted her to make the next move. Was he guarding his emotions as carefully as she was guarding hers? How long could they both ignore desire before the tension snapped?

They dined in a converted warehouse at Fisherman's Wharf where the seafood was delicious. After dinner they wandered like tourists, browsing in shops, admiring the street musicians and enjoying each other.

"I have an appointment tomorrow," Zachary said as they strolled hand in hand.

"I should have known you wouldn't come to San Francisco just to speak at a dinner."

Chuckling, he led her to a bench that faced the bay where they could see the tall spires of sailboats reaching like bony fingers toward the night sky. "It might take most of the day, I'm not sure."

"Another secret?"

"No, actually the same secret." He slipped an arm around her shoulders. "I'll tell you about it soon. I want to get everything together first."

Leaning her head against the crook of his shoulder, Tannis felt complete peace. "I'm the last person in the world who would pressure you to reveal a secret before you're ready."

"I know." His hand found its way to wind in her hair. "That's why I can keep it. Can you find something to do tomorrow?"

"I'd like to go to the electronics show."

"That's good. You can tell me what the competition's about to unleash."

"Mmm-hmm," she murmured dreamily.

"Are you asleep?" He leaned his head against the top of hers.

"Close. My body's on East Coast time."

"Come on." He stood and pulled her up from the bench. "Let's get this East Coast body to the hotel."

Zachary asked the cab driver to let him out a few blocks from the hotel the next afternoon. He wanted a walk to help him put his thoughts in order.

The unbuttoned edges of his jacket flapped in the wind as he paced, thinking. He'd met with Starfire's board of directors for hours, working out the details of the sale. He'd insisted on job security for Delilah and a retirement plan for Avery, the only two employees he wanted to protect.

Except Tannis. What was he going to do with Tannis? He couldn't let her go back to Conway, even if she wanted to. She had to have a job so she could maintain her sister's care and pay off Conway. Maybe, he thought, considering the details of the sale of Wizac to Starfire, maybe he still needed a personal assistant.

When he knocked on the door of Tannis's room, she had just returned from the convention center.

"How was the show?" he asked when she let him in.

"Terrific. Every cartoon character known to man now exists in a large stuffed version that talks and moves exactly like your Storyteller." She sat on the bed and kicked off her shoes. "If I were you, I'd sue."

"Not worth the effort." Leaning against the chest of drawers, he unknotted his tie. "Any AI projects?"

"Nothing more advanced than what you read about in college textbooks." She arched and flexed her feet, rotating her ankles in slow circles. "I should have worn sensible shoes."

"Yeah," Zachary mumbled, wondering how she could make aching feet seem sexy.

"Oh, everybody's talking about the new NASA project. They're all ready to kill each other for the contract."

"Starfire's already got it." When she looked at him quizzically, he tapped a finger to his temple. "The Wizard always knows."

"I think I'm starting to believe that."

"How about a nice quiet dinner here at the hotel, and I'll tell you how I know?"

"Is that part of the secret?"

"Maybe." With a sly smile he moved toward the bed and pulled her to her feet. "Go soak those lovely toes in a hot bath and knock on the wall when you're ready."

The hotel restaurant was classically formal: thick carpeting, elegant brocade chairs, white linen table cloths, English bone china and delicate crystal. Tannis watched the glow of candlelight shooting golden sparks into Zachary's eyes as he sipped his Scotch. He lowered the glass to the table and ran his finger around the rim, shifted in his chair, placed his hand on the table, then began to toy with the silverware.

Nervous? Tannis wondered. Was he apprehensive about something? Reaching across the table, she covered his large hand with hers to still it. "Want to tell me about it?"

He turned his hand over and closed it around hers, stroking with his thumb in the gesture she had come to expect. "I spent the day at Starfire corporate headquarters."

That much she had already guessed, and she had speculated that he had spent the previous Monday at their branch
in Cambridge. But why?

"They want to buy my company."

He paused, watching for her reaction, she knew, but she
carefully disguised any flicker of emotion on her face. "Do
you want to sell it?"

"I'm giving it serious consideration." As he mentally
cataloged his reasons, he raised his other hand to their
joined ones, enveloping hers with his wide palms and long
fingers. "Their offer is sizable, more money than I would
have imagined in the early days. They've agreed to all of my
stipulations. I could play in my lab for the rest of my life."

Tannis realized that he was listing the advantages for
himself as well as for her. "What are the drawbacks?"

Before answering he studied her face, but still she re-
vealed nothing. "I keep coming back to one question. If it's
worth that much to Starfire, isn't it worth just as much to
me?"

"Only if you want it. I'm not sure that you do."

"For the past few months, I haven't been sure about
anything." His gaze drifted around the room as he gathered his thoughts, then settled on Tannis again. "Running
the company isn't as much fun as it used to be. In the beginning it was exciting and challenging. Now it seems that I
spend all of my time settling arguments and solving problems."

"You're good at that," she said quietly.

"I'm better at other things."

His probing eyes held her as thoughts circled in her mind.
She knew he wanted her to tell him how she felt about the
offer, but she didn't want to influence his decision. Obviously he had conflicting emotions about it. So did she. But
what could she say? Her own future was uncertain enough.
She certainly couldn't make suggestions concerning his.
"When do you have to tell them?"

"I asked for a week. That's how I know about the NASA contract. They don't know for sure that they have it, but it seems that way. They want to finish the legal work on the purchase before they move into the space project."

The waiter arrived with entrées. Although Tannis pulled her hand away from Zachary's, his gaze never left her face. "Stop looking at me as if you think I have the answer," she pleaded when the waiter had left.

"Can't you give me your thoughts?"

She picked up her fork, pushed food around on her plate and put the fork back down. "The company has made you wealthy. You've earned respect in the industry. It seems to me that you aren't as happy as you could be, but I only have one month of your life to base that observation on. I don't know what other forces are affecting you right now, what motivation brought you to this point."

Picking up his Scotch, he sipped slowly, then turned the glass in his hand, staring at the golden liquid. "I disagree. I think you know me better than any other person." He carefully set the glass on the table and looked deep into her eyes. "I can see myself converting the farm into a sophisticated lab. Working when I feel like working. Sitting in front of the fireplace when I don't. Walking in the woods. Growing roses. Can you see that, too?"

Tannis stared in stunned silence. Yes, she could see it. Leaning over his shoulder at a terminal. Curling beside him with a good book. Walking with her hand in his through the snow or the burst of spring life. "Zachary... why are you asking me this?"

Oh, God, I've frightened her, he thought. He'd frightened himself as well. Why did he suddenly have to know what she thought about his future? "For some reason, I feel that you understand me. I'd like to know what you think about the life I just described."

She thought it was wonderful. She thought it was exactly what he needed to make him happy. And suddenly she

wanted that life, too. Desperately. "Yes." Her voice held a
slight tremor as she faced his probing eyes. "I can see all of
that for you."

Awed by these strange new feelings that had just taken
charge of his heart, Zachary glided past further discussion
of the topic. He picked up her fork and placed it in her
hand. "Eat your dinner. If you're going to run all over San
Francisco with me tomorrow, you need lots of energy."

Somehow Tannis managed to get through the meal.
Zachary entertained her with an endless list of places they
should explore. She voiced her preferences, and they worked
out a schedule, but most of her mind dwelled on a startling
new realization. Whatever future Zachary chose for himself, she wanted to be a part of it.

When they stopped outside her hotel room, she knew that
he wanted her to invite him in, but the emotions bombard-
ing her were too intense. She had to be alone to explore this
incredible revelation. She was falling in love with him. Falling? No, leaping, plunging, diving headfirst with her eyes
closed. Oh, God, she didn't stand a chance! She turned to
him as he leaned against the door frame with his hands in his
pockets and offered a cheerful smile. "I better get a lot of
sleep tonight if I'm going to keep up with the hectic pace you
have planned for tomorrow."

His hands clenched into fists in his pockets as he wondered what excuse she would have used if they didn't have a
busy day ahead of them. He knew she was pushing him
away because he'd gotten too close. He also knew that he
could take his hands out of his pockets, pull her against him
and kiss her until her defenses crumbled, but she'd probably resent him for it. "There's a vibrant, exciting woman
inside of you, Tannis. I've seen her. You ought to let her out
more often. She might surprise you with what she can do."

Without another word, he left her in the hall, not even
glancing back when he stopped to unlock his door. Tannis

stared, shocked and confused, until he closed his door behind him before she went into her own room.

Her first reaction was defensive anger. What the hell did he know about the woman inside her? She paced the room furiously, stripping off her clothes and tossing them to the floor. Did he ever have to sit beside his sister's bed and watch her waste away to nothing? Did he ever have to stoop to extortion by pond scum like Conway to keep his income? Did he ever have to deny his feelings because he'd betrayed the person that he wanted to love?

That last thought stopped her cold, both physically and mentally. She did love him, damn it. And there *was* another woman inside. Yanking the covers from the bed, she stretched out fully nude, contemplating her feelings. The person she had been before Meredith's illness bore little resemblance to the one she had become. And Zachary had reached inside her and found that better part of her that had been hidden for so long.

What was she afraid of? He was nothing like Mark. He already knew about Meredith, and he didn't want to run from it. He'd given her a chance to redeem herself when he should have had her arrested. No other person in the world would have done that. Maybe he had more faith in her than she had in herself.

Damn! She *was* in love with him. Turning in the bed, she placed her hand against the wall. She could knock on it, she knew, and he would be back at her door in thirty seconds. She knew exactly how exquisite it would be to make love with him all night, to wake up in his arms. It was too damn frightening. She had to remind herself that she was there with him because he didn't trust her to stay in Boston alone.

With immeasurable pain twisting her insides, she slowly drew her hand away from the wall. But tomorrow, she promised herself. Tomorrow, she would let that woman inside of her out of her cocoon. And she'd do her best to keep her out.

* * *

They raced each other down the hall when they returned to the hotel less than an hour before the dinner was scheduled to begin. Tannis leaned her back against the door, panting, and tried to calm her breath.

Zachary braced one hand on the door beside her head and laughed. "Out of shape," he teased, pinching the flesh at her waist. "Chubby."

"Chubby!" She placed her hands against his stomach and patted. "You're the one who had to have sourdough bread after lunch!"

"Right. It was good." He kissed her quickly. "Let's skip the dinner."

"You're speaking at the dinner."

"I'll call and tell them I have laryngitis."

"Really, Wizard?" Her hands slid around his waist and met behind his back. "If you had laryngitis, how could you call?"

"I'll send a telegram."

"We came to San Francisco because you agreed to speak at this dinner."

"Wrong." Grinning, he shook his head. "We came to San Francisco because I wanted to spend the weekend with you."

As Tannis looked up, stunned by that admission, he lowered his head and kissed her deeply, thoroughly, with all of the passion and longing that had been building during the long, frolicsome day. Her lips parted, his tongue invaded as they both gave and took.

Zachary broke away with reluctance. "Dinner," he breathed on a long sigh, resting his forehead against hers. "Thank you for letting that woman inside of you come out today. She had a good time. Please don't put her away."

"I won't." She smiled up at him, her eyes shining. "I promise."

"Knock on the wall when you're ready."

* * *

When they finally made it to dinner—fortunately being held in their hotel—the first course had just been served. As guest speaker, Zachary had a seat at the head table with Tannis beside him. She really wasn't hungry since they had eaten almost constantly all afternoon.

Zachary was an entertaining speaker, injecting humor and wit into his vision of the future of the industry. When he sat down beside her, she leaned closer to whisper in his ear. "If you decide to sell, you could have a career on the college-lecture circuit."

His smile lit his eyes. "I told you there were other things I do well." He squeezed her hand. "I could show you more."

The promise in those words heated her skin as they mingled with the several hundred computer specialists after the program. Like the crowd at Jackson Hunter's birthday party, everyone knew Zachary. Everyone wanted to speak with him. Finally alone, they were about to leave when Tannis heard someone call her.

"Ms. Robbins! I don't believe it!"

Tannis spun to meet a familiar face. "Jonathon!"

"Jonathon Wallace," the man said to Zachary, who took his outstretched hand and shook it. "We went to college together." He turned back to Tannis. "But which one are you? Don't tell me. I know a sure-fire way to find out." Jonathon grasped her shoulders and plundered her with an exploratory kiss. "Hmm, Meredith. You always were the better kisser. Though Tannis was not without talents of her own."

Wide-eyed, Tannis stole a glance at Zachary, who watched the scene with a frown. As her vivacious mood shattered, she made a snap decision to go along with the mistaken identity.

Oblivious to the turmoil he'd touched off, Jonathon gushed, "You never guessed that I was on to you, did you

Meredith?'' He shifted to Zachary again. ''She used to send Tannis on dates with me if she got a better offer.''

''Did she?'' Zachary's voice was cool enough to frost the air around them. ''I'll have to remember that.''

''What's Tannis doing these days?''

Quick-witted, Tannis came up with an answer that defied denial. ''She married a goat farmer and moved to New Zealand.''

''No kidding? I bet she has the whole farm run by computer.''

''She does.''

''Tell her I said hello. Nice to see you again, Meredith.''

''Thank you,'' Tannis mumbled as Jonathon faded into the crowd. She stared after him, unwilling to meet the questions in Zachary's eyes.

''I think it's sheep in New Zealand, not goats. Isn't that right, *Meredith*?''

''It was the best I could do on the spur of the moment!''

When she didn't look at him, Zachary grasped her shoulders and forced her to face him. ''We wouldn't want you to ruin your excellent record by telling the truth.''

''The truth is too hard to explain.'' She averted her eyes from his. ''And too painful.''

''You didn't tell me that you were identical.''

''It never came up.''

His eyes narrowed and hardened like stones. ''Just like it never came up during your job interview that you were spying for Conway?''

When she stared in stunned silence, he continued, ''You get indignant if I act like I don't trust you, then you stand beside me and lie to an old friend about who you are?'' Anger and betrayal flamed in his eyes. ''Come to think of it, how do I know which one you are? I haven't had the advantage of kissing Meredith to make the comparison.''

"Just drop it, Zachary." Her anger was as great as his, but she had no wish to fight in the middle of the hotel banquet room. "I was actually enjoying myself until—"

"Until what?" he interrupted. "Until your past came back to haunt you?"

"Zach?"

They both turned at the sound of the sultry voice. Tannis stared at the gorgeous blonde with the huge silver eyes.

Oh, God, Zachary thought. Now whose past has come back to haunt? "Hello, Rebecca," he said in a grim, tight voice.

"You know I usually avoid these stuffy dinners like the plague." She fluttered lashes that were long and thick. "But when I heard you were speaking, I just had to come and see you." She tilted her head toward Tannis as if she were only a momentary distraction. "You won't mind if I steal Zach from you for a minute?" She linked her arm through his. "It's been such a long time."

Zachary looked over Rebecca's head at Tannis, who glared at him. "No," he answered bitterly. "She won't mind at all."

Smiling, Rebecca led Zachary to a quiet corner of the room. He said nothing to Tannis as he walked away from her.

Tannis stared as Rebecca fawned over Zachary. Then the fury set in. She knew we were arguing, Tannis thought. She waited for that moment to interrupt us! Well, that's just fine. They deserve each other. Every Wizard needs a Sorceress at his side! And this one certainly seems anxious to have the job. She dragged her eyes from the couple and headed for the door.

"You've done so well, Zach," Rebecca purred when she had him to herself.

"Surprised, Rebecca?"

She formed her mouth into a flirtatious pout, plucking at the fabric of his sleeve with slender fingers. "You don't still blame me for coming out here? You would have done the same thing.''

"No, I would have moved heaven and earth to be with the person I loved." His eyes shifted to follow Tannis as she left the room. Angry and hurt, he judged from the lack of bounce in her step.

"If you loved me so much, why didn't you move out here with me?"

"Come on, Rebecca. Your deductive reasoning is better than that." He looked at her again, wondering why he'd ever thought she was kind, exciting or beautiful. Everything about her paled compared to Tannis. "I don't really see the point to this conversation. Excuse me."

He started to move, but Rebecca tightened her fingers on the arm she held. "Where are you going?"

Carefully he pried her fingers loose and straightened his sleeve. "To move heaven and earth for the woman I love."

Painstakingly, Tannis removed her clothes, folded them neatly and placed them in her suitcase. Dressed in a diaphanous white nightgown, she went to the window and looked out at downtown San Francisco brightly lit against the night.

Pressing the palm of one hand against the cool glass, she felt a heaviness settle in her heart. They'd had such a good day, unencumbered by the mistrust and doubt that had lain between them. She'd actually come close to believing that the feelings she'd discovered last night when Zachary discussed his future might have a chance to grow.

Until Jonathon turned up. Why couldn't Zachary understand that by pretending to be Meredith, she saved herself the painful explanation?

She'd quelled her initial reactions to Zachary because she'd been sent to betray him. Then he'd coaxed her to behave as his lover when it had been her greatest fantasy to become just that. Once having given herself to him, she'd had to flee to protect her tortured heart. And the crowning insult—he'd brought her to San Francisco because he didn't trust her to be out of his sight.

The most frustrating part of the entire experience was that she didn't deserve his suspicion. Truly dire circumstances had propelled her into this charade, and she wasn't sure there was any way out.

Now Zachary was engaged in a cozy tête-à-tête with Rebecca, undoubtedly the woman Jack Hunter had mentioned. Most assuredly the woman Zachary had almost married. Whether she had the right to or not, Tannis felt possessive and jealous and betrayed.

Zachary paced around the lobby of the hotel, the wheels in his mind turning faster and faster. Was it true? Was he in love with Tannis? He must be, or he wouldn't have been so upset when she'd lied to the college friend.

One thing he was sure of—he'd never been in love with Rebecca. Over the years he'd wondered how he would react if he ever saw her again. Given their occupations, their paths were bound to cross. It surprised him that when it finally happened, all he wanted to do was to get away from her as quickly as possible.

Because of Tannis.

Now Tannis was upstairs in her room alone. And he wanted to be with her. With a purposeful stride, he approached the clerk at the front desk. "Is there someplace nearby where I can buy a rose?"

Chapter Ten

Zachary paused outside Tannis's room and grimaced at the pitiful rose in his hand, but under the circumstances it was the best he could do. His greenhouse was three thousand miles away. Perhaps Tannis would see the humor in the situation. He raised his hand and knocked gently.

Muffled sounds of footsteps filtered through the door, then the slide of the chain and the click of the bolt. When she opened the door slowly, the tension was so thick he could feel it. The filmy white nightgown and matching robe that she wore did serious damage to his control. He tried a smile. "I'd like to talk."

She looked him up and down, but didn't move. "Go ahead."

"Inside? Please?" When she still didn't move, he pulled his hand from behind his back. "I brought you a rose."

"Oh, Zach!" Tannis tried to stay angry, to remember that she hurt, but the poor rose looked absolutely awful. The long stem was limp, bent almost in half. The red petals, tinged with black around the edges, barely hung on. The leaves were wilted. Even the thorns looked tired.

Zachary grinned. "You have to admit my heart was in the right place."

Tannis shook her head in disbelief and smiled in spite of herself. "Come in."

Taking the flower from him, she went to the table and propped it in an empty glass. The contrast between the healthy blossoms he'd gifted her with before that had unfolded their petals in flourishing splendor and this dying one that had no chance at survival almost brought tears to her eyes. "It looks so sad," she mumbled softly.

"The gift shop had closed." Zachary stood beside her, suppressing the urge to wrap his arms around her. "The desk clerk pulled it out of a discarded centerpiece in the garbage. You should have seen the other ones."

She turned around, touched that he would go to so much trouble for her. "Thank you."

"You're welcome." He waited until she sat on the edge of the bed and then turned one of the chairs to face her. "I've been prowling around downstairs for a while, trying to think, but my usually ordered mind has failed me."

Tannis watched him as he sat down and propped his elbows on the arms of the chair. He was struggling to find words, she knew, but his eyes were still. This time, the thinking wasn't in his mind. It was in his heart. She waited.

"I hurt you downstairs, and I didn't mean to. I want to trust you, Tannis. I believe you when you say you never would have given Conway anything important. Still, I know I have to be careful because I get confused when I start to think emotionally instead of logically. When you let that man believe that you were Meredith, something snapped inside me."

"I have to explain that to you."

"No, you don't."

"I want to." She linked her fingers together in her lap and stared at them. "Meredith and I were fairly old before we realized we were two separate people. Perhaps it seems wrong to you, but it seemed quite natural to us to switch places if it was necessary or even convenient. We never did it maliciously.

"Jonathon was a casual acquaintance whom I'll probably never see again. It was easier to let him think I was Meredith than to explain the long sad story. If it had been someone close, someone who cared about us, I would have told the truth. Can you understand that?"

Nodding slowly, he studied her. All of her defenses were stripped away leaving only the fragility that he'd always known lay underneath. She was so beautiful with her eyes wider and bluer than he'd ever seen them. He wanted to take her in his arms and shield her from every ugly thing in the world. Was that love?

Standing up, he shoved his hands into his pockets and wandered aimlessly about the room, sorting his thoughts. "What you said on the plane is true. I am dense sometimes because I can't handle emotions. I understand a lot of things that average people don't, but love can't be broken down into bytes. It scares me, and I don't know what to do about it."

When he turned to face her, she saw a wealth of emotion in his eyes, struggling to make the proper connections in his mind. She wanted to help him, but she wasn't sure she understood her own emotions at that moment. "Zach—"

"No, wait. I have to say this. It's important." He started to pace again but kept his eyes on her. "The truth is, I'm not sure I know how to recognize love. I was wrong with Rebecca, and I didn't see it in Delilah, although the more I think about her, the more I'm convinced you're right."

Tannis followed his movements with her eyes, his words tumbling over and over in her mind. All of his life he'd been different, unable to relate to the people around him. She'd seen him as strong, intelligent, successful, powerful. She'd never thought of him as emotionally unskilled. It made her heart ache. "What happened with Rebecca?" she asked gently.

He leaned against the dresser, one leg crossed over the other at the ankle. "She had to make a choice between me and her career. She chose her career."

Tannis paled, a heartbreaking tremble working its way through her system. He'd lost the woman he loved because she wouldn't put him first in her life. Would he accept that Meredith had to come first in hers? "Couldn't she find a way to balance the two?"

He gave a sarcastic laugh. "I gave her a way. She was offered a job by a major computer company out here. I had to stay in Boston because I was just getting the Wizac off the ground. All of my contacts and financial backers were in Boston. I offered her the same position with my company, but she said she couldn't pin her future on a fledgling company that might not make it. She had to take the sure thing."

He shrugged, as if dismissing the incident as unimportant. "I think I was more hurt that she didn't have faith in my computer than that she didn't want to stay with me." His gaze drifted around the room, then settled on Tannis. "If I really loved her, wouldn't I have found a way to make her stay? If she really loved me, wouldn't she have believed in me?"

Tannis shook her head slowly almost unable to comprehend that he'd ever come up against something that he couldn't properly analyze. "You do know what love is, Wizard."

He frowned at the name. "I don't feel very wise right now."

"You are." She held out her hand. "Come here."

Crossing to the bed, he took her hand and sat down beside her. With his thigh brushing against hers, he cradled her small hand between both of his. She tilted her head to look into the kindest, most compassionate eyes she'd ever seen. "Why do you take care of your nephews?"

"They're my brother's children. I want to protect them."

"Because you feel obligated?"

"No, because..." He sighed, mumbling slowly. "Because I love them."

"Avery told me that you bought your mother a condo in Florida. Why did you do that?"

"She's my mother, Tannis. What does this have to do with—"

"Everyone has a mother, Zachary. Not everyone buys her a condo. Why did you?"

"I wanted her to have it," he answered softly. "Because I love her."

"Why did you move in with Jack after his wife died?"

His eyebrows arched in surprise at that. "That old codger talks too much!"

A slow smile eased across Tannis's lips. "There's a point here, Wizard. Are you getting it?"

"You're showing me that I do love my family and my friends." His eyes moved impatiently. "But that isn't the same as the love between a man and a woman."

"No, it isn't." Here was the part that gave her trouble as well, but she thought she was beginning to get a better grasp of it just by talking with him. "But in any form, love is still an illogical emotion. Yet from what I've seen, you handle it quite well."

Deep in thought, Zachary searched her eyes. Maybe she was right. Maybe he could handle love better than he thought. Maybe it was completely normal to be apprehensive. "Are you afraid of love, Tannis?"

"Terrified."

"Good." Wrapping his arms around her, he aimed his lips toward hers. "Let's scare the hell out of each other."

Tannis giggled against his mouth as they fell back on the bed, but soon the giggles gave way to gasps and sighs. When before passion had been spontaneous combustion, now it was a gently glowing ember. With caressing lips and stroking tongue, Zachary tenderly nurtured it into flame.

Just a kiss, Tannis thought. It's just a kiss. But, Lord! What this man could put into a kiss. He *was* a wizard, creating flash fire with a mystical touch. She wanted to feel skin, had to feel skin. Her hands sought to pull his shirttails free of his trousers. When she ran her fingers across the flesh on his stomach, she felt him shiver and heard a low moan escape from him.

Seizing her hands, Zachary pulled his lips away and sat up, gazing down at her. Slowly he tugged, and she rose beside him. As his hands skimmed up her arms to her shoulders, she inhaled deeply. When his long fingers slid the robe free, she exhaled with a shuddering sigh.

Zachary's gaze dropped to the bodice of her gown, and his breath was lost. It was transparent lace, hugging the curves of her breasts, dipping into the valley between those ivory globes. His hands followed his eyes, capturing the pebbled peaks between his fingers. As his thumbs brushed lazy circles around her hardened nipples, he returned his eyes to her face.

She was braced on her flattened palms, her head thrown back, her hair streaming in an auburn cascade down her back, her lips parted, her eyes closed.

"Tannis, look at me."

Her lashes fluttered, and she met his eyes, darkened now to the deep green of emeralds. He raised his hands to frame her face. "The other time was urgent passion. This time, we'll make love." He stood up and shrugged out of his jacket, his eyes never leaving her. "Take off your gown."

With his words fluttering in her heart, she did as he asked and watched him drape his clothes over the chair, layer by layer. The play of muscle under skin as he moved fascinated her. She'd learned every inch of his body by touch the other time, but she hadn't looked at it, really looked at it.

Broad shoulders, long legs, bronze-toned skin, dark blond hair—thick on his chest, light over his arms and legs. Lean-muscled and supple, he moved with confident ease. When he turned to her, fully nude, she lay back on the pillow and waited.

His eyes moved over her with an intensity that she could feel. Her skin heated beneath his appraising gaze. Her nipples hardened, her stomach lurched, her pulse pounded. He came to the bed and knelt beside her, brushing her hair away from her face.

"You're beautiful," he whispered.

"You are."

A hint of a smile turned his lips. "Men aren't beautiful."

Lifting her hands, she dragged her fingers through the hair on his chest. "This one is."

When she found his flattened nipples in their nest of curls, he groaned and closed his fingers around her wrists. "Love me, Tannis," he said on a ragged breath. "I want you to love me."

She rose up on her knees before him and slid her hands around his neck. Pressing her soft curves against his hard planes, she lifted her chin. Their mouths met and clung. His hands splayed across her back, molding her closer.

His lips left hers to roam the lines of her cheek, down her neck, into the soft hollow of her throat. Whispering her name, he bathed delicate kisses over her shoulders, then moved downward.

While the other time their passion had raged like wildfire, this time it flowed like molten lava. She wanted him, needed him to fill the aching void within her. As if he read her thoughts, his hands cradled her hips and lifted her. Then he eased her down to join them as one.

He began to move, slowly at first, then faster as his hands worked her hips to meet his thrusts.

Tannis didn't have to move. Zachary controlled the motion, stroking her with exquisite heat. She felt the crest approaching and gripped his arms, dropping her head onto his shoulder.

"Tannis, no! Look at me."

She jerked her head up and met his eyes. They were wild with desire, gleaming with passion.

"Stay with me, love. All the way."

Even as he spoke the words, her body began to convulse around him. He felt the tremors and gripped her tighter, driving into her with primitive need. Tannis held on, her own shudders still racking her body as she felt his release throb into her. She never closed her eyes.

Fully sated, Zachary slid his hands up her back and gradually eased her down to lie on the bed. He stretched out beside her and ran a hand over her stomach, her skin slick with their mingled sweat. Nuzzling in the damp tresses beside her ear, he whispered against her skin, "Exquisite."

Turning, she found his eyes, glittering green, an eloquent expression of the pleasure they had given each other. Was this love? He might have trouble sorting and filing it emotionally, but she had no doubt. She loved him, had wanted to love him from the beginning.

Where was it going to lead? That was the question. He still couldn't give her his complete trust, though she believed him when he said he wanted to.

With any other man, she might have been angry, but after the things he'd told her earlier, she understood. It wasn't all because of Conway and the plot she'd participated in. Zachary wouldn't trust his emotions with any woman.

Zachary shifted and drew her close to his chest. "Maybe if I hold you tight enough, you won't leave me while I'm sleeping."

Trailing her fingertips down his spine to caress his hard-muscled buttocks, she felt his shivering response. "Maybe you won't sleep."

With a deep-throated groan, he rolled her to her back and stoked the still-glowing embers to flame.

* * *

Later, they slept, with arms and legs entwined, until the telephone rang.

Tannis sat up quickly and reached for the receiver on the bedside table, vaguely aware that Zachary stirred beside her. "Hello!"

"Ms. Robbins, I'm sorry. I don't know what to do." The voice rushed anxiously across the wires. "I can't find Zach. I've been calling his room all night."

"Avery?" She sat up, tucking the sheet around her. "Calm down. It's all right. He's here."

"Oh, thank good—" Avery broke off, his voice flooded with embarrassment. "Ohhh...oh, jeez, Ms. Robbins. I'm sorry."

"It's all right, Avery. Just a minute."

She handed the receiver to Zachary, who was fully awake now, sitting up. "Avery, what's wrong?"

Tannis watched him as he listened. She knew he was upset and laid a hand on his arm.

"Did they see anyone?" Zachary asked into the phone. "All right, what time is it...? Wait until nine and call Mrs. O'Malley. You have the number...? She has the keys and knows how to turn off the alarm. Ask her to go with you and check things out. Call me from there." His eyes met Tannis's and he chuckled. "I don't know, Avery. Try both rooms."

Stretching, he replaced the phone in its cradle, then leaned back against the headboard. "Someone tried to break into my house."

"What happened?"

"I have a security system. Apparently the intruder fled when the alarm sounded. The system automatically alerts the police. They couldn't find anything, but they called Avery anyway. He's going to get my housekeeper and go over there."

"Conway again?"

"Maybe. Could have been just an average burglar looking for silverware or a VCR."

Or it could have been Pete. She knew from the look in his eyes that he thought it, too. And that notion hurt him. Wrapping her arms around his chest, she snuggled against him, with his heart pounding beside her ear.

He held her for long, silent moments, losing his fingers in her hair, thinking. The break-in attempt disturbed him. His security system was excellent, but nothing was foolproof. He didn't like it that someone had gotten that close to Pandora. And who knew that he had his major project in his home lab anyway? Only Jack . . . and Tannis.

As his fingers stroked gently, he considered the woman in his arms. What did he know about her really? Only what she told him. His emotions urged him to trust her, but emotions could distort reality. He still had to be careful. Making love was not the same thing as being in love. Though with Tannis, he couldn't see how to separate the two.

They slept again, and again were awakened by the telephone. This time Zachary reached for it, talking quietly while Tannis snuggled deeper under the covers. When he hung up, he reached for her.

Just the touch of his fingers heated her flesh. Tannis turned toward him and molded her body against his. "Is everything all right?"

"Mmm." He nuzzled the side of her neck. "Perfect."

"I meant at home."

"Ms. Robbins—" one hand trailed up her rib cage to cup her breast "—you worry too much."

"And—" she stopped to gasp with pleasure "—and you don't worry? You can't fool me, Wizard. I've learned how to read your eyes."

"Really?" His thumb flicked across the taut peak of her breast. "What are they saying now?"

Lifting her dark lashes, she gazed into the polished jade and smiled. "Too easy. I've seen that message in them a thousand times. You want to make love to me."

"Lucky guess," he mumbled, and took her again to that special place she'd discovered in his arms.

"Zachary." Tannis threw one leg across his torso and slid her body atop his chest. "You have to get up."

"Again?" He opened his eyes and cocked an eyebrow at her. "I don't think my hard drive can take it."

"Your hard drive is in excellent shape." She ran her tongue across his chest from nipple to nipple, teasing, tasting. "I meant you have to get out of bed. We have a plane to catch."

"No."

"No?"

"Let's stay for a few days. I don't want to go back."

He's serious! Tannis thought with amazement. He really wants to stay. "You have to take care of the break-in at your house."

"Avery took care of it. Nobody got in. Let's stay."

Automatically, with instincts bred from habit, she thought of Meredith. "I visit my sister every Sunday."

"Even when you're out of town?"

"I haven't been out of town before. I thought we'd be back in time for me to go." She felt the sickness of disappointment tighten her stomach as she thought of her final scene with Mark. As understanding as Zachary was, would he accept her choice of sister over lover? "I've never missed a Sunday."

His thumb stroked lightly over her cheek as his eyes searched hers with a look that was cautiously guarded. "I won't ask you to miss this one, but is that the only reason you don't want to stay?"

Moving out of his arms, she rolled to the side of the bed and sat up, her back to him. "Meredith comes first in my life. She has to come first."

Trembling within, she waited—waited for Zachary to tell her that he couldn't accept it, that he had to come first, that Meredith could not be a factor in their relationship. She heard the rustle of sheets behind her and imagined him getting up, leaving her, saying that he would not play second to an invalid sister. Instead she felt his arms surround her from behind.

"Is this what your fiancé did to you, love? Did he force you to make a choice?"

Closing her eyes, she dared not even to breathe. It was too much to hope that he understood and accepted. "More or less."

Tightening his arms around her, he pulled her back against his chest. "Don't you know me well enough to realize that I understand and respect your dedication to taking care of your sister?"

Lifting her hands to his arms, she felt tears welling in her eyes. "Yes, I do. It's just hard to believe."

"Believe it." He lowered his head to kiss the top of her shoulder. "Remember it." He wanted to say more, to offer more assurances, but he wasn't certain he could do it yet. "Go take a shower. I'll call room service for coffee."

The flight home was just as nerve-racking for Tannis as the earlier flight had been, but again, Zachary diverted her thoughts. When he picked up the Jaguar at the terminal, he drove her home and carried her bags inside.

"I'm not sure you're safe here alone," he said, taking her luggage to her bedroom. "Conway's getting more desperate or he wouldn't have tried breaking into my house. I'd feel better if you at least had a burglar alarm."

"We don't know that it was Conway." Following him, she tossed her purse on the bed. "Anyway, he won't hurt me. I'm his inside source."

Zachary turned to grip her shoulders in a fierce rush of protectiveness. "Don't underestimate him. I've seen the vicious way he crawls over people to get what he wants. Until this is over, I'd like you to stay with me."

She read the concern in his eyes, and it touched her heart. She might have agreed with him if not for the phrase "until this is over." What about when it was over? Where would they be? She would still need a job when he was finished using her to catch Conway, and he would still be reluctant to trust his emotions. If he wanted her to be with him, why couldn't he say that instead of disguising it with concern for her safety?

Shrugging out of his embrace, she turned away and distracted herself with hanging her coat in the closet. "I don't think that's necessary."

He shoved his hands into his pockets and braced a shoulder against the wall, wondering what he'd done to cause the sudden coolness in her tone. "Do I have to insist again?"

She banged the closet door with more-than-necessary force and spun toward him. "Do I have to question your motives again? Since your office was vandalized, you don't want me out of your sight."

"I just don't want you to get hurt," he protested.

"Fine! Then go home and leave me alone. Your inability to trust me is hurting!"

"It has nothing to do with trusting you."

But she pivoted sharply and stomped out of the room, leaving Zachary to stare after her, stunned. Why in the hell couldn't he understand women as easily as he understood microchips and circuits? For a few minutes he fumed, listening to her slam cabinets and rattle dishes in the kitchen. It was true he didn't want her out of his sight. Not because he was worried about what she might do, but because he wanted her with him. All of the time. Forever.

Damn it! He was in love with her, and he was going to tell her whether it was the smart thing to do or not. To hell with logic! This time he was going with emotions!

He forced his temper to cool before he went into the kitchen and found her staring into an open cabinet, as if she couldn't remember what she was looking for. "Tannis . . ."

"Still here?" She closed the door and turned around, only to find that she was trapped against the cabinets.

Zachary placed one hand on either side of her on the countertop, effectively locking her within his arms. "Yeah, I'm still here. And I'm going to stay here until you get over being mad and start thinking logically again."

She looked up ready to hurl an insolent remark, when the telephone rang.

"Want me to get that for you?"

"No!" Tannis shoved against his chest and ducked under an arm to get away. "It might be Conway."

With a furious scowl on her face, Tannis grabbed the receiver. "Hello!"

"Well, Ms. Robbins. I thought your cozy little weekend would put you in a better mood. What's the matter? Are you falling in love with him?"

Her eyes shot to Zachary a few feet away, signaling him to join her. "That's none of your concern, Mr. Conway."

Zachary was beside her in a second. His hand covered hers on the receiver, holding it so they both could hear.

"You're getting closer, I presume."

"You'll have to be patient, Mr. Conway. He's not a man who trusts easily." She sent Zachary a pointed glare on those words. "But I am getting closer. Someone tried to break into his house last night. One of your henchmen?"

Conway's oath was explicit. "Why didn't you mention the security system when you told me about his private lab?"

Zachary's fingers tightened around Tannis's hand with a viselike squeeze. His face went white. Tannis stole a glance at him, unable to speak or move. Just breathing was a lost art.

"Ms. Robbins?"

"I . . ." Her throat was tight with shock and fear. "I forgot."

"Details cannot be forgotten."

With effort, Tannis ignored the fury seething from Zachary and concentrated on her role. "Why didn't you wait until I could get into the lab on my own? You're making him suspicious."

"Insurance, Ms. Robbins. I'm not convinced that when it comes right down to it, you'll do the job. You find out the code for disconnecting the system. Then you can keep him busy while someone else goes into the lab."

"I'll try."

"Do more than try."

As usual, Conway ended the discussion with a harsh click. Zachary let go of Tannis's hand, and she hung the receiver on its hook on the wall.

"Why did you tell him about my lab?"

God, he looked dangerous. She had never heard such anger in his voice. He hadn't been this mad when he'd caught her at his terminal. Unconsciously, she backed up until she hit the counter. "I didn't tell him."

"Tannis!" How in the hell could she lie to him when he'd heard the conversation? His fury was so great that he thrust his hands into his pockets to keep from hurting her. "Damn it! Stop lying to me! Hasn't anything been the truth?"

"Everything has been true! I never lied to you!"

She searched for a way to convince him of her innocence. Then it hit her. "Oh, God," she whispered, trembling with fright. "I did tell him."

"Which is it?" he demanded. "Did you or didn't you?"

"I did! But I didn't mean to. It was after your office had been vandalized. I was furious with Conway because I couldn't bear the pain in your eyes when I walked in and found you sitting on the floor. Without thinking, I told him it had been a waste of time because the secret project was in your private lab."

He stared at her in silence. She took a step closer. "Zachary, I haven't betrayed you. Think about this logically. You showed me Pandora. If I'd wanted to get more information, I could have used the sexual chemistry between us then. I got into your computer system, but I didn't take anything. You heard him say he's not convinced I'll come through for him. I've done everything you asked of me." Her hands clenched into fists as she shook with anger and frustration. Hellfire! "Why am I bothering to defend myself? You don't trust me! You never have!"

She saw the firm set of his jaw, the furious movement of his eyes. He was processing information as rapidly as a computer, as logically. But feelings were getting in the way. "What isn't his concern?"

"What?"

"When you first answered the phone, you said, 'That's none of your concern.'"

"Oh." Clasping her upper arms with her crossed hands, she turned away from him. A rush of color burned her cheeks as she stared at the floor. "He asked me if I was falling in love with you."

The breath rushed out of him. His heart stopped. Every muscle in his body tightened. "Are you?"

Slowly, very slowly, she dragged her eyes up to meet his gaze. Polished jade. Flashing with angry sparks.

"No, don't answer that," he said quickly before she could speak. "I don't know whether I want you to say yes or no." The lines on his face hardened. His eyes frosted. "I couldn't believe you anyway."

Without another word, he headed for the door. Tannis couldn't move. Her heart was broken. Her pride was destroyed. Even anger couldn't stir her blood. She just stood and watched him walk out.

Zachary drove home with emotions roiling inside him. Methodically, he checked every room of his sprawling house for signs of intrusion. Nothing was out of place. Nothing was missing. The security system he'd designed had stopped the burglar. This time.

Satisfied that everything was all right, he went to the basement lab. The heavy steel door had a deadbolt lock, but he kept the key in the kitchen. That would have to change, he thought as he started down the stairs. A quick glance around assured him that no one had been there. Nothing was disturbed.

Absently, he went to a large box of spare parts and rummaged around for a circuit board and plastic casing. Taking the items to a long worktable, he started to build with only part of his mind on the task.

The other part was on Tannis. He desperately wanted to believe everything she claimed, yet he couldn't trust his heart over his logic. Even if he hadn't heard the entire conversation, he'd known since the break-in that she was the only one who could have told Conway about the lab. Not even his staff in R and D knew that he had a lab in his basement. Well, that wasn't entirely true. A handful of people knew that he tinkered around at home, but only Jack and Tannis knew that he had a phenomenal project underway.

Picking up a pair of wire cutters, he tapped them on the tabletop, analyzing the situation from every angle. There were two clear options: she was either still spying for Conway or she wasn't. If she was, there were a number of things she could have done that she hadn't even tried. She hadn't told Conway about Pandora. She hadn't asked any questions. She hadn't gone to bed with him at a time when he would have eagerly handed over all of Pandora's disks—he'd been that anxious.

In reality, she hadn't done much of anything in the way of espionage. Which was reason enough for Conway to doubt her allegiance. To keep her safe, they should probably give him some kind of information that would convince him she was on the job.

Wait a minute! He dropped the wire cutters with a loud clunk. Why the hell did he care whether Conway doubted her or not? She was a spy. Trying to steal from him. But even though she'd had opportunities, she hadn't stolen anything.

Except his heart.

Damn it! He couldn't think straight. Nothing fit! Nothing! Never in his life had he been so frustrated. Emotions were crowding his mind, making logical thought as indecipherable as a foreign language.

Damn her to hell, he *would not* care!

Then why was he building a burglar alarm for her?

What she really needed, Tannis decided, was a good cry. But she couldn't muster a single tear. She felt empty and cold. Every emotion in her heart had drained out when Zachary had walked out the door. She didn't know if she would ever see him again.

"It isn't fair!" she shouted to the apartment in general, and punched a pillow on the love seat for emphasis. She'd done everything he'd asked, spending weeks trying to juggle her emotions, pretending to Conway that she was a spy, yet remaining loyal to Zachary.

But nothing in her life had been fair for the last two years. Whenever she felt sorry for herself, all she had to do was think of Meredith lying helpless and pale in that hospital bed. At least she herself was alert and vital, experiencing life, feeling emotions.

Too many emotions. How could she have been so negligent as to let such important information slip to Conway? She'd worked cautiously to give him insignificant facts that wouldn't hurt Zachary. In heated anger, she'd offered him everything.

She couldn't blame Zachary for his reaction. As if it weren't bad enough that he thought she was bent on betrayal, she had to hand him the evidence! He'd never believe in her innocence now. Even if she could find a way to prove it, she doubted that he would let her try.

What a fool she was!

Hours later, Tannis sat at the kitchen table. Her financial records were spread out around her, and she was circling want ads in the Sunday newspaper. Bartender. Probably make great tips, but she couldn't mix anything more complicated than bourbon and water.

She knew she didn't stand a chance of getting a job in the computer industry, but she had to find something. Zachary certainly wouldn't keep her as his assistant, and Conway would have no use for her once he found out she'd been fired. Staring at her meager bank balance, she wondered how long she could go without food. Didn't Tibetan monks live on bread and water?

Maybe she could cultivate a busy social life so that she'd have enough dates to buy her dinner every night. Hellfire! She must be really close to the edge to consider that. It seemed dangerously close to prostitution. Now there was a lucrative profession, but she'd starve for sure. Who'd pay to sleep with her?

A knock at the door brought her thoughts from the absurd. Glancing at her bank books as she pushed back her chair, she wondered how far she would go if she really got desperate. Was prostitution much different from what she'd done for Conway?

When she looked through the peephole, she couldn't believe what she saw. A grim-faced Zachary holding a plastic box and a paper bag. For a moment, she debated ignoring him, but her heart thumped wildly in her chest.

She opened the door.

Chapter Eleven

May I come in?''

She wished she couldn't see the pain in his eyes. And she wished it wasn't there because of her. "Why not?"

Stepping back, she let him enter, then closed the door, taking her time about turning the lock and sliding the chain. When she turned, their eyes met and held. Tension crackled between them. A light tremor fluttered through her body. She'd thought she'd never see him again, yet here he was. But he still looked angry. Her gaze fell to the box in his hand. "What's that?"

He looked down, as if he'd forgotten that he held anything. "A burglar alarm. I think you need it."

"Zachary, you—" She cut off her protest midsentence. Why was he still being kind to her? She didn't think she could stand it. Her voice was a gentle whisper. "You didn't have to buy an alarm for me."

"I didn't. I made it." He wanted to throw it down and drag her into his arms. "I have to attach it to your telephone. Do you mind?"

"Go ahead." Waving an arm toward the kitchen, she followed him. "Does it call the police?"

His back was to her as he pulled tools from the paper bag. "No, it calls me."

"Oh." Because she couldn't stand and stare at him when she wanted to fling her arms around him, she went to the love seat and picked up a magazine, pretending to ignore him. She had turned only a few unread pages before he finished.

"I have sensors for your door and windows. It should take about fifteen minutes."

"Fine."

When he passed the kitchen table, his gaze swept the papers spread out there. He saw the newspaper with red-circled ads and stopped. "What's this?"

She glanced nervously from him to the table and back to him. "I thought I'd start job hunting tomorrow."

Something ugly kicked him in the gut. His voice was tight. "You have a job."

"Conway certainly isn't going to keep me on the payroll if I never give him anything."

"With me." The words were deathly quiet. "You have a job with me." He turned and went into her bedroom.

Tannis was frozen in disbelief, but only for a second. Then she flew after him. "You think I'm selling your secrets to Conway. You couldn't possibly want me to work for you!"

Slowly he turned from the window, his motion carefully controlled. "I want you, Tannis."

"Like hell! If I walked back into that office, you'd probably have Delilah taking inventory of the pencils and paper clips."

One part of his brain acknowledged that they were both running on raw emotion, but he ignored it. His temper ignited. "Take a look at your track record, Tannis. How many lies have I caught? How many have gotten past me? Let's not forget that I caught you at my R and D terminal."

"Let's not forget that if I wanted to, I could get back in again. Why haven't I done that?"

"No, you couldn't. I changed the code."

With a gasp, Tannis recoiled as if he'd struck her. Wrapping her arms protectively across her chest, she turned away. "Oh, yeah. You really trust me."

The hurt in her voice made him cringe. Laying the sensor and the tools on the windowsill, he stepped behind her to rest his hands lightly on her shoulders. "Tannis, I'm sorry. That was before..." He stopped short of saying before he'd fallen in love with her. "Before I understood everything."

"Do you, Zachary? Do you understand?" Hot tears welled behind her eyes, and her lips trembled. With conscious effort she calmed down. She turned around and looked up at him through dampened lashes. "Do you believe that I didn't realize I'd told Conway about your lab?"

"Tannis..." Too late he realized that it had been a mistake to touch her, to hold her this close when he could see the light sheen of tears in her eyes, breathe the delicate scent that was now familiar, feel the flutter of breath that drifted between her parted lips. God, he wanted to kiss her, to pull her against him and make everything disappear except for the fire that raged between them. But, because it wasn't logical, he didn't. "Forget it, Tannis. No harm done."

No harm done? Her eyes were wide with incredulity as she watched him go casually back to the window and pick up his tools. No harm done except it had been another strand in the web of his distrust. No harm done except it had ruined the final moments of an otherwise perfect weekend. No harm done except despite everything, she wanted to drag him to the bed and tell him, show him, that she loved him. Except he wouldn't believe her, so why bother?

Mumbling an inaudible curse, she picked up her suitcase, plunked it on the bed and started to unpack. In a few minutes Zachary left the room to install the other sensors. Tannis was storing the empty suitcase in the closet when he came back.

"I'm finished."

She didn't turn around. "Fine."

"Come into the kitchen so I can show you how it works."

"I'll be there in a minute."

He hated the cold, unfeeling sound of her voice. How had they lost the magic that had woven them together in San Francisco? How could they get it back? "Tannis, I do want you to keep working for me. You're the best computer specialist I've ever met."

Her spine stiffened as she recognized the words she'd given him at the end of her first week in his office. She turned and found him leaning against the door frame, his thumbs hooked through the belt loops of his jeans, his eyes wary. "Considering the company you keep, probably not. But close."

Studying the blue frost in her eyes and the determined set of her chin, he shifted tactics. "I have a plan for trapping Conway. If you can hang on for another week, this mess should be behind us. Once Conway is dealt with, I think we can work out the other things between us, don't you?"

That depended on whether he trusted her or not. Once Conway was dealt with, would he find some other reason for blocking his emotions? "What's the plan?"

"I'm working on some surveillance equipment. You'll meet with Conway and get him to admit that he tried to bribe you. I'll be monitoring the conversation. We'll have the evidence on videotape."

"Then you'll hand this tape over to the police?"

He nodded.

"Why don't I just tell him that I refuse to spy anymore, and we can forget the whole thing?"

"Because I'd kind of like to see him pay for what he's done to me. To us. Wouldn't you?"

Tannis dragged a hand through her hair, pulling it away from her face. "What I'd really like is to wake up and find out that the whole last month of my life has all been a horrible dream."

Stiffening, Zachary pushed himself away from the door frame. "All of it?"

She averted her eyes, but kept her chin thrust out in determination. "All of it."

Zachary took a step toward her, bringing him close enough to touch. What he wanted to do was take her shoulders and shake her until she shouted that she loved him. Instead, he kissed her.

It was desperate and swift. As his arms went around her, his mouth closed over hers with a hardness that marked possession and greed. His tongue ravaged her with deep strokes that were hot and hungry. Savage heat swept through her.

He broke his lips away long enough to probe her with his eyes. "No, not all of it."

Then he took her lips again.

Cursing herself, Tannis kissed as hungrily as he. Damn him! Damn him for making her want so much. Barely more than twelve hours ago, on the other side of the country, she'd gotten out of bed with him, yet her body longed for him as if it had been months. She put her hands around his neck and pulled him deeper into the kiss.

Logic fled. Zachary's hands slipped under her arms and lifted her from her feet. Even as he carried her to the bed, she was already tugging at his sweater. As soon as he laid her down, she finished the job, pulling it over his head and tossing it blindly aside.

Kissing him with feverish need, she felt his hands grope beneath her sweater to capture her breasts. Stroking, kneading, he drove her to frenzy. Then he jerked her sweater off, and they were skin to skin.

Her nipples—aching and swollen—brushed against the silky curls of his chest, causing her to moan. She yanked at the snap of his jeans as he yanked at hers, then they both struggled to remove the final barriers.

Now, she thought as Zachary kicked the clothes away, now she could catch her breath before the conflagration consumed her. But she couldn't. His hands were everywhere, followed closely by his lips. Then he was on his knees between her thighs. And then he was inside her.

Gone were the tender strokes he'd shown her. Gone was the patience. He thrust within her now with a ferocious need that portrayed the power she'd always known to be restrained within the gentle man. Far from matching it, she could only ride with it.

In moments she couldn't think. She could only feel as he drove her to a peak towering far above any he'd taken her to before. She clung to him as if the inevitable descent would surely kill her. When he plunged for the final time, crying out her name, she screamed.

Exhausted and spent, Tannis lay beneath him, trembling as his heart pounded against her chest, then gradually slowed. She would probably have bruises in the morning, but she didn't care. There had been no pain.

Zachary lifted his head, giving up the soft pillow of her hair, and searched her eyes. "Did I hurt you?"

She smiled. "No."

Rolling to his side, he held her close, letting emotion flood his senses. Nothing mattered. Nothing except the passionate, vibrant woman who had come into his solitary life and given it meaning. This was what he needed, what he lacked. Success, money, fame—all were empty dreams without a partner to share them.

Cradling her face with one hand, he looked deep into her eyes. "We *will* work everything out, Tannis." He stroked his thumb across her lips. "We have to because I love you."

Tannis closed her eyes and let the precious words circle her heart. If only that could be enough. Her lashes fluttered upward to meet his waiting gaze. "I love you, too."

Zachary's tender smile brought the twin creases to frame his mouth. "Then you don't wish the last month had never happened?"

"I wish it had happened differently."

"But it didn't. We can't change that." Zachary threaded his fingers through her silken hair and pressed a kiss to her forehead. "Can you hang on for a few more days, love? We'll settle everything by the end of the week. I promise."

She wanted to protest, but how could she when his skin was still warm from their loving? When she still tingled from head to toe? "All right," she murmured. "I can make it."

"We're together now," Zachary said, settling a sweet kiss on her lips. "That's the important thing."

But nothing was resolved. And Tannis wasn't sure that anything would be different by the end of the week. Even if she helped him catch Conway, would he ever totally trust her? Would he always wonder if she'd chosen the path of least resistance? She felt his breath against her neck, deep and regular. As sleep pulled at her, she started to form an alternate plan, one that would completely absolve her. She was a bit of an electronics wizard herself.

And that was when she realized that although it was Sunday, she had not gone to Greenbriar.

After a quick breakfast, Zachary went home to change, and Tannis went to the office, still dwelling on her plan to prove her innocence. Despite the fact that he'd confessed his love, she had to be sure that it was complete. Unless Zachary knew unequivocally that she'd never intended to betray him, she couldn't allow herself to accept that love, though she wanted it more than anything else in the world.

At her desk, she shuffled through the ever-thickening file of notes on the math project under Delilah's usual glare. It was odd, Tannis thought, but she actually felt sorry for the woman. To have been in love with Zachary all these years, working beside him day in and day out, knowing that he didn't even realize it, must have been supreme torture. Tannis had to admire Delilah's devotion and persistence. She wondered if under the circumstances she would have held on that long. But knowing the man, she conceded that she would have.

Shoving those thoughts aside, she made a mental list of the supplies she would need to pull off her scam. To be convincing, only Wizac software would do. As much as she hated the thought of "borrowing" from the supply closet at the end of the hall, she knew the end result would vindicate her.

She would not, could not, allow herself to think about the danger involved in her scheme. More than anything, Tannis wanted to freely accept the love Zachary had both voiced and shown last night. She wanted the future he had outlined in San Francisco. Duping Conway was a necessary step toward that acceptance. It was marvelous to experience Zachary's love, but she had to know that she also had his trust.

During the long, anxious day, Tannis ran her plan through her mind, checking for flaws. She was counting heavily on Conway's greed as an advantage for her. Whenever her thoughts headed toward the risk, she had only to swivel in her chair to see Zachary's head bent over his work. He was worth it. The promise of love was worth it. Proving herself was worth it.

Her obligation to Meredith, she knew, still posed a possible threat. Despite the fact that she had begun to accept that her sister's condition would not change, there would still be choices to make concerning her welfare. But Zachary had promised that he understood and respected her fierce dedication to her twin. Mark's vicious words no longer taunted her. Zachary was a thousand times the man Mark could ever be.

At the end of the workday, she went into Zachary's office where he still sat at his desk, working out his own plan to catch Conway. Steeling her nerves, she put on a bright smile as she approached him. It was the last time she would ever have to pretend with him.

"It's after five, Wizard."

Zachary glanced at his watch, then tossed his pencil down and moved his shoulders to work out the kinks. "So it is. Are we alone?"

Her blue eyes sparking, Tannis nodded.

"Good. Come over here." When she rounded the desk, Zachary reached for her, pulling her into his lap and enclosing her in his strong embrace. His lips found hers and plundered unmercifully, absorbing her taste, her scent, her texture. "Mmm, I've wanted to do that all day."

Resting her forehead on his, she sighed. "Me, too, but neither of us would have gotten any work done."

"Right." Reluctantly he pushed her to her feet. "I've got about two more hours' worth to do here. Want to help me? We can have dinner afterward."

"Umm, I've got some errands to do." She told herself that it wasn't a lie. "Why don't I meet you later?"

Zachary nodded. "How about my house around eight o'clock? I'll cook."

"The Wizard cooks!" Tannis exclaimed, feigning shock.

"Hey! Who made the toast this morning?"

"Who *burned* the toast, you mean."

Zachary shrugged. "You distracted me." Pulling open the top drawer of his desk, he rummaged around until he produced a key, extending it to Tannis. "Here. In case you get there before I do. Oh, and you'll need the code for the security system."

"I don't want to know the code." Tannis took a step backward, shaking her head as she shunned the key. "Don't tell me."

"Tannis..." Zachary leaned forward and took her hand.

"No." She withdrew again, her eyes meeting his with anguished plea. "Zachary, please."

For a moment he studied her face, certain his suspicions, though well-founded, had driven her to this defensive state. Slowly he curled his fingers around the key. "All right. I'll make sure I get there before eight."

"It's all right." The tension eased from her face. "If you aren't there, I can wait in the car. I don't think I want to be alone with your cat anyway," she added with a smile.

"I'll be there." He dropped the key into the drawer, stood and drew her into his arms. He kissed her with a promise for later. His lips molded to hers in awareness of how much he loved her, needed her. Arousal hardened him at just the thought of holding her pliant body beneath him, and his hands moved to cup her breasts. Skimming his lips across her cheek, he whispered in her ear, "Why don't you bring a change of clothes?"

Liquid heat shot through her. Later, she promised herself. Later this can be complete. She forced her body's response to cool. "Mr. Spencer!" With hands against his chest, she pushed back and raised huge innocent eyes to him. "Are you propositioning me?"

A wide grin brought the dimples to slash his cheeks. "Trying my best."

She slid her hands up his chest to lock behind his neck, and pulled him into a quick kiss. "I'll let you know if it worked. Eight o'clock."

Zachary stood smiling as she walked to the door, then called her name. When she turned, he spoke softly. "Be careful."

A portentous shiver scampered through her. Did he know? Of course not! she chided herself, and gave him a sweet smile. "You, too."

Zachary had most of his plan to catch Conway worked out and was making a brief sketch of the equipment he would need to build when he heard the elevator open in the hall. Engrossed in his work, he paid it no heed, thinking in a far corner of his mind that it was the cleaning crew.

When a shadow fell across his doorway, he looked up. A surge of emotions swept him as he acknowledged his brother's presence with a curt nod. "Pete."

Pete took a few tentative steps into the room. "How are you doing, little brother?"

"Fine." Green eyes locked on green as Zachary dropped his pencil and leaned back in his chair, the creak of the springs sounding unusually raspy in the uncertain silence. "How are you?"

"Oh, I've been better." Pete shoved his hands into the pockets of his jeans and sauntered to the window. "Nice view."

Impatient, Zachary picked up the pencil and ran it between his fingers, following his brother's movement with inquisitive eyes. "You didn't come here to check out my view."

"No." Pete turned, looked at Zachary, then away. "I've got to tell you something, and it's going to make you mad as hell. I figure you might throw me through the window, so I thought I'd see if it was gonna be an interesting fall."

Zachary shook his head. "It's safety glass. I probably couldn't send you through it, but it might hurt when you hit it." Pete didn't respond or look at him. "Why don't you sit down and tell me about it."

Accepting the offer, Pete settled into the chair directly across from his brother and crossed one long leg over the other. "I, uh . . ." His gaze skittered around the room, then met Zachary's. He sighed with defeat and resignation. "I trashed your office."

A muscle jumped in Zachary's jaw, the only outward sign of emotion. "I figured that." Though the pain of betrayal wrenched his gut, he truly wasn't surprised. "Did you also try to break into my house?"

Pete nodded.

"Why?"

"Why else?" He lifted his shoulders in a slight shrug. "I needed money. Someone offered me the job. I took it."

"Richard Conway."

Pete's brows arched in surprise. "You know that, too?"

"I know he's after me. You aren't the only person he's sent to make my life difficult."

"Damn." With a long sigh Pete raked a hand through his hair and shifted uncomfortably. "I thought if I came to warn you, I might be able to take a step toward redeeming myself."

Dropping his gaze to the paper on his desk, Zachary made idle doodles with the pencil. "Well, I appreciate the thought." Light strokes on the paper became bold, furious swipes. He threw the pencil down in disgust. "How much do you want?"

"Nothing!" Pete answered in a burst of defensive anger that he quickly cooled. "I didn't come here for money. Not this time."

Zachary's eyes narrowed, on guard, as he watched his brother rise and move nervously around the room. The struggle to maintain a semblance of pride was evident on his face. Just this visit, Zachary knew, was not made without great personal cost.

Pausing beside the bookshelves, Pete ran one hand across the neatly aligned spines. "I'm at rock bottom, but I've been there before. When Conway approached me, I thought it was a quick way to make some easy cash. Then I thought, this is Zach. This is my brother that I'm running a scam on." He turned, his eyes an eloquent statement of his inner turmoil. "Whatever else I may be, I'm not a man who sells out his brother."

Zachary looked away, remembering growing up together, remembering all the times he'd bailed Pete out of trouble, remembering his frustration when he'd gone to the farmhouse. "You could have come to me," he said quietly. "You know I would have helped you."

"After all the trouble?" Pete's voice was barely more than a whisper. "You'd still help me?"

"Yeah."

"Why?"

Leaning back against the chair, Zachary let his shoulders slump and sighed. "You're my brother. That won't ever change. I grew up in the shadow of the best pitcher ever to throw a curve ball. I never stopped idolizing him."

"Me?" Straightening, Pete turned, face-to-face with his brother. "You idolized me?"

"All my life."

"You're the one." Pete shook his head in disbelief. "You always did everything right. I thought you were perfect. I wanted to be like you."

Two pairs of polished jade eyes met and locked. This time, Zachary shook his head. "And I wanted to be like you. I won every scholastic award there was, but I couldn't throw a curve ball. I could plot the trajectory, calculate the speed, figure the odds that a batter would hit it, but I couldn't throw it."

As the brothers stared at each other across the expanse of the office, a lifetime of emotion passed between them. Pete blinked against tears that welled behind his eyes, and Zachary swallowed a lump that clogged his throat.

"So do you have any plans?"

"Well—" Pete shifted, moving along the front of the shelves "—I had some thoughts about spending time with Sylvia and my sons, but she vetoed that in a hurry."

"I know. She told me."

When Pete came to the baseball sitting on its shiny brass pedestal, he raised one hand to stroke it almost reverently. Then his fingers curved around the smooth sphere, and he picked it up. "So I was thinking about heading down to Florida. Mom will probably let me stay with her for a while. Until I find a job."

He tossed the baseball from hand to hand with practiced ease, as if he still pitched every day. "I used to be pretty good with my hands. Remember that tree house I built for Brian? And the wagon I made for Justin?"

Zachary nodded, watching the ball go back and forth.

"There's a lot of construction in Florida. Maybe I can find something to do."

This was the first positive step that his brother had taken in years. Zachary rushed to encourage it. "I think that's a good idea. How are you going to get there?"

Any answer Pete may have given was delayed by the buzz of the telephone. Zachary glanced at the instrument, then reached for it. "I need to answer this. It's my private line."

"Sure." Pete nodded, still tossing the baseball.

Zachary picked up the phone. "Hello."

"Zach! Thank God you're still there."

"Delilah? What's wrong?"

"I know you think I'm wrong about Tannis, but I've really got her this time. If you get over to her apartment right now, you can catch her in the act."

"What act?" An ominous weight of foreboding settled in his stomach. "Delilah, what are you talking about?"

"She's a thief!" Delilah declared, her voice at a nervous pitch. "I told you, but you wouldn't believe me. Now I can prove it. Get over here right now."

"Delilah, slow down. Start at the beginning."

She drew a deep breath. "I saw her go to the supply closet. She took some disks and put them in her pocket."

"Blank disks? She probably wants to work at home."

"Zachary! Stop being blinded by lust and listen to me! I followed her. She stopped at a phone booth and made a call. Then she went to an electronics store, came out with a package and drove home. I sat outside for a while, and I was just about to leave, but you won't believe who she just let into her apartment."

Fear clutched Zachary's stomach in a deathly grip. "Who?" His heart ceased to beat as he waited an interminable second for the answer.

"Richard Conway."

"No!" Zachary's free hand came down on the desktop in a powerful fist. "Damn!"

"See?" Delilah's tone was smug. "I told you she was a thief."

"She's not a—never mind. I'll be right there. Don't go near her apartment. It could be dangerous for both of you."

He slammed the phone down, cursing as he jumped to his feet. "There's trouble," he said to Pete. "I have to go."

Pete's fingers tightened around the baseball. "Should I come with you? Do you need help?"

Stopping in the act of shoving his arms into his jacket, Zachary looked at his brother, still athletically muscular, still light on his feet. "It couldn't hurt."

"Let's go." Instinctively, Pete shoved the baseball into his pocket and followed Zachary to the elevator.

As soon as Tannis admitted Richard Conway into her apartment, the courage that she'd been strengthening all day began to flag. He strode into the room, his eyes on her with the keenness of a hawk. He had a hungry look about him that she knew was dangerous. But she also knew it would play into her plans. Ordering herself to think of the end result, she calmed her jittery nerves.

"You said you had something big for me. What is it?" Conway demanded.

"I'll explain it to you. Wouldn't you like to take off your coat and sit down?"

"I'm taking a risk by coming here." Keeping his coat on, he perched on the edge of the love seat, a few feet from her. "Get on with it."

"I've seen the Sorceress," she lied.

"The Sorceress!" He spat the words at her. "I'm not interested in his toys!"

"You are interested in this toy. He's taken the Storyteller several steps closer to reality. It's incredibly lifelike. It moves and talks. The material has the texture and warmth of human skin. I swear, if it were the right size, you'd think it was a real person."

Conway looked skeptical. Tannis knew she had to make the bait more alluring. "The Sorceress is only a toy, but it's the prototype for other similar projects." She paused for effect. "He's making androids."

Conway's eyebrows shot up. "Robots!"

"Unbelievably realistic. It's going to revolutionize industry. He wants to mass market them as a labor force. Baby-sitters, waiters, salesclerks—the possibilities are endless."

"He's perfected this?"

Preposterous! Tannis saw the gleam of greed in his eyes and knew he was buying it. "Absolutely. Why do you think he's so secretive about it? And you know the Wizard. If anybody can do it, he can."

Conway raised a hand to rub his chin, and Tannis could almost see the dollar signs in his eyes. He was silent for a moment as he gazed at her thoughtfully. "You have proof?"

"Of course, I have proof."

"Where is it?"

"Where's my reward?" she countered.

Conway laughed derisively. "You don't expect me to give you money without something concrete."

"You offered to write off my debt and give me a bonus in exchange for information about Zachary Spencer's new project. I've given it to you. Make good on your offer."

"I offered you a bonus for *useful* information." Conway shifted impatiently. "Without schematics and programs on this project, the knowledge is worthless."

Bingo! She had his admission in his own words. Now she only had to play out the hand. "Everything you need is in his computer. I've copied it onto floppies." Pulling open the drawer of the small end table beside her, she took out a square, thin object.

Conway stared, that hungry look creeping into his eyes again. "It's all on one disk?"

Tannis leaned back into the corner, her face a portrait of serene confidence, though inwardly she was anxious to end this charade. "No, I'm only giving you one disk—just enough to convince you. Before I give you everything, I want to see some money."

A sardonic smile crawled across his mouth. "You're neither stupid nor naive, Ms. Robbins. I see a long, productive relationship between us."

It was all Tannis could do not to laugh in his face. She had the confession. Now all she wanted was to get Conway out and hightail it to Zachary's house with the evidence. "I don't think so, Mr. Conway." Shoving the disk at him, she stood up. "Take this and go. Once you're convinced of its authenticity, you can contact me about my money. Then I'll be out of your life."

"Not so fast." Conway stood, too, and took a step closer. "Don't be so anxious to get rid of me." His eyes filled with a lecherous look as he swept his gaze over her tight jeans and bulky sweater. "There are other aspects of this relationship that we haven't explored yet."

Tannis's eyes widened in fright. Never in her wildest dreams had she considered this unseemly twist to the scenario. She tried to back away, and found herself hemmed in by furniture. Conway took another step and laid one palm against her cheek. Her nerves of steel melted, and she flinched.

"What's wrong, Tannis?" Conway rasped. "Where's the tempting vamp who crawled all over Spencer at Jackson Hunter's birthday party? You're putting out for him, aren't you? Why won't you share your favors?"

Fear shook Tannis to the bottom of her soul. How could she bluff her way out of this? She called up control. "That was necessary." She gave him a level gaze. "This isn't."

"Yes, it is."

Conway slid the fingers on her cheek to hook behind her neck, intent on pulling her against him. Panicking, Tannis placed her hands on his chest and shoved. He teetered on his feet, but regained his balance before she got past. Grabbing a handful of her sweater, he also caught wires. There was the sound of tape being stripped away from flesh as Tannis gasped, frozen in fear.

"What the hell?" Conway muttered, his face twisted with confusion. Then realization dawned. He yanked Tannis closer by the wad of knit in his hand and jerked it up to expose the recording device now hanging loosely around her middle. His features contorted with rage. His eyes hardened to cold gray steel. "You double-crossing tramp!" he screamed, and shoved her down on the love seat. Then he reached into his coat pocket and pulled out a gun.

Chapter Twelve

Zachary rounded the last corner to Tannis's apartment with excessive speed that made the Jaguar fishtail wildly. Having spent most of the breakneck drive giving Pete a brief rundown of the situation, he allowed fear to muddle his thoughts in the final seconds.

Oh, God! What was Tannis up to? Trying to catch Conway by herself, he was sure. Was it his fault for doubting her? As dangerous as that theory was, he had to hope he was right, because the alternative— Damn! He couldn't stand to think of the alternative.

Whipping into the parking lot, he spotted Delilah in her car several doors past Tannis's apartment. He pulled into the space beside her and was out of his car before the engine had silenced.

Delilah got out, too, and met him at the front of the Jaguar. "They're still in there." Her eyes shifted to the disembarking passenger. "Pete!" She looked nervously from one anxious face to the other. "What's going on?"

"I'm not sure." Pushing past her, Zachary strode hurriedly to Tannis's door with Pete close behind. He pressed his ear against the entrance and heard the muffled sound of a slap and Tannis's cry of pain.

His face pale, his features rigid, he grasped Delilah's upper arm, dragging her a few yards from the door to avoid alerting Conway to his presence. "Go call the police."

Delilah's eyes were wide and round. "And tell them what?"

"I don't know. Murder, kidnapping, anything that will get them here quickly. Hurry!" With a none-too-gentle shove, he sent her on her way and sped back to the doorway where Pete stood listening.

"Sounds like Conway's gone berserk," he whispered to Zachary. "Door's not locked. I tried the knob. Is there a back way?"

Swearing under his breath, Zachary shook his head. "Just windows."

"A window is all I need."

"There's an alarm, but it's probably not on."

"No problem." Pete took off at a run to the back side of the building.

With his hand on the doorknob, Zachary paused, considering his entrance. Quietly or like gangbusters? Like the entire United States Cavalry, he decided, and flung the door open with enough force to make it smash against the wall.

For one fleeting second, Zachary beheld the image of an enraged Conway bending over a cowering Tannis, pointing a gun at her heart. A gun! By the time that sight registered, Conway straightened, startled by the noise. He was livid when he saw who it was.

With one eye on the weapon, Zachary took a cautious step into the room. "Put the gun down, Conway. There's no need for violence."

"Close the door and shut up," Conway ordered, with the gun still trained on Tannis.

Zachary stared him down, debating whether Conway was desperate or deranged enough to actually pull the trigger. With Tannis's heart as the target, he decided not to force the issue. Moving slowly, he closed the door.

Though a surge of relief had swept Tannis when Zachary burst through the door, it was replaced by despair when she realized that he had placed himself in danger with her. Conway kept the gun aimed at her, but his gaze jumped back and forth between the two of them.

Zachary moved closer, directly in front of Tannis's position on the love seat. Conway was between them but to Tannis's right, his back to the bedroom.

"Stop right there, Spencer," Conway ordered.

Zachary obeyed, knowing that he had only to stall for time. Was Pete through the window yet? Were the police on the way? How could he get Tannis out of the line of fire? "This battle is really between you and me, Conway. Tannis is just a pawn. Point that gun over here."

As Zachary took another challenging step closer, Conway swung the weapon toward him. "Either way, Spencer. You first or your girlfriend. Makes no difference to me."

"No!" Tannis screamed, and leapt from her seat, propelling herself to stand between Zachary and a bullet. "He didn't know what I was doing. Don't hurt him."

"Tannis!" Zachary put his hands on her waist to push her out of the way, but Conway's threat was deadly.

"Freeze!"

Immediately Zachary and Tannis obeyed the command, both staring at the barrel of the gun, each anxious to shield the other.

"Touching display of bravado, Ms. Robbins, but totally worthless. You see, now I have to kill both of you." Conway's eyes had taken on a glazed look, indicating that he had finally gone over the edge. "A lover's quarrel will be appropriate, I think. And a murder-suicide."

Looking past Conway's shoulder, Zachary saw Pete in Tannis's bedroom. He gently squeezed his hands on her waist in an effort to communicate reassurance.

"Good plan, Conway." Seemingly oblivious to the tension, Pete sauntered into the room, lightly tossing the baseball up and down in one hand. "But where do I fit in to the plot? You can't shoot all three of us. Not without chancing that one of us can get to you before you fire the third time."

The baseball never stilled as Pete positioned himself at Conway's side, turning his body and planting his feet firmly. Zachary had seen his brother knock milk bottles off the backyard fence thousands of times. He recognized the pitcher's stance and knew what Pete meant to do. His hands tightened on Tannis, ready to shove her aside as his mind quickly calculated ball speed and reaction time. He couldn't suppress a hint of a smile. It would work. He knew it.

Moving only his eyes, Conway held the gun steady, leveled at Zachary. "Oh, this is rich, Spencer. I love it!" His voice held a perverted glee that marked his obsession with destroying Zachary. "Both your brother and your girlfriend have betrayed you, yet here they both stand ready to defend you. How do you inspire such loyalty?"

Pete chose Conway's moment of distraction to let fly with the baseball. Zachary saw the motion and dived to the floor, covering Tannis with his body in case the old pitching arm had lost its precision. But Pete's aim was true. The baseball hit the gun with lightning speed, knocking it from Conway's grip. Then Pete lunged, wrestling Conway to the floor.

Dazed from the fall, Tannis was aware only that her face was pressed into the carpet. A great weight was on her, and she couldn't breathe. Then the bulk lifted, and she turned her head. Conway, too, was facedown on the floor, his hands locked behind him in Pete Spencer's grip. She saw Zachary retrieve the gun from where it had flown and hand it to Pete, who pressed it against Conway's spine.

For the last hour, she had been running on adrenaline. Now, the danger passed and she began to tremble. Then

Zachary's arms were around her, and she let her mind go blank except to absorb the sound of his soothing words, the familiar feel of his protective embrace and the faint scent of cherry tobacco. On the edge of awareness, she heard sirens.

Zachary tilted her head, framing her face in his hands as his thumbs stroked gently across her cheeks. "If I weren't so glad that you're alive, I'd wring your stubborn neck for pulling such a dangerous stunt."

Staring into the emotion-filled depths of his eyes, she shook her head slowly. "I'm sorry," she whispered.

"We'll discuss it later." He bent his head and kissed her lightly, then drew back as the sirens screamed louder. "Sounds like the police finally got here. Tannis, we're going to tell them the truth—that Conway bribed you to spy, that you couldn't do it, that you agreed to help me catch him."

Searching his eyes, she asked, "Do you believe that's the truth?"

He dropped his hands from her. "There was no doubt," he said in a stiff voice. "But if there had been, it would have vanished when you stepped in front of a gun for me."

Tannis squeezed her eyes shut against tears that threatened to spill, but they flew open again at the sound of a loud knock on the door.

"Come in!" Zachary called, then turned back to Tannis. "Can you stand up?"

Nodding slowly, she let him pull her to her feet as two uniformed police officers entered her apartment. A dozen questions suddenly flooded her mind. She turned astonished eyes to Zachary. "How did you know I was in trouble?"

With a tight smile, he gestured past her shoulder with a nod of his head. Tannis turned and saw Delilah peering into the doorway, a frantic look on her face. "Delilah?" Tannis gasped in disbelief.

"It's a long story," Zachary explained. "Let's only tell it once."

For over an hour the police questioned and the group answered as the sequence of events unraveled. Conway was handcuffed and taken away. The taped admission Tannis had obtained was secured as evidence along with the gun and even the baseball. At last the police departed.

Delilah, who had scowled throughout most of the ordeal, stood up, nervously jingling her car keys. "I guess I'll go now."

When Zachary rose and escorted her to the door, she tried to make a quick getaway, but he touched her shoulder, and she turned back, her large dark eyes filled with tears.

"'Lilah, you probably saved Tannis's life. I don't know how to thank you for that."

A trembling sigh escaped her as her gaze drifted past Zachary to where Pete and Tannis sat talking quietly. "Don't bother, Zach. I wasn't trying to save her. I was trying to discredit her." She looked back at him, the tears sliding down her cheeks now, leaving long black trails of mascara. "You really love her, don't you?"

He nodded, not knowing what to say. How could he have worked with this woman for seven years and not realized how she felt? Perhaps he'd subconsciously blocked it from his mind.

With no adequate words remaining, Delilah walked away. Zachary softly closed the door.

Walking back into the living room, he pulled keys from his pocket and tossed them to Pete. "Wait for me in the car. I'll be out in a minute."

Tannis stared, aware that her mouth dropped open. She forced it to close as Pete gave her a wink and walked out. Her widened eyes took in Zachary, disheveled, pacing, and—good God!—angry? Tannis folded her hands in her lap to stop their trembling. It didn't work. "You're leaving?" she asked in a voice so tremulous she didn't recognize it.

He thrust his hands into his pockets and turned to her, his face grim. "Yes."

Her gaze crawled over him, taking in every familiar nuance and gesture. A muscle worked in his jaw, a sign that he was suppressing reaction. His hands were in his pockets because he was fighting the urge to touch her. Why? She asked him. "Why?"

He shrugged to show indifference. "Conway's in jail. You have the alarm. You'll be safe." You don't need me, he added only to himself, but wondered if it showed in his eyes.

Disbelief, confusion, torment. Tannis saw the beautiful end to her dangerous plan crumble before her eyes. "You're mad at me. Mad because I wanted to catch Conway by myself."

Silence. But she saw his hands tighten into fists inside his pockets. Where was the patience he'd always displayed? The understanding? The compassion? She wanted to cross the room and put her arms around him. Fear and confusion wouldn't let her. "I did it for you, Zach. I wanted you to know—no doubts—that you could trust me."

His eyes were moving, moving. Then they stilled. He walked slowly to the door, opened it, then turned back. "You want to know what you could have done for me, Tannis? You could have believed in me. When I told you I love you, you could have believed it."

"But I . . ." She trailed off, no proper words coming to mind.

Then the door was closed and Zachary was gone.

Gone? Tannis swept her gaze around the room, so achingly empty without Zachary's commanding presence. Now that Conway was no longer a threat, he was gone? Now that she'd risked her life to prove herself worthy of his love, he was gone? Gone because she hadn't believed in him?

Rebecca hadn't believed in him. She'd chosen her career over his love because she hadn't believed in him. Tannis still held enough reason in her jumbled mind to understand why her action had hurt him. But didn't he have the capacity to understand why she'd felt it was necessary?

Pain. It started as a light tremble in the pit of her stomach, then her chest felt tight, her palms started to sweat, her heart thudded, slowed, amplified. How could everything have gone so wrong? How could she have misjudged his reaction to her plan? Was his love for her so tenuous that he could withdraw it that easily?

You're better off without him, she tried to tell herself. That rationalization had worked when Mark left, but not now. Oh, God! Not now! The pain of losing Mark compared to the pain of losing Zachary was the discomfort of a hangnail likened to having her heart cut out. Without anesthesia. With a rusty blade.

She could survive it, she knew. But not easily.

Hours later, Zachary walked through the greenhouse that jutted off his kitchen, seeking relief from the ache in his heart. Logical thought hadn't done it. Most of a bottle of Scotch hadn't done it. Why did he think that the place where he'd gathered almost every rose he'd given Tannis could do it?

At the very least, the night and the events had rebuilt a bond with his brother that had been missing for too, too long. After a lengthy discussion over glasses of Scotch, Zachary had offered Pete the chance to stay at the farmhouse, earning his keep by taking care of the many repairs the old house needed.

He'd given Pete a check large enough to purchase a secondhand truck and all the supplies he needed. First thing tomorrow, he would head for Mystic Grove. Or, Zachary thought more realistically, he would cash the check and vanish again. He didn't know which. This wasn't the first time Pete had seen the error of his ways and vowed to correct them.

But it made little difference. Despite the bond, Zachary was past hoping that his brother would change. He accepted that he would always take care of him. Just as Tannis accepted that she would always take care of Meredith.

Neither of them knew if their efforts with their siblings would ever be rewarded.

In the darkness he continued past the long rows of plants, past the potting table, to an enclosed terrace that looked out on the backyard. As he sat in a white wicker chair, the scents of a myriad of blossoms assaulted him, bringing to mind Tannis's delicate fragrance. His photographic memory called up a picture of her face when he'd given her the large bouquet of roses. There had been such simple joy in her eyes that morning.

That image faded, replaced by one of her skipping through the airport in San Francisco. The girlish animation, the carefree spirit were almost as haunting as the intensely passionate wanton woman he had found beneath her surface. Making love with Tannis had ruined him for any other woman's touch.

There was only one woman he wanted, one woman he would ever want. The pain he'd felt at the initial discovery of her deceit, the pain he'd felt at her lack of faith in him were but gentle aches compared to the pain of just imagining his life without her.

So how did he get her back in his life? Forever. He'd hurt her tonight, he was sure, as deeply as she'd hurt him. He was beginning to understand why she'd felt compelled to hatch her plan alone. This last month was probably the first time in her life her integrity had been challenged. It had been vital to her that she prove herself. It didn't mean that she didn't believe in him. It meant that she wanted him to believe in her.

He stood up quickly, intent on going to her immediately to tell her that he understood, but the Scotch caught up with him, making him sway on his feet. No, not tonight. But tomorrow. He'd see her tomorrow. And he would take extra care to make it a beautiful, memorable moment. One they would cherish all of their lives. Together.

But there was one more obstacle that he hadn't counted on. After a frantic morning of seeing Pete off, running errands, creating the mystical environment he wanted at home, he called the office.

"You're kidding," Delilah said in answer to his inquiry. "Tannis hasn't been here all morning. I assumed she was with you."

"No." Stunned, Zachary tried to think. Where could she be? "If she comes in or calls, tell her I'm looking for her. Tell her it's important."

"Zach? Are you all right?"

Zachary sighed. His desperation must be evident in his voice. "I will be when I find Tannis. I think."

I hope, he amended as he hung up.

Next, he called her apartment, but she didn't answer. Where could she be? Shoving emotions out of the way, he put his unequaled intellect to work on it. She would be upset, confused, depressed. What would she do? Talk to someone? Who? If she had a close friend, he didn't know about her. Family? Just Meredith.

Meredith... Identical twins, closer than sisters. Genetic equals. Would she go to Meredith? It was worth a try, but again he was at a loss. Where was Meredith? He wasted agonizing minutes as he paced and cursed himself for not pressuring Tannis to reveal more details about Meredith.

There was one sure way to find out everything he needed to know. It would require time and patience, two commodities that he had in short supply. He had promised the FBI he would never do it again, but when he'd made that vow, the welfare of the woman he loved had not hung in the balance. The mental debate lasted only a second before he unlocked the basement door and headed for a computer terminal.

It took him all afternoon, but he found her.

He'd worked through a maze that began with Tannis's bank account, detoured past an unrelenting operator who would reveal only that Meredith Robbins had been moved to another facility sometime during the night, and ended with an intensive care unit at one of Boston's largest hospitals.

Muttering curses, Zachary fought the beginnings of rush-hour traffic, trying to get to Tannis. An endless stream of thoughts flooded his mind as he dodged cars and cruised through yellow lights. Something was wrong with Meredith, but what? He couldn't imagine, but whatever it was, Tannis needed him. If he hadn't left her last night... He had to stop thinking about that.

Finally he reached the hospital, parked quickly and sprinted to the doors.

Tannis was the only person in the intensive-care waiting room. Dressed in faded jeans and a soft sweater, she sat on one end of a worn sofa, her face in her hands, her shoulders shaking. It struck him that her posture was almost exactly the same as the night he'd found her at his R and D terminal. Defeated. Forlorn.

How long had she been here? he wondered, then quickly followed with, why hadn't he been with her? Pride. Stubborn, masculine pride. Slowly he crossed the room and sat down beside her. When she didn't move or acknowledge his presence in any way, he said her name softly.

Lowering her hands, she seemed not altogether certain that she hadn't imagined his presence. "Zachary," she breathed on a whisper of disbelief.

One look at her haunted, red-rimmed eyes, and Zachary wrapped his arms around her. She lost the last vestiges of control and began to cry.

"Shh, it's all right, love. I'm here." He cradled her against his chest, rocking her and speaking soothing words. He gave her all the comfort and strength he had, asking no questions.

After a moment she raised her head, wiping tears from her cheeks with the back of her hand. "I don't care how you found me." Her voice trembled with emotion. "I'm glad you did."

"Me, too." He ran one hand through her hair. "I've been looking for you all day."

Hope bloomed in her heart, but she didn't dare let it grow. From the moment she'd received the phone call from Greenbriar, she'd shoved her despair over Zachary to the far corner of her mind. But periodically, it had eased back out to add to her turbulence. "Why?"

Why. He put one hand against her cheek, stroking with his thumb. "Because I was a jackass last night and I wanted to beg your forgiveness. Because you laid your life on the line for me and I was fool enough to walk away. Because I couldn't stand even one night without you. I love you, Tannis."

Staring into the polished jade eyes, she felt tears stinging again. "I love you," she whispered. "Zachary, I'm so sorry. I was so concerned with proving to you that I was trustworthy, I never considered how it would make you feel."

"Don't even think about it." He reached for a tissue from a box on the table beside her and dabbed at her moist eyes. "We have no more secrets, no more reasons for any."

Crumpling the tissue into a ball in one hand, he pulled her into his arms. Tannis breathed in the familiar cherry scent and felt him press a kiss to the top of her head.

"Tell me about Meredith. How is she?"

Tannis sighed and pushed away from him, leaning her back on the frayed lumpy sofa cushion. "I got a call at about two-thirty this morning. On routine rounds, one of the nurses noticed that her pulse was erratic. They kept a close watch on her for a while."

Her gaze was fixed on the pale beige wall across the room, her eyes motionless. "Once, her heart stopped completely, then started back up again really fast. Dr. Moore decided to transport her here for intensive-care monitoring. Since she's been here, it's stopped again. Twice. But when it starts back up, it's strong."

Zachary read her fear in the inflection of her voice and her expressionless eyes. One of his arms circled her strong yet fragile shoulders. "They don't know what's wrong?"

Tannis shook her head. "They let me see her for ten minutes every four hours."

"When can you go in again?"

"Six o'clock."

Zachary glanced at his watch. Just under an hour. After that he was going to take her home and make her rest.

But they didn't have to wait that long.

At five-thirty Dr. Warfield came into the waiting room. "Good news, Tannis. She's calm and steady now."

"What does it mean?"

"I don't know." When the doctor glanced at Zachary, Tannis introduced the two men. "All day her heart rate has varied from nearly two hundred beats per minute to as low as seven. But for the last half hour or so, she's been hammering away steadily at about eighty."

He sat down in a chair adjacent to Tannis. "Whatever it was, it appears to be over."

Tannis's sigh of relief was long and heartfelt, but her look was still anxious. "But we don't know if it will happen again."

"No." He crossed one leg over the other, glanced from Tannis to Zachary, then back to Tannis. "Dr. Moore told me that you believe you experienced Meredith's symptoms of the tropical disease when the infection was at its worst although you were in Boston at the time."

"Yes," Tannis answered cautiously. "We often experienced each other's pain if it was extreme." The look in her eyes dared him to dispute her, but apparently he had no intention of doing that.

"Well." Dr Warfield cleared his throat nervously. "Would you mind telling me what you were doing last night?"

Tannis's mouth dropped open in astonishment. She glanced at Zachary, who smiled encouragingly and gently squeezed her shoulder, then she looked back at the doctor. "My heart was breaking."

She shifted her gaze back to Zachary. "But it was pulled back together about a half hour ago."

Dr. Warfield's grin was sheepish. "I wouldn't want to be quoted in any medical journals, but I think you and Mr. Spencer may have just saved your twin's life."

Animation sparked in Tannis's eyes for the first time in twenty-four hours. "And if I keep talking to her, Dr. Warfield, I'm going to pull her out of this coma."

"You won't get any argument from me. Stranger things have happened. We'll keep her for observation at least until tomorrow, but I think we can move her out of intensive care if she remains stable. Would you like to see her now?"

"Yes! Can Zachary go with me?"

"Oh, please." Dr. Warfield smiled. "I insist on it."

When they approached the glass enclosure where Meredith lay hooked up to the machines, Tannis paused and searched Zachary's eyes. "Are you sure you want to do this? Some people find it a bit...spooky...that I talk to her."

"I'm sure, love." His hand squeezed hers. "It can't be any spookier than what I'm doing with Pandora."

"All right."

She smiled and advanced to stand beside Meredith's bed. Still holding Zachary's hand, she grasped her twin's hand with her free one. "Meredith, I'm back. Zachary is here, too." She turned to him. "Would you say hello to her?"

Intrigued, he studied both faces for a moment. Identical. Uncanny. "Hello, Meredith." He shifted his gaze back to Tannis. "You've told her about me?"

"Everything."

He accepted that with no qualms. After all, he talked to a cat. Some people might argue that his habit made far less sense than hers did. They stood for a moment in a silence broken only by the electronic sounds of the monitoring equipment. The fact that there was another person who looked exactly like Tannis intrigued him, but more intriguing was the sharing of feelings between them. He'd read about the unique bond of identical twins. Now he wanted to know more. "Tannis, do you really believe she hears you?"

She turned her head from her sister to Zachary. "I'm sure she does."

The unexpected. The unexplainable. He thrived on it. "How?"

"How do you think?"

As he stared at her, she realized his mind was searching for every fact he'd ever read about identical twins. She knew the moment he found the relevant one. "Telepathy," he said on an awe-filled whisper.

Tannis nodded her confirmation. "I think so. Maybe it's just my subconscious, but I think she hears and understands everything I say to her. And I think she responds."

He turned his head to look at Meredith, then turned back to Tannis. "Fascinating."

"You don't think it's crazy?"

Shaking his head, he smiled. "No crazier than my computer asking me if I'm in love with you."

"Interesting analogy, Wizard." She leaned her head against his shoulder and sighed. "But I'm too tired to explore it."

Dropping her hand, Zachary put his arm around her and drew her close to his side. "Will you let me take you home, love? My home. You need to rest. And I have a surprise for you."

"Surprise?"

He grinned. "Indulge me."

"All right." She turned back to Meredith and squeezed the hand she held. "I'm leaving with Zachary now, Merrie. But I'll be back in the morning. Just rest and get stronger."

Reaching forward, Zachary covered Tannis's hand that rested on Meredith's. "Don't worry about Tannis, Meredith. I'll take care of her heart and yours. We'll both be back in the morning."

Tannis turned her face to Zachary, her eyes clouding with tears at the wealth of love this man displayed.

He loves you, Tannis. Don't hold back.

They both turned their eyes to the still form on the bed and stared. "That one wasn't your subconscious, Tannis," Zachary said quietly. "I got it, too."

By the time they got to Zachary's house, it was completely dark, but he turned on no lights as he led her down the hallway to the kitchen.

"Where are we going?" Tannis asked, feeling strangely that she should whisper.

"You'll see," he answered softly.

He was a man who loved surprises. She had no urge to spoil this one with questions or protests. When they crossed the kitchen, Zachary opened a door that she had noticed but not looked beyond the other times she'd been in the room. A tingle of anticipation crept over her as she followed Zachary through the opening.

Too dark to see, she relied on other senses. There was no sound, but the scents were overwhelming. Rich earth, the perfume of flowers, the pungency of organic loam. A greenhouse. Of course. No surprise there. He reached for a switch, and lights twinkled in some of the larger plants. Tiny white lights, more delicate than Christmas decorations, flickered like fireflies.

"Zachary..."

"Shh!" He squeezed her hand. "Don't break the spell. There's magic here tonight. A wizard and fairies and a beautiful sorceress. Can you feel it?"

She breathed the heady fragrance of the flowers and heard the rustle of leaves as they passed. "Yes," she whispered.

He led her through the greenhouse to an enclosed terrace with walls of glass and seated her in a white wicker chair. Perfect, he thought, and turned to the matching table.

"We were supposed to have champagne." He pulled matches from his pocket and struck the flame to light tapering candles. "But it took me so long to find you that the ice has melted."

Champagne? "Are we celebrating?"

Oh, God! He hoped so. "Maybe."

As the wicks flared, he blew out the match and turned to sit opposite her in an identical chair. Their knees just brushed in the small space he'd allowed. Perfect, he thought again, and looked at her.

The flickering candles sent radiant beams to shimmer through her hair, turning the dark auburn to blazing copper. Her eyes were large and luminous, her lips slightly parted and moist, glistening in the play of light across her face.

"I've never seen you more beautiful than you are right now." His tone was reverent. "I never want to lose this image."

What was he up to? she wondered as she stared back, not answering. There was an impatience behind his eyes that he barely restrained. A heat. A hint of passion. His gaze electrified her. "Zach?"

"Shh! Don't disturb the magic. The Wizard knows what he's doing."

He picked up a rose from the table and held it in his long fingers, twirled it, looked at it. "I have to give Starfire an answer." He lifted his gaze back to hers. "Have you given it much thought?"

Starfire! This is about Starfire? Champagne, candles and a long-stemmed red rose are about Starfire? Her heart pounded, almost exploding. She had thought for a moment that he was heading toward something else. But his eyes... Suddenly her heart calmed. She smiled. "Yes, I've thought about it."

Again he twirled the rose. "And what do you think?"

"I think it's your decision to make."

Never taking his eyes from hers, he shook his head. "It's our decision. What should we do about it?"

Her eyes widened to shimmering blue circles as she realized that he *was* leading to where she had thought, but he was leaving it all up to her. Could she do it? Believe in him, she told herself. Don't hold back. Yes, she could do it. "I think we should convert the greenhouses into labs. Work when we feel like working. Sit by the fire when we don't. Walk in the woods. Grow roses. Can you see that?"

"Ms. Robbins." It took every ounce of control he could summon not to shout with joy. "What are you asking me?"

"Wizard." She was sure her heart had burst apart and even now was pumping its last drop of blood through her body. "I think I just asked you to marry me."

"I'm almost sure you did." He twirled the stem again and extended it to her. "The sorceress gets the rose."

She took it in her hand and brought it close to her face. "Wizard, you didn't answer the—" With a startled gasp she broke off when a diamond winked at her, catching the light and throwing it back from every facet. "Oh, Zachary! This is no ordinary rose!"

The dimples deepened, framing his smile. "You are no ordinary sorceress." Leaning toward her, he slid the ring from the blossom and lifted her left hand. "Are you saying yes?"

"Are you?"

"Yes," they said together.

He pushed the ring onto her finger. "There are conditions I want to be certain you're aware of."

Anything. She'd agree to anything as long as he never let go of her hand. "What are they?"

"You'll let me give you a salary for working with me on Pandora."

"Zachary! I'd do that for nothing! I'd pay you for the privilege if I had the means."

"Perhaps, but I'll feel a lot more comfortable when your debts to Conway are paid in full."

Tannis was deeply touched. He'd overlooked nothing in planning their future, even realizing that she'd balk at using his massive fortune to pay her debts. "Believe me, that's one of my top priorities, too."

He cupped her face with both of her hands, gazing deep into her eyes. "I must warn you that I have a brother who is going to be a financial and emotional burden probably all of our lives."

"I have a sister in the same condition." She returned his probing gaze. "Are you sure you can be comfortable with the knowledge that I will always put Meredith's welfare before yours?"

One thumb grazed across her lips. "No, and I don't have to. When you were willing to take a bullet for me last night, you did put me before Meredith. How could you pay her expenses if you'd been shot?"

She stared into his eyes as that knowledge sank in. "It never crossed my mind."

"There is one rule that I must insist on concerning Meredith."

A troubled frown creased her brow, and she felt a twinge of panic. "What?"

But he still smiled. "Don't ever send her to be with me if you get a better offer."

Wicked mischief played in her eyes. "You would never know."

His fingers stroked lightly on her cheeks as his mouth moved to seal their promise with a kiss. When his lips hovered a breath away from hers, he whispered, "The Wizard always knows."

* * * * *

Author's Note

Although it is not uncommon for an expert in the rapidly growing field of computer science to be nicknamed a wizard, Zachary Spencer is a product of my imagination. So are the company called Wizac Electronics, the Wizac computer, the Wizac Storyteller and Pandora.